THE LAST HUMANS

THE LAST HUMANS

GREGORY D. LITTLE

Cursed Dragon Ship Publishing, LLC

6046 FM 2920 Rd, #231, Spring, TX 77379

captwyvern@curseddragonship.com

This books is a work of fiction but deals with real life issues including suicide. Any resemblance to actual persons or places is mere coincidence.

Cover © 2022 by Stefanie Saw

Developmental Edit by Kelly Lynn Colby

Copy Edit by S.G. George

ISBN 978-1-951445-27-0

ISBN 978-1-951445-28-7 (ebook)

For Dad. Thank you. I love you. We miss you.

O hostile Earth, if any still live beyond our walled
    city, our fortress, our prison, we beg for aid! We
    are the suffering souls of Coldgarden, once
    Calgary. Show us proof that we are not the last of
    humankind.

Show us we are wrong to despair.

-*Inkwell graffiti, paraphrasing the automated
    Coldgarden distress call, running continuously for
    the past ninety-eight years. Author unknown.*

CHAPTER 1

THE BAR WAS in the part of Watchfire where people were least likely to be eaten. The heady mix of that sense of safety with the subtle seediness of its dim lighting and aging décor ensured the Prison City steady crowds every night of the week. It had been a favorite haunt of Iazmaena and her friends for years: drink, vent, repeat as necessary.

Tonight, everything was all wrong. Their favorite booth in the corner, normally cozy, hemmed Iaz in like a paddock. It wasn't just her. Steffi clearly didn't even want to be there. That was fair. Most extremely pregnant women didn't frequent dive bars, and three was an awkward number when two of them were in a relationship.

Besides, not so long ago, they'd had a fourth.

Worst of all, though, was Damon. Iaz's boyfriend kept staring into the middle distance with haunted eyes, brows slightly furrowed, mouth slightly frowning. His skin was even paler than usual. Damon had good days and bad days. This was definitely one of the latter.

"Do you want to leave?" Iaz asked him softly, hoping he'd say yes. Steffi dutifully pretended not to notice the turn the conversation was taking.

He came back to himself and plastered on a soft, fake smile. "No, babe. I'm good."

Iaz suppressed a guilty wince at this lie. She'd barely had time for him in the waning months of the campaign, even while watching him struggle. *Just one more day and I can get him the help he needs.* It hadn't been the reason she'd decided to run, but it certainly helped.

"Is this about your appointment today at Gene Sequencing?" she asked, guilt-ridden into following up.

This was apparently the limit of Steffi's polite pretense that she could not hear. Iaz couldn't really blame her. It wasn't as if Steffi had anyone else to talk to, ever since Ali ...

Regardless, the scientist perked right up at mention of her professional nemesis. The lengths of grayish, vat-sequenced meat she'd been poking at unenthusiastically lay forgotten on her plate.

"What's this about Gene Sequencing?" Steffi's voice was a mix of exasperation and alarm. "Damon, why are you going there?" She turned to Iaz. "You know better than to let him."

Iaz ground her teeth. "They don't always give you a choice, Steffi. Or have you forgotten how that whole operation works?" She kept her voice low with an effort. Steffi had always possessed a mothering streak, but she seemed to be peaking early in the case of her actual child.

"Hey," Damon said, "tonight is supposed to be about celebrating. Pre-celebrating. Whatever." He hoisted his glass and—without waiting for them—downed it in one gulp then reached for the first of the next round Silvio, the bar's owner, had brought them without asking.

"Whoa there," Iaz said, feeling a pang of envy. She could stand to toss back a drink like that. Or three. "Slow down." She'd meant it to be fondly exasperated, but the scowl that flashed uncharacteristically across Damon's face gave her pause. Then it was gone, his usual good humor returned.

"That one was mostly empty," he said. "Can't do a proper toast with a mostly empty glass. Now, as I was saying, let's all lift our glasses to the future magistrate of Watchfire, Iazmaena Delgassi!"

He'd raised his voice, and a ragged cheer went up from the bar's regulars, with lifted glasses all around. Regulars only, thank the gods below. Silvio had seen to that. By law, no campaigning was permitted the night before an election, but that didn't stop the press from trying to hound the candidates into saying something they'd regret the next day. Iaz's new aide, Johe, was running interference on the press for her tonight, but they'd get wind of where she was if she stayed out long enough.

"Thank you, everyone," Iaz said. The cheer seemed to call for some acknowledgment. "Still just your friendly ward police chief, though, at least for one more day." Hopefully that would be innocuous enough when it inevitably leaked out. Iaz, Steffi, and Damon dutifully downed their glasses: Iaz's already mostly empty, Steffi's just water. Damon grabbed another from the center of the table.

"Hey now," Iaz said, her voice a tight hush. She didn't like the idea of her boyfriend getting sloppy drunk on the night before her election. And there was that pang of envy again.

But all Damon's exuberance had fled him. "To an absent friend," he said, gesturing at the empty fourth seat at their booth.

Fuck it. Police routinely drank hard, and it made her look like one of the people. "To Ali," Iaz said hoarsely as she hoisted the final shot from the table's center. She swallowed the bracing, brown liquid around a lump in her throat.

Damon downed most of his, then handed the tiny amount remaining to Steffi. Blinking back tears of her own, the amber-skinned woman lifted the glass in salute to their dead friend's seat, took the tiniest of sips, and reached to hand back the rest.

The glass shattered as it hit the table hard. Damon had fumbled the handoff. All three leaned away from the shards scattering across the surface. Steffi was out of her seat like a shot, gripping Damon's arm with one hand while she examined it for cuts .

3

"Are either of you hurt?" she asked, voice brisk with medical authority as she reached into her coat pocket for the cryoband Iaz knew she always kept on-hand.

And this was the other side of Steffi the Mother, and how Iaz knew her friend would be an amazing one: being willing to grab the unprotected skin of a possibly injured man in Coldgarden. She could be absolutely fearless when the moment called for it.

All conversation around them had ceased at the sound of shattering glass. It was not a sound heard often in the city. And for good reason.

"I'm fine," Damon said.

Steffi clearly didn't trust him, for she kept up her close examination of his arm. "What about you, Iaz?"

"I'm good. No hypermutations tonight," she said loudly and jovially, trying to cover how shaken she was.

Minor cuts or wounds weren't usually enough to trigger the mystery affliction to go from dormant to active. If they were, the entire city would have succumbed long ago. But freak incidents had happened, and once one person went active, the malady's strange sympathy effect could spread easily to anyone in close proximity. Every citizen of Coldgarden knew a person who knew a person whose cousin had fallen, scraped their knee, and then wound up incinerated by the lancers to keep from losing an entire city block.

"Real glass?" Steffi said angrily as she released Damon's arm.

She made no effort to keep her voice low, much to Iaz's annoyance. Silvio was rushing over from the bar.

Steffi added, this time in an actual hush, "If you don't say something to him, I'm going to have to file a report."

Grimacing, Iaz gestured that she would take care of it.

"I am so sorry," Silvio said, sweat pouring down his wide, pale face. His eyes darted between Iaz and Steffi. Steffi was the angrier of the two, but Iaz carried the authority here. He settled on Iaz. "A left-over from an old set. Must have slipped through our tossing out when we switched to compglass."

4

Irritation flared in Iaz again. It was a bad excuse. "I'm impressed, Silvio," she said, her volume low but her words hard. "It was quite the survivor. Real glass has been banned for a very long time in the city. Just how long ago did you make this switch?"

"I ... well ... yo-you know how expensive compglass is, Ward Chief. We're trying—"

"More expensive than getting shut down forever because of a Mutagen Prime outbreak?" Silvio's face fell at Iaz's words, and she modulated her tone. Time for good cop. "Get it taken care of. Tomorrow. I don't want to have to write you up."

"Yes, ma'am. I surely will," Silvio said, bobbing his head and looking very relieved. "Though if I may say so, ma'am, unless the polls are very wrong, it would be your successor writing me up. Surely, a newly minted magistrate won't have time to waste on my little corner bar."

"That's right," Iaz said, "and who knows if my successor will be as nice to you as I am?"

"Excellent point, ma'am," Silvio said, going pale again. "Now, I can move you all to a different table while I get this cleaned up."

"Carefully," Steffi said. She still looked angry. "Extremely carefully."

Finding the entrance to the bar mercifully free of press, Iaz and Damon walked Steffi to her apartment just across the ward's border with Illuminance. Despite the visible presence of both the police and the lancer corps, Coldgarden wasn't ever truly safe to walk alone at night.

Moving from ward to ward required producing their passports for the lancers at the walled checkpoint. Steffi both lived and worked in Illuminance, so she was ushered in easily. Iaz's status as a ward police chief granted her access to all wards, even though her official jurisdiction ended at the borders of her native Watchfire. Damon was an Inkwell resident but also Iaz's guest.

Iaz endured with good grace the exclamations of recognition from the young lancers she'd soon be the boss of as the trio was ushered through. The change as they passed from Watchfire to Illuminance was stark, the income disparity between the wards written upon the very architecture. Behind them, the lumped husks of cracked composicrete that made up Watchfire's much older buildings contrasted with Illuminance's sleek, well-maintained, lace-steel structures piling upward into the night sky.

Lighting grew more regular, shadows shrinking from vast swathes to slivered wedges. Iaz couldn't help but note that all three of them relaxed somewhat at the change. Being farther from the city's edge meant being safer.

As if to punctuate the feeling, a clutch of eight lancers jogged past, anonymous in blue-gray armor and helmets. They held their multi-charge explosive lances uniformly propped against their left shoulders and moved with the air of urgency.

They were never far, these reminders of what lurked outside Coldgarden's wall. Revenants. It wasn't that the creatures stole into the city nightly. Every citizen could cite the statistics the government touted daily: "Only one fatality in the past six months!" It was just so much easier to imagine the nightmarish creatures' chitinous, hooking limbs reaching from those wider shadows in the city's poorest wards, and Watchfire was literally the border between the entire city and the vast, depopulated world beyond.

The silence after the lancers' passage caught and held, and none of the trio seemed capable of resurrecting conversation. Ali would have darted in with a lighthearted dig or the perfectly timed quip that had the others laughing themselves out of their moribund mood. But Ali had, on a night very much like this one and not that far away from here, been dragged off and eaten by a revenant.

Ali had been the one fatality.

"Good night," Steffi said ten minutes later as she keyed open the armored outer door to her apartment building. "Get home safe, you two!" Hugs made awkward by her pregnancy followed. Iaz got a whispered, "Good luck tomorrow."

She waited to see if Steffi would make some comment about Damon and Gene Sequencing, but the other woman held her tongue. For now. Iaz had no doubt Steffi would take up the fight again at the earliest opportunity.

Maybe it was an effort to forestall that eventuality that caused Iaz to bring it up herself on her walk back. "Tell me about how it went today."

"You know how it went today," Damon said.

Iaz could tell he was trying not to sound sullen. It just wasn't working.

"Dr. Libretta is not Dr. Kasmus," Damon said, relenting. "My old meds were working. I don't understand why Gene Sequencing had to stick their noses into it." He looked pained. "You've seen how I'm getting. It's not just that I'm reverting to how I was before. It's worse, Iaz."

"How?" she asked, pressing.

He never liked to talk about his depression, but Iaz had sworn she wouldn't let him just fall in on himself out of some ridiculous fear of burdening his loved ones. Damon had no family. If he couldn't unburden himself to Iaz, who else was there?

"I can't describe it." He noted her look. "I mean it. I can't! It's like..." And she could see the struggle on his face as he tried. His pale skin grew red with the effort of trying to verbalize his pain. "I try to explain, and I can't! I don't know what's wrong with me. This isn't depression. I know what that feels like. It's something else." Even saying that much seemed to drain him.

Iaz's suspicions of Gene Sequencing, normally latent, immediately flared to Steffi-level. "After tomorrow," Iaz said, "I'll have more clout. We can get answers. We can get—"

"Can we?" Damon interjected. "I'm not so sure. You'll be a magistrate, yes. But Gene Sequencing answers to the archon. And we

7

already know he has no reason to love you or the fact that you're about to unseat one of his toadies."

"My personal history with the archon doesn't matter."

"Of course, it matters," Damon said. "He had it in for you then. Why not now?"

"The archon probably doesn't even remember me."

"You want to bet on that?" Damon asked, his voice suddenly low and dangerous. It brought Iaz up short even as the thunderhead of his face transitioned to something bordering on resentfulness. "I don't even know why you decided to run for magistrate."

"You know why," Iaz said, unable to keep from sounding defensive. "You raised a glass to her tonight."

"You were talking about it before Ali died," Damon countered. "Even if you've told yourself otherwise so your personal story about your rise to glory holds together for the press."

"Hey!" Iaz said, trying to keep a lid on her temper. *Gods below, I need another drink.* "I'm trying to be understanding here, but you need to knock it off with the low blows."

"I'll knock it off when you start paying attention to what's going on around you," Damon retorted.

Iaz took several deep breaths. "I just have to get through tomorrow. Then we're going to get to the bottom of what's going on with you, whatever, or *whoever,* is causing it."

"No," Damon said. "You're not."

He stopped walking, and Iaz realized they'd arrived back at the border. Damon's gaze drifted over to the tram station.

"I think I'm going to take the tram back to my apartment in Inkwell," he said. "You need your rest tonight. It will be a big day tomorrow."

"I don't think that's a good idea," Iaz said, though in truth, she'd had about as much as she could stand of Damon tonight.

"Trust me. It is. Because I'm probably going to be sick from all that booze, and the last thing you have time for tomorrow is cleaning that up. I'm fine," he said, forestalling her further complaints. "I'm a big boy."

And she decided she could trust the intensity in those brilliant blue eyes of his.

She would never know how things might have gone differently if she hadn't.

CHAPTER 2

THE VICTORY PARTY WAS OVER, the champagne bottles drained dry. Iaz should, by rights, still be schmoozing up her biggest boosters, gladhanding supporters and volunteers, and relishing her crushing victory over soon-to-be-former Magistrate Indred. Already she was bracing for what would undoubtedly be an epic hangover on her first day of the job.

But Iaz was not at her own party any longer. Nor was she passed out in her bed in a too-empty apartment. Iazmaena Delgassi was in Inkwell, going to confront her boyfriend regarding his failure to show up at *her own thrice-damned election.*

She had walked the run-down hall in a run-down building leading to his apartment, all the way at the end, many times. But never had she been filled with such a confusing mixture of emotions. There was worry, of course. How could there not be? As much as Damon matched the stereotype of the flighty artist, this was not like him. But she'd spoken to him throughout the day, and he'd assured her he would be there as soon as he finished up the piece he was working on. She'd told herself that her trepidation over their near-argument the night before had been just one more wasted worry over nothing.

Then the appointed time of his arrival had come ... and gone. And there had been no response to her increasingly irritated and worried messages. Poor Johe was once again running interference, monumentally harder on this night of all nights. Iaz had even left her new security detail behind, for which she would undoubtedly catch hell.

She hadn't wished to get angry. But this had been her big day, the culmination of months and a vindication, proof that Ali might not have died in vain after all. And Damon Blackburne, the most important person in her life, had been nowhere to be seen. Even Steffi, fit to burst and in obvious discomfort, had showed up to lend her support. So Iaz felt a touch of anger was warranted.

Besides, anger was always more pleasant than fear.

She got her wish in the worst possible way, for anger fled entirely when she saw Damon's apartment door ajar.

Her hand went for the police-issue sidearm she no longer carried. *Shit.* No time to worry about that now. She crushed her other cop instinct as well—to call this in. She wasn't sure why, but she didn't let herself dwell on it.

The door squealed as she pushed it open, which shouldn't have surprised her but made her jump all the same. It nearly swung into Damon's easel, Iaz catching sight of its edge just in time to stop short. Made of glossy true wood, the easel had cost Damon an entire commission. What was it doing there, so close to the door? Like it was waiting for whomever found his door open and investigated.

She didn't appreciate the thought.

"Damon!" she called. There was no response.

Upon the easel sat a canvas illuminated by the hallway's lighting. It was covered in broad, dark strokes highlighted with vibrant, iridescent hues. He was painting revenants again. Iaz didn't have the heart to tell him she hated those paintings. How could she tell her boyfriend his skill in capturing the mutable, insectile madness set her teeth on edge?

She closed the door behind her, plunging the room most of the

11

way into darkness. The squeal of the hinges was no easier to bear the second time. Iaz stalked across the tiny living room with all the careful grace of those pretending a lack of inebriation. All remaining illumination came from the bedroom door, cracked open as the front door had been, allowing a right-angled wedge of light to cascade out, both beautiful and unsettling. Iaz was about to call out his name again when she heard the sound.

It was a creak but not of floorboards. The sound of a rope under tension. Iaz stood rooted to the spot for just a moment. Then she charged through the door, noxious dread speeding her movements.

Damon was in his bedroom, dangling from a short length of rope from the ceiling light fixture, a tumbled chair beneath his bare feet, which did not quite reach the ground. The noose had bunched the high collar of his shirt tight around his constricted throat. His face was slack and purple.

He twisted slowly, as though caught in a nonexistent breeze.

Iaz staggered as she beheld him. Blood crashed in her ears. She hesitated, desperate hope that she wasn't too late warring with the bone-deep fear of any citizen of Coldgarden when faced with the dead: Mutagen Prime, hypermutation. Any bodily harm could begin the process, where the body's attempt to repair itself ran wild, spiraling off into biological madness.

She crushed her fear. This was *Damon*. He could still be alive!

She held her breath as she lowered him down, some distant part of her aware of how silly a notion this was. Iaz was no Steffi, but a few heartbeats of examination were enough to tell her he was past coming back. She pinched the fabric of the high, tight collar away from his throat anyway, hoping the relaxation of pressure might inspire him to find his way back to breathing. He didn't respond at all. She heard no heartbeat, dared not feel for a pulse around the tortured skin of his throat.

He wore that collar for me, a crazed voice inside her said. *To keep the skin from breaking. To keep me safe when I found him.* This thought nearly pushed her over an edge so high she would fall forever, and she felt her cop brain sliding in to take over.

Slow down. Assess the scene. The collar of the shirt was important. Purely internal injuries—*like a broken neck, like a crushed trachea, oh gods below*—did not prompt the hypermutation process as quickly, but it began on all dead bodies eventually, burning through what reserves of stored energy they had left before at last falling still. She had to get someone here to sterilize the place.

She stood, trying not to think of anything because thinking would doom her. She was pulling out her handheld to put in the necessary call when she saw something on the dresser, just in front of the mirror, and paused.

Since when did Damon own a gun? They were rare in the city, an unnecessary risk of major injury and hypermutation. This one looked so close to police-issue that Iaz almost wondered if it was hers. Yet it was the placement of the gun that chilled her.

Someone had sat it upright, balanced upon the bottom of its grip, held up only because the muzzle was braced against another standing object. That object was Damon's picture of Iaz and himself, the one she'd framed and given to him because he'd liked it so much, even though she thought she looked better in other photos.

It was specifically Iaz's face the muzzle pressed against in the picture. Yet even this paled with the other thing, the thing reflected in the mirror. Someone had painted words on the wall with the door. The mirror reversed them, and in her current state of numbed shock, she couldn't read without turning to see them properly.

They'd been painted hastily, in the same dark shade Damon had used in his revenant painting. They completely changed who Iaz planned to call to deal with this.

You want to bet on that?

CHAPTER 3

MARRI WAS NOT NORMALLY afraid of the tunnels beneath the city. As far as she knew, she was the first to dare Underguts after it had been closed off all those years ago, years before she was born even. Dark and cramped and twisting as they were, only she'd been bold enough. *Desperate enough*, a little voice whispered, one that spoke often and was shushed just as often.

Others had followed her lead, of course, had copied her idea about searching the tunnels for their treasures. Marri's Mice were first and best. And she at last caught sight of the particular mouse she was looking for.

"There you are." Marri was pleased to see by the light of her LED's ragged red splotch that Bry did not wilt as he once would have. Though in this one instance, it would have been better to see him wilt a little.

Because while the tunnels had been empty of dangers when she'd started this practice, recently that was no longer the case. That was why she'd restricted her mice to a much smaller search area, however difficult that made finding enough to trade. It was also why she'd been so angry when she'd heard the rumor from some of the other mice that Bry had violated her invisible border, the one that separated "probably safe" from "probably not safe."

"What are you doing this close to the city edge?" she asked, giving him a little shake for emphasis. Not too hard. Several years older, she could hurt him by accident if she wasn't careful. She worried this kind of approach might break him back down. Of all her mice, Bry needed his backbone built most. Just not like this. This part of the tunnels was where the revs came in sometimes.

"It was slim pickings," he said, defensive. "A couple of off-brand handhelds and a few battery packs. Been like that for a while. I didn't want to come up empty."

"Rains will be starting soon. That will wash new stuff our way. So," she said, preparing her trap, "where are we?"

"Huh?"

"How many turns to home? Which turns? How many paces between each?"

"I know my way back," he said, bristling. Then the expected wilt. "I think."

"You think."

"Never been this far out before," he whined.

"Yes," Marri said. "That's the point." She was about to lay into him some more when she heard the distant scuttling. Both children fell utterly silent.

Revs.

Trying to stay ahead of panic, she motioned Bry to remain still, and saw by her light the fear on his face. Marri strained her ears, trying to soak up every sound. It was impossible to tell how many there were. Only idiots tried to guess the number of revs by their footsteps, since the number of feet was always changing.

Besides, one rev was too many.

More important than how many was where they were and which direction they were moving. Sound was tricky down in these forgotten sewer tunnels. The further out from city center you went, the worse shape the disused pipes were in. Some were cracked open, others blocked entirely. That left the mice with a maze of passages where sometimes there was no way through, and though Marri had known this area well once, changes happened all the time.

She listened a bit longer. One tunnel over. Maybe two. The sound was closer to a vibration in her feet than something coming through the air, which might mean no connecting passageway. Also, it seemed to be getting farther away.

"Did you even find anything out here?" she asked, working back up to her tirade. All the mice seemed to think the great score that would keep them fed forever was just one more bend around the tunnel. Marri dimly remembered feeling that way, once.

"No," Bry said, glum. He gestured to a patch of greater darkness at the side of the tunnel where part of the pipe wall had fallen away into some depth. "I was thinking about climbing down there to check it before I gave up."

Marri closed her eyes and willed down her anger. How could any mouse be so brave at facing mortal danger and so scared of facing Marri at the same time?

"Do not ever think a thought like that again," she said levelly.

"But last week we barely had enough to trade for food," he protested. "And we still need supplies for the lair! And Mote needs medicine!"

"What good will medicine for Mote do me if you break your leg? Or neck? You'd just trade me one problem for another."

Bry said nothing, just sulked.

"Someday," Marri said, forcing patience into her voice, "you'll get old enough and smart enough to know I'm always right. And the reason you'll get that old and that smart is because I'm watching out for you, and I'm always r—"

She stopped as Bry put a trembling hand on her wrist. She heard it, then. More revenant scuttling from a different direction. Much closer, which was bad. From the direction she'd come was even worse.

And getting closer still, which promised disaster.

Think fast. Two options. Head closer to the city edge, risk running into the first group they'd heard, or ...

"Into the hole," she hissed. "Lights out."

They thumbed off their lights, which made backing into the hole much more dangerous. Not knowing how deep it went or what was at the bottom, they couldn't just jump in. The edges of the hole were not exactly gentle, either. Marri forced her mice to wear thick coveralls and gloves no matter the weather. Without them, they'd surely have scraped themselves, and then who knew what might happen?

It was a tight fit, for Marri especially, but they managed. She tried to still her breathing and mostly succeeded, right up until her feet met empty air and she realized she was supporting herself entirely by her arms and hands. Hoping Bry was strong enough to hold himself up, hoping she herself was, Marri hung there, waiting. She prayed a silly prayer to Undel Underguts that nothing would reach up from that hole and drag them down into it.

She could barely hear the weeping Bry, who was trying so hard to keep silent.

They came in a pack, as they usually did. Between six and ten of them, she guessed, scuttling on their giant, insect legs. In this total darkness, Marri couldn't see a thing. But she'd seen revs before, enough to imagine in detail the group that passed them.

The scuttling sounds paused every so often. She'd seen this as well, at a safe distance, seen them stop and sweep featureless, egg-shaped heads back and forth, scanning for prey. It was almost like smelling, scenting the air, but she'd always heard they had terrible noses. She'd never seen noses on them at all. Or eyes. Some said they saw from inside their mouths, but Marri had never even seen mouths on them, just those perfectly smooth heads. She wondered, not for the first time, just how they ate their human prey.

She imagined their segmented black legs sweeping the tunnels with clawed tips. During happier times in the Mousehole, Marri would tell scary stories, saying their claws were like tongues, and they could taste morsels of little children even through tunnel walls. Now the memory made her want to puke. She couldn't seem to stop shivering. Surely they could hear the hammering of her heart?

If they find us, I'll lead them away, give Bry a chance to escape. This thought made her feel much better.

Then the pack was past and moving on. Marri waited until they'd rounded two more corners before she hauled herself back up, Bry following her lead. He'd been so quiet, so still, for a moment she feared he'd fallen without a sound.

"Come on," she said hoarsely, trying for confidence and failing. "We're gone."

CHAPTER 4

YOU WANT TO BET ON THAT?

Iaz tossed in tangled sheets, half awake, half in a nightmare.

She had painted over those words as soon as she'd made her call. The gun she'd examined to see if it might be traced, but of course, its electronic ID had been tampered with.

The body was disposed of discretely, a favor owed to Iaz from her days on the force owed no longer. There would be no funeral for Damon Blackburne. Not for a long while yet. Not until she could understand what he'd done and what it meant.

He'd always struggled. Iaz knew better than most his bouts of depression, his battles with his inner demons. The way they kept emerging in his art was clue enough of that. But he'd never been delusional. Never paranoid.

Until that night, Iaz would have said the latter about herself as well.

A message, painted like a reminder of something she had not grasped. A gun propped up, aimed at her likeness's forehead like a warning.

And now, awake or asleep, the painted words and the propped gun drummed through Iaz's mind like autumn rains. Even more than the memory of him dangling there. Words meant for her. A gun pointed at a picture of her. She dreamed of him asking her those words again, this time with the barrel of the gun leveled at her actual forehead.

Maybe the truth of his death or the injustice of covering it up were too much to bear. Maybe that was why it had to mean something. But the words, the gun, they gave her focus. The words had been some of the last Damon had ever said to her. Tossed off in anger, or so she'd believed at the time.

An answer to her statement that Archon Teodori probably didn't even remember her anymore.

And Damon had been behaving so oddly ever since his first appointment with Gene Sequencing.

The half-conscious dream ended when Damon's slowly spinning corpse opened its mouth and emitted an electronic buzzing and vibration. Iaz sat bolt upright in bed, sobbing, scrubbing at herself to clean away the feeling the dream left in her. Her hands shook as she kneaded her forearms with them. In her dreams, Damon was a permanent fixture. But she saw him awake sometimes, too. He wasn't really there. She knew that. But she saw him.

She felt an overwhelming need to wash herself of this horror, but something was buzzing at her. *My handheld.* Someone was trying to reach her. Iaz glanced first at the handheld, then at the clock and grew alarmed.

Sloughing off the remains of sleep, Iaz snatched the phone from where it lay on the bedside table. "What is it?" Her words sounded foreign to her, muddied, as though both the language and the voice were not her own. It was just the confusion of sleep and the dryness of her throat, but for a moment it sounded more like Damon's voice in her head. She shut her eyes against tears she wished would just dry already.

"Magistrate, it's Johe." Her assistant was simultaneously the most likely caller and the most frightening. Fiercely protective of her time and her rest, Johe would have deferred all but the demands of catastrophe. "I'm so sorry to wake you, ma'am, but there's been an incident."

"Tell me what happened." Iaz had to work hard to keep irritation down. It was not being wakened; rather, it was the dream, the sense of having been caught in the act of something illicit. A tremor pulsed through her.

"Revenants, ma'am. Inside the walls."

Five little words froze all Iaz's petty thoughts and shattered them. *Ali all over again.* And Johe was still talking, still pushing information at her when she couldn't even process five fucking words.

"They got in through the condemned tunnels in Underguts. Normal enough, but they cut power to a quarter of the city somehow." The tiniest hint of worry wormed through his voice.

Iaz growled a curse. "Isn't that always the way? I told Undel! I warned him on my first day this could happen." It had been all of two weeks since she'd taken office, but still Iaz understood better than most that the revenants got in from time to time. *I should have already gone public with these concerns.*

"You did warn him, ma'am, and I have a feeling the rest of the council be willing to listen after tonight." Johe's voice bloomed with the pride of being associated with her.

It made Iaz feel sick. Her hands would not stop shaking.

"What's the damage? Beyond the power outage, I mean?" Iaz had to get control. She rose to pour herself a drink.

"Nobody can tell with so much of the city dark. All the diagnostic meters in the affected region are non-functional."

"Are you at Heart Hall?" The liquor burned sweetly, the promise of calm.

"Yes, ma'am. The first of the magistrates are starting to trickle in." She heard the competitive edge in his voice, the urgency. Iaz smiled grimly before realizing he could not see her.

"I'll be right in." She hung up, willing the tremors of her hands to calm as the alcohol seeped in.

All this insomnia and anxiety meant she should probably see a doctor. But as Damon had proved, every doctor in the city ultimately led to Gene Sequencing. Damon, who had gone to Gene Sequencing for a handful of depression treatments and wound up killing himself. And Gene Sequencing answered to only one person.

YOU WANT TO BET ON THAT?

There was no telling what patient information might not be so secure when certain people asked. Snarling reflexively at thoughts of the archon, Iaz downed the rest of her glass and rushed to get dressed.

CHAPTER 5

SIX OF THE twelve magistrates had arrived, and Heart Hall was beginning to look less cavernous and more bustling. LEDs powered on, banishing the shadows into the spaces behind its rib-like pillars of dark wood.

Johe Istuil was bouncing on the balls of his feet with anxiety when Magistrate Delgassi strode in. Upon catching sight of her, he forced himself back into a semblance of calm.

Despite the short time since the call, Magistrate Delgassi looked almost immaculate. Her long auburn hair was pulled back in a thick tail, and her hazel eyes were bright and intense, marred only a little by the slight blurring of darkened sockets. She always looked so tired.

"Which wards?" was the first thing out of her mouth once her eyes had found Johe. She made a beeline for him and her seat at the table while awaiting his response. Above them, the lights dimmed for several moments, then brightened again to a heightening of concerned babble.

"Latest reports say the outages are confined to north quadrant segments of Watchfire, pushing inward under Inkwell and finally Sparks."

"If they've made it all the way to Sparks, that would explain the power outages."

"Yes, ma'am." Underguts contained large sections of mostly unusable sewer tunnels, eventually abandoned in favor of high-efficiency recyclers and cisterns after the Loss. "But if you follow the track of outages, they could be heading right for Haleness, or even Heart."

"Right beneath us, in other words," Magistrate Delgassi said grimly.

It sent chilling rivulets through Johe to consider. The revenants had succeeded in a mass invasion only once, just after they'd first appeared ninety-eight years previous. It had cost the city nearly everything to beat them back. Since then, small incursions were a fact of life, mostly in Watchfire, the city's encircling ward, but very occasionally, revenants troubled themselves to push deeper.

Johe had accepted Magistrate Delgassi's offer of a job in part to escape the endless push to join the lancer corps that fell upon Watchfire natives like himself. Yet even now, the horrid creatures might be scuttling beneath the floors, whatever passed for their ears burning as they listened to the humans above speak of them.

"All right," Magistrate Delgassi said, "give me as much of the fine detail as you—"

"I call," interrupted the booming voice of Archon Teodori as he strode into the room, flanked by five magistrates and their aides, "an immediate vote to impose rolling blackouts on the city until the power situation is resolved. We must prevent a general panic and keep people in their homes where they will be safest."

The archon's retinue of loyal magistrates formed a phalanx behind him, approaching the table only after he took his place at the head. Taking his position at Magistrate Delgassi's shoulder, Johe could not help but notice the flat stare she transitioned from the archon to level at Magistrate Undel. There was little doubt whom she blamed for this catastrophe.

"Second," came the voice of Magistrate Bennefred, Teodori's most devout toady.

"Very well," the archon declaimed, his posture ramrod straight and radiating command. "All in favor?"

Every voting hand went up.

"So be it." Teodori then turned to a man Johe did not recognize, one of his many underlings. "Power will be allocated in four-hour blocks, one third of wards in any given block. See to it immediately."

The man nodded and turned without a word.

"Now, we need a status update," Teodori said, and raised a forestalling finger in Iazmaena's direction.

Her mouth froze in the act of opening. Johe could feel the tension rising from her like a heat haze.

"Begging the Magistrate of Watchfire's pardon, but I'd like to hear from the Magistrate of Foundation first." Though it was the legal name, only in this chamber or during other official functions was Underguts ever referred to as Foundation.

Magistrate Delgassi's mouth closed reluctantly. Across the table, Magistrate Undel puffed his chest up like a strutting bird unaware he'd misplaced the plumage on his head. He lifted his tablet and adjusted his glasses self-importantly on a round, bulbous nose to read it.

"Esteemed Archon and colleagues, according to my best information, approximately two hours ago a breach occurred beneath the northwest boundary of Watchfire directly adjacent to Inkwell, allowing an undetermined number of revenants access to condemned sections of Foundation. There are no reports of any sightings or surface breaches at this time, and we can only pray that our outdated barriers separating the tunnels from the surface hold." His eyes turned down, saddened by what he had to say next. "Regardless, this is an appalling security failure on the part of Watchfire, and I—"

He was forced to stop when Magistrate Delgassi lurched to her feet, hissing like a column of steam. Even Johe started. Her hazel eyes flashed, and ferocity boiled from every pore. An angry red flush rose in her cheeks.

"With all due respect to my colleague, one of my first acts since taking office was to warn this body that such an attack was a matter of time, given Magistrate Undel's steadfast refusal to block up or impose any sort of quarantine measures on the condemned sections of Foundation. He has ignored or outright denied every one of my requests to work with him on this matter!"

"Now see here, young lady!" Undel puffed up even further and dropped all pretense of decorum. "If I can quote from the revised city charter, 'defense against revenant incursion is the sole responsibility of Watchfire and its residents. Patrols against incursion are to be performed on a regular basis in *all* vulnerable areas—'"

"Enough!" Her bark brought a halt to the man's building pontification. "Enough," she repeated. "We can blame each other later. Right now, we have to ascertain where the revenants are and kill them or drive them off. I have three lancer Ferret Squads on standby at Foundation entrances near the outage areas. Archon, I call a vote to enable these squads to enter Foundation with the intent of removing the revenant threat by any means necessary."

The archon looked both perplexed and angry. "You mean that's not being done already? I hardly see the need to put such to a vote—"

"Second," came the whip-crack voice of Magistrate Graysteel of Illuminance. The harsh lines of her face spoke of grim determination and steadfast resolve, as they always did. Johe didn't think he'd ever once seen the woman smile.

The archon glared in her direction briefly, then turned his ire back to Magistrate Delgassi.

"Magistrate Delgassi," he said, his frown transforming the strong lines of his face into a portrait of menace, "you will tell me why you haven't already deployed your lancer squads. That should have been your first act upon being informed of the crisis."

One of Teodori's pet magistrates muttered something he didn't have the nerve to speak aloud.

"All respect to the archon," Magistrate Delgassi said, "but such an act would constitute a violation of sovereign Foundation territory, as Magistrate Undel has so frequently reminded me, and therefore requires an emergency vote of the entire presiding council and yourself."

"What are you talking about?" the archon said, his voice thunder. "We settled that bit of bureaucratic boilerplate in your first session. You and Undel were to work out the terms of the access treaty between you."

Johe, almost too late, saw where this was going and frantically began pulling up documents on his tablet while trying not to be too obvious about it.

"And I have tried, Excellency, many times. The exact number would be?" Magistrate Delgassi turned to Johe.

"Six times in the past two weeks, Excellency," Johe said, his voice reedy as adrenaline washed through him.

The grateful look on Magistrate Delgassi's face as she held his eyes only served to warm Johe further.

"None received any response. All attempts to bring the matter up in the three sessions since were deferred. And," he added for extra color, "Foundation is the only ward that has not agreed to the removal of bureaucratic blocks to counter-incursion action by the lancers since Magistrate Delgassi took office."

Magistrate Delgassi smirked at his additions and gave him the tiniest of winks.

Johe's heart soared.

The archon's rage shifted. Undel was a member of his coterie, the unofficial majority he had built himself since taking office a decade ago and held onto right up until the moment Magistrate Delgassi had ousted her predecessor. In the wake of her victory, Teodori had only the slimmest of majorities backing him. A blunder of this magnitude by one of its members could put him in a bad light.

"Magistrate Undel, we will discuss this when the crisis is past. At length. In the meantime," the archon said, turning back to the Council, "all in favor deploying Magistrate Delgassi's teams?"

The ayes overwhelmed him before he could finish.

"Do it," he snapped. "I want a status report in half an hour, and I want those tunnels flushed in two. We'll reconvene at that time. In the meantime, see to your individual wards. Adjourned."

Magistrate Delgassi didn't even need to look Johe's way as the meeting broke up. He was already electronically stamping the orders for the prepared mission plan. He received acknowledgment from the team leads in seconds. Magistrate Delgassi stood, looking angry but satisfied, for now.

"Nicely done," she said softly, still flushed with anger, her eyes never leaving the archon as he crossed to the door, coterie in tow. "Perhaps, we can leverage something out of this disaster."

Still riding high from his own part in the performance, Johe hid a smirk. He had a better idea, but it was not one he needed to put to her just yet. She was always lost in her own head, thinking about the work, no doubt. Never her own image. That was what he was there for, in part, whether she knew it or not.

Magistrate Delgassi went off to join the babble of frenzied conversation rising as the district leads moved into the situation room, awaiting word of the operation. Johe took the opportunity to lag behind, opened up a new document on his tablet and began composing a press statement.

Above them, the lights flickered once again.

CHAPTER 6

THE LIGHTS FLICKERED in Stefani's birthing suite. Exhausted, she barely noticed. She just kept waiting to hear her baby cry for the first time. But the microphone piping in the sound feed from the little portable scanning chamber next to her bed remained resolutely silent.

She could call out to the monitoring nurse, demand human intervention in the expert machine's process, but she did not want to be one of those panicky new mothers. And the nurse was on call for the entire hospital, the only human present at this hour and only there in the improbable event the expert machines reached an impasse and an alert was triggered. Everything was fine. The autodoc would inform her if that wasn't the case. Still, only the calming drugs kept her resolve firm.

Baby Ella's first squall coincided with the next flicker of lights, and Stefani took in an enormous breath of relief.

During that glorious space of release, the autodoc's articulated arm and its many nimble fingers finished knitting up Stefani's incision. The chill of mutagenic suppressing spray, felt even through the numbness, began to ebb. She'd have more of the substance applied to her incision tonight than she'd ever be granted access to for her lab

29

work. Brute-force as it was, it was too valuable—and too expensive—to use for anything but major medical procedures where cutting into someone was unavoidable.

Beyond the compglass window enclosing the tiny chamber, the scan continued, and Stefani's trepidation found something new to grip. It was supposed to be a formality. The birth of a child always presented a chance of Mutagen Prime shenanigans. It was why births always took place under the supervision of only the autodoc robotic systems. Family and loved ones there for the delivery could observe remotely. Even the father, if there had been one, wouldn't have been let in. And Ella's birth had no visitors. Stefani had made the decision to have Ella herself, neither wanting nor having time for a partner in the process.

Still, it was hard going through this night alone, hard thinking of Ali, gone three months now. Ali had promised she would help Stefani raise the baby when she came, jokingly and yet not, the way Ali always did. Ali always kept her promises, too, right up until she no longer could.

Iaz had offered to come to the birth, of course, but the few moments she'd found to talk to Stefani via video since her election had shown a haggard woman who needed her every moment of time just to stay afloat, so Stefani had declined. She could have asked Damon, she supposed, but Damon without Iaz would have been strange. In any case, she hadn't heard from the man since the night before the election.

So it was Stefani alone watching when the warning popped up in block red letters. The one every new parent dreaded. MUTAGEN ACTIVE.

"No." The word was reflex deeper than thought. Stefani barely had time to read it and to begin processing the import when the warning was replaced.

NORMAL—DORMANT.

Then it reappeared. MUTAGEN ACTIVE.

NORMAL—DORMANT.

Mutagen active.

On and off it flickered, as Stefani vacillated between panic and relief with equal speed. She found she'd pressed her hands plaintively against that impenetrable window, ignoring the tugging sensation the movement produced in her sutures. *My baby. My sweet baby. No.*

Error: Attempting to resolve discrepancy flashed up at last. Her panic clarifying, Stefani was seized with a sudden, terrible certainty. In a few moments, the machine, unable to resolve this dichotomy, would summon help from the nurse. The nurse would contact an on-call doctor. And Stefani knew what the doctor, out of an abundance of caution, would order. Swift removal by Gene Sequencing. Stefani would never get to hold her child.

Would never see her again.

Stefani had seconds to act. She resided in Illuminance, a place where Grand Project scientists such as herself were granted an absurd amount of authority. Here, she was nearly as powerful as Iaz was in Watchfire. Her ID chit looked the same as any doctor's in this facility, but Stefani Palmieri's chit afforded her far more control over the same systems.

That included this autodoc and its scanning chamber.

The chamber's ID chit slot beckoned, asking its wordless question.

With trembling hands, she answered in the affirmative, reached further, inserted the chit, and overrode the autodoc's attempts to resolve the discrepancy.

As if the world condemned her action, the power flickered again.

Normal—Dormant appeared on the screen. This time, it did not switch back.

"Dr. Palmieri?" a young woman's voice came over the intercom. "Your system threw an error that showed up on our terminal here. Shows normal now, though. Is everything all right?"

Stefani almost blurted out what she'd done but forced herself to remain calm. She was covered in cold sweat unrelated to childbirth.

They can't know. They'll take her away from me. My beautiful baby. Whatever this is, I have to deal with it myself.

And she could. In that moment, she was absolutely certain of this fact. *I'm the head of the Grand Project to study Mutagen Prime. If anyone can solve this, I can.*

"Must have been the power flickers," Stefani said, amazed at how steady her voice was. "Everything looks normal from where I'm sitting."

"That's good to hear," the voice came back, obviously relieved. "To be honest, this is my first night on duty, and I would have been freaking out otherwise." Her laugh was shot full of nerves. "I probably shouldn't say that sort of thing."

"Your secret is safe with me," said this new Stefani, capable of lying with absolute impunity.

"I appreciate it," the young woman said, her laughter more genuine now. "Oh, and congratulations! She's beautiful!"

CHAPTER 7

TWENTY MINUTES after and forty meters below a meeting none of them had attended, Lance Captain Karl Yonnel oversaw the hasty assembly of a forward command post for his Ferret Squad in what the mapping systems had listed as the most obvious choke point. Assuming they actually knew where the revenants were, of course.

For which Karl was still awaiting confirmation.

Set in a junction between four smaller tunnels joined at odd angles, Karl needed half his force just to guard all the ingress points. But this was the only space that had enough room for the sensor equipment needed.

"Do we have anything on sensors yet?" Karl asked.

"Negative, Lance Captain." Lance Corporal Zelizer knew her business when it came to the portable equipment, so this answer was a bad sign.

"Do enlighten me," Karl said.

"This stuff is designed to do exactly what we're asking it to do, but the returns I'm getting are all over the place. Sometimes there's nothing at all. Sometimes I'd swear there were dozens of revenants all around us. I've never seen anything like it, sir."

The damp air of the tunnel seemed suddenly stifling to Karl. "And *are* there dozens of revenants around us?"

"No way, sir. I'd stake my rank on it."

"You're staking all our lives on it, Lance Corporal. So please tell me the basis for your certainty."

"Well, Margie there, Lance Lieutenant Sellers, sir." Zelizer gestured at the young lancer working the portable comms array. "She's linked up with the three forward phalanxes. She'd be a trifle more upset if we were getting word about revenants in those numbers. Hell, we'd hear them, sir. According to these returns currently, they're right on top of us. Practically in this room."

"Well, let's hope the powers that be didn't spend too much on that sensor," Karl said. "Keep at it. There must be some way to clean up that signal into something that resembles reality." A bullshit order, but one of the prerogatives of command was issuing orders and then expecting the soldiers to find a way to make them happen even if you couldn't see how yourself.

Distant booms of lancer fire echoed into the command center. Fewer booms than Karl would consider apocalyptic in number, so that was something.

"Contact!" Sellers called out, repeating what she was hearing. "Center phalanx. Three revs up, three revs down. Unknown number retreating." She blew out a relieved sigh. "No casualties."

"Count it and map it," Karl said to his staff. Revenants tended to cluster. They needed to form a better picture of where those clusters were. He turned back to Zelizer. "Any improvements on sensors?"

"The three we killed were definitely visible before they died," Zelizer said. "I think."

"Very reassuring."

"Sorry, sir. It's a mess."

"Well, as long as the phalanxes hold position and the maps are accurate, we should see any that attempt to come through with our own eyes."

"Yes, sir."

"Additional contacts," Sellers reported, her words punctuated by more distant booms. "They're pushing harder this time. Along all three phalanxes." Her youthful face was pinched with worry when she looked at Karl. "Reporting multiple casualties, sir. They caught us by surprise."

"Don't force a stand. Tell them to fall back to the designated choke points and make the revs come at us single file. Zelizer!" He turned to the specialist as Sellers relayed his orders.

"I don't know," the woman said. She sounded rattled, which in turn rattled Karl. "There's sensor ghosts everywhere! And then sometimes they turn out to be real."

"Something to do with the tunnels?"

"These sensors were designed for the tunnels. I don't know what's different today. If I didn't know better ..."

Karl pressed. "Talk, soldier."

"I'd almost swear they were using some sort of ... of tech to confuse our sensors!"

"Revenants don't use tech," Karl said, wondering if it was time to reevaluate that axiom.

"I know, sir," Zelizer said.

"No one's blaming you, soldier. They're throwing something new at us, so we have to adapt. Can you clean up what you're seeing?" Karl asked. "Figure out a way to tell the ghosts from the revenants?"

"I've been trying, but I can't see anything to distinguish them. I'll have to have the computer analyze the results when we get b— contacts in the safe zone! Two contacts, closing fast."

"Rear guard!" Karl bellowed as a pair of *children* darted in from one of the side tunnels.

A girl and a boy, the former nearly a teenager, the latter several years younger. Both wore filthy, battered coveralls and oversized work gloves.

Several lances were leveled to blow their little heads off almost before Karl could bellow, "Hold fire! Civilians!"

Gutter mice, he thought, disgusted by the name even as it leaped to mind. Gutter mice were the worst kept secret of Foundation. Poorest of the city's wards, many of its homeless and disaffected children had formed loose gangs. They were considered not much better than rats by much of the populace.

"Kids," Karl said, speaking with all the authority he could muster to draw the attention of those wild eyes, "where on Earth did you come fr—"

"They're right behind us!" the girl shouted.

Simultaneously, Zelizer bellowed, "Many contacts! Six! Eight! Right on us!"

"Rear guard!" Karl shouted again, watching the girl and boy angle hard toward the egress tunnel out of the corner of one eye. Then skittering black shapes shining with iridescent hues in the glare of the flickering spotlights dragged his attention back, and lances discharged. Karl's helmet took the edge off the punishing sound.

Heartbeats later, at least two of the shining black beasts were down, but some of Karl's were too. One revenant perched atop Zelizer's station, and Karl knew his desperate turn to engage the creature would be too slow. The revenant, as if in triumph, stabbed its foreclaws through the console readouts, tore open a mouth along its featureless head, and screamed.

"Oh, gods below," Zelizer moaned, seemingly transfixed, her gaze lost as she stared into that horrible mouth before it closed over her head and savagely twisted.

Karl at last brought his lance to bear upon the revenant which had killed Zelizer. With icy, controlled anger, he calmly vaporized the back of its screaming head. Around him, the decapitation strike by the revenants faltered. It hadn't been an overwhelming push by any means, but Karl was glad he'd kept plenty of lancers in reserve. The sensors' malfunction—if malfunction it had been—had left them unprepared for the sudden appearance of such a force.

"Report!" he shouted as the last revenant died.

"Phalanxes held, Lance Captain," Sellers said. She was still manning the comms station, but her lance was shorter by several shots. "They have casualties, none fatal, and the revenants appear to be pulling back."

"Thank you, Sellers. But I meant locally," Karl said.

"Six of ours down," said one of the sergeants. The man's voice was shaking so badly Karl couldn't identify it. "Including the sensors officer. All dead," he said with perverse relief. They wouldn't have to put anyone down before hypermutation claimed them. This place was now an extreme biohazard.

"Mutagen protocol," Karl said to the few who hadn't already taken that step. Karl himself had not. *You're getting slow, old man.* He triggered his helmet to cover the exposed part of his face. Breathing became at once harder and safer. They'd all have to decontaminate upon returning to the barracks.

"Confirmed," Sellers said. "Phalanxes report a complete withdrawal of remaining revenants."

A relief to hear but also a worry. A broken rank would have neatly explained how the revenants—and the children—were able to get to the command center untouched. Now he had more questions than answers. Karl was half-tempted to send someone to chase down those gutter mice and offer food and shelter in exchange for eyewitness reports. But he didn't dare divide his forces now. He had to hope that pair would find their way back to wherever they called home.

"Final field estimate is twenty revs total," Sellers said.

Karl did a quick count. "We got more than half the bastards then." At least eleven revenant corpses against just six of his. *If the kids hadn't run past, giving us that moment's warning, we might all be dead.*

But there was nothing to be done. He turned to look at poor Zelizer, her final mission one of confusion, frustration, and a sense of failure. He couldn't imagine much worse of a way to go, except a bad wound festering with hypermutation, your own brothers and sisters forced to put you down.

Zelizer's console was wrecked, all her experience lost. Any

secrets she might have divined in her final moments would remain that way forever.

"Prepare for incineration protocol," Karl said over a lump in his throat.

It never got any easier.

CHAPTER 8

THE ARCHON'S voice thundered over the loudspeakers, reflecting off the warren of buildings surrounding the square. "My fellow citizens, I have come here today to speak to you again on the subject of the revenant incursion and subsequent power failures of one week ago."

Teodori was in rare form today. He chose to speak in front of the magisterial facade of the university library in Illuminance whenever he wanted to sound wise, and when he wanted to sound wise, he tended to pontificate.

The day was bright and pleasantly warm. The sky shone a blue so cloudless and brilliant that the visible wedges of it looked like gemstones. Encompassing those wedges of sapphire was the great spoked partial dome of Canopy, arcing majestically over the city. While the bulk of the city's food was grown along the wall, the rest came from Canopy. Its verdant greens and splashes of citrine color marked it for the great wash of life-sustainment it was. There were times, Iaz reflected, when it was easy to forget all the darkness that waited outside the walls of this final bastion of humanity.

Only Teodori's speech seemed determined to sour the moment.

"As I vowed," Teodori said, "after the breach, I commissioned an emergency inventory of all Foundation tunnels that lead outside the city safe zone, a joint effort led by Magistrate Undel and Magistrate Delgassi."

From her chair to the podium's immediate left, Iaz smiled at the crowd to scattered applause. Moving by rote, she turned and gestured at Karl Yonnel, the lance captain who had led the most successful of the counter-incursion teams and whom she'd tapped to represent the lancers, the citizen-soldiers of Watchfire, and by extension of all of Coldgarden. Yonnel looked more uncomfortable than Iaz felt. He was going to be even more uncomfortable when she let him know she was promoting him to lance commander of the entire corps. She wanted one of her own selections in the position, not someone beholden to her predecessor.

"And today," Teodori intoned sagely, "I can tell you that the study has identified those key vulnerabilities and that they are being dealt with even as we speak. Together, we must remember the brave sacrifices of those lancers who perished in our defense. With their noble sacrifice and the successful efforts of the last week and of the weeks to come, we will ensure there are no future breaches of Foundation!"

More applause. Civilian deaths or not, that night had been terrifying for the entire city, and the archon was giving them what they wanted to hear.

Too bad it was a lie.

Theories still abounded for why the revenants would steal so deeply into the city's underbelly and not burst upward onto the streets to spirit anyone away as they normally did. The gods below knew they'd had enough time before Iaz had been able to order the lancers in. Unregistered residents might have vanished, but no listed citizens had been taken, and in the turbulent wake of such fear, that was all these people would care about.

But to say that their vulnerabilities had all been mapped in a week was patently false. The joint effort, really Iaz's solo effort given Undel's status at present, had only begun to map out the open pipelines and culverts. Even of that small fraction, the vast majority were deemed sufficiently threatening to act on.

The safe answer was that every disused pipeline that opened to the trackless expanse of wilderness beyond the city was a potential entry vector for future revenant attacks. They would have to block up or guard them all, at least until the mapping really was completed. Which was the only reason she was not too angry at Johe for forcing this issue with his press release regarding Undel's refusal to work with Iaz. What was about to happen was necessary. Watchfire simply did not have sufficient manpower or authority to deal with this alone.

As Teodori waxed philosophical about the first duty of government being to protect its people, Iaz noticed Steffi in the crowd trying to catch her eye. Baby Ella was nowhere in sight, which struck Iaz as odd. Still, Steffi smiled broadly and waved, so everything must be all right.

Iaz did not wave back, considering the setting. A muted return smile with eye contact was the best she could manage, and she hoped the strain did not show.

I need to make time for her soon. This thought was—she was ashamed to admit—not purely selfless. The truth was she needed Steffi's help.

Iaz's friend wasn't alone among familiar faces. Damon stared out at Iaz from the crowd as well, at least until Iaz blinked and he vanished. Far from supportive, his face was accusing. Living people needed her help now. The dead would have to wait. *But not much longer,* she swore to his shade.

"And now, I bring you sad news," Teodori said. Iaz forced herself to focus. It was nearly time. "Our esteemed Magistrate Undel, after many years of tireless dedication, has decided to retire from public service. We shall dearly miss his leadership and his willingness to sacrifice in the times we face today."

Iaz struggled not to roll her eyes. This entire leadership establishment was so duplicitous, so false-faced, it made Iaz's stomach cramp to consider it. She avoided looking back into the crowd, fearing she might see Damon again.

"Given the circumstances of the last few days," the archon said, "the city council and I have decided that in this time of transition, it would be prudent to restructure matters in regards to the defense of Coldgarden."

Here it comes.

"Watchfire has long been the line of defense between the good people of this city and the revenant threat. But as we learned that fateful night, there is one border this city possesses that Watchfire does not yet encompass. Therefore, effective immediately, Watchfire and Foundation wards are to be consolidated under the name of Greater Watchfire. With Magistrate Undel's retirement, the new ward will be placed under the sole governance of Magistrate Iazmaena Delgassi. Why don't you all join me in applauding our youngest magistrate? I know she will do a fine job representing even more of our good citizens."

And this solves the problem of your nearly lost majority, fearless leader, Iaz thought hatefully.

Teodori's voting majority was the crux of the matter. He'd had a majority plus one spare vote—eight to five—before Iaz's election had removed Gaspard Indred, who had always been his creature, and made the vote seven to six. Left with no margin now, the loss of Undel's vote to Iaz would have left Teodori with only six votes in the council against seven any time the remaining magistrates united against him.

But while city dictates did not allow there to be more or less than thirteen votes in the council, they said nothing about distribution beyond each magistrate have one vote. And regardless of how many wards she oversaw, it was not *Iaz* who was getting an extra vote. Instead, the archon could—and would—bestow the extra vote upon himself, and his math problem was solved, the proper seven to six asymmetry restored. Archon Teodori would still possess all the power where it counted. Iaz almost had to applaud the finesse of his solution.

Now she was left with twice as many people to represent, all of whom barely knew her in the role, if at all. As if reflecting her own uncertainties, the applause to the pronouncement was scattered and confused.

Swallowing her frustration, Iaz rose at the archon's beckoning and walked lead-footed to the podium to speak.

CHAPTER 9

EVERYONE BUT MARRI was asleep when Mote arrived at the Mousehole, the partially collapsed basement they'd claimed near their favorite entrance to the 'Guts. It had only been meant as a temporary space while they gathered supplies, but Marri feared those plans were ruined forever now.

The money they'd made from Bry's excursion had been enough for the medicine Mote had needed. Marri had sent him, newly recovered, into that entrance to spy on what was going on down there. When the proper knock came and Marri opened the door, the look on the tiny boy's face had told her everything.

"Lancers," Mote recounted. "A lot of them. I hid where I could hear everything. You were right. They're sealing the tunnels."

It all made Marri sick at heart. This much attention on Underguts made their scavenging impossible. Even when the lancers were gone, the blocks would remain. And little mice that could not produce treasures could not trade for food, much less build themselves a long-term home.

There's no choice, she thought. *I'll have to set them to searching the surface, stealing if they have to.* Most surface salvage went to bigger, stronger people than Marri and her mice. The sickness in her heart swelled. Stealing was so much more dangerous than Underguts had ever been until that awful night.

Marri swore Mote to secrecy. The others didn't need to know how bad things were yet. It wouldn't hold for long. Mice loved to squeak.

With Mote bedded down in his ratty blanket in the corner, Marri allowed herself the indulgence of quiet tears. It wasn't fair. Underguts had been perfect. Once their new lair had been built, they'd have been set for years, long enough to let the older ones get big enough to defend the littler ones while competing on the surface.

It was all this new woman's fault. Mote had confirmed what the rumors on the street had told Marri. Undel was gone. "Retired," they said. The street had been buzzing with the big speech at which Undel and the archon, the boss of bosses, would appear. And the rumors had been right about what would happen there.

Marri had worshiped Undel for years, praying to him but never once laying eyes on him. Now she never would. It didn't matter. He was out, and the new woman was in. Delgassi, Mote said, but her name didn't matter either. She was just a monster stealing food out of the mouths of starving mice.

Marri had to think. She'd survived years of thieving when it was her alone, but she was fast and quiet and smart. She loved her mice, but none of them could match her. They could never hope to keep the rest fed without access to the 'Guts. But Marri would abandon none of her mice.

I'll die first.

She realized she'd been pacing, expertly threading her way through the sleeping mounds of her mice, only when she found herself paused in front of the supply corner. Stacks of sheet metal, welding torches, and more. Nearly everything they'd needed for real security.

Whenever Marri found herself with extra after feeding and clothing and caring for everyone, she added to the pile. There was a place in the 'Guts she'd found. With some considerable work, it could have been fortified and transformed into their permanent lair. No run-down Mousehole, but an underground fortress, centrally located beneath the city yet hard to find. Secure against revenants and lancers alike.

Now she felt the dream tumbling down, as ruined as the building they cowered beneath. It felt like a foolish thing to have ever dreamed at all.

Turning away and stepping silently back through her sleeping mice to her own pallet, Marri felt like she was drowning. How? How could she ensure her little children, her little mice, were fed and warm and safe?

She woke from nodding off some time later, the idea having occurred to her in that between-space, not awake and not asleep. It was crazy. Impossible. But she knew, even as she thought of objection after objection, that she had to try.

CHAPTER 10

IT TOOK Stefani Palmieri several long, deep breaths to steady her nerves after the buzzer on her apartment door rang. No one had been to visit since Ella's birth. By rights, she shouldn't be letting *anyone* in here. Ella should be under observation at Gene Sequencing. Or worse.

No. Stefani would not leave her baby with those ghouls, no matter what the law said. And this wasn't just anyone coming to visit them. It was Iaz.

As a last-ditch effort to find calm, Stefani checked the baby monitor feed on her handheld. Her perfect little angel lay in her crib, fitfully sleeping, and Stefani's heart was fit to burst. Thus fortified, she opened the door, trying to feel the delight she displayed at seeing Iaz standing there beaming back with an equally false smile.

"Come in and make yourself at home, stranger," Stefani said by way of greeting. She fought down a wince at her use of the word stranger. It felt a little like too much truth. *So much has happened to me that I haven't told her.* And, judging by the other woman's face, the reverse was true as well.

"Have we really not seen each other since before the election?" Iaz asked. "This has to be some kind of record for us."

"Well," Stefani said, desperately trying to keep the tone light, "between birth and political ascendancy, I guess a lot has happened." She gestured them both into the living room, palatial by most standards, the soothing, blue-gray walls decorated tastefully with angular artwork.

Iaz's smile slipped as she walked, and her eyes reminded Stefani of lancer combat veterans. She winced inwardly at the thought of actually saying as much, though. Iaz had been drummed out of the service far too quickly to have developed any stare so haunted.

"So, how is the new job treating you?" Stefani asked. It was the most casual way she could think of to ask the question.

"It certainly isn't boring," Iaz said. "Even coming to visit you means I have to convince my security detail to wait outside the building. But some things are worth the trouble." The wink was almost the old Iaz, but Stefani was suddenly too anxious to enjoy it. Her palms went sweaty at Iaz's mention of security, and she fought to hide her sudden discomfiture. *Easy, Palmieri. They're protecting your friend. They aren't here for you.*

"Well, I appreciate the effort even more then," Stefani said.

"Gods below, Steffi, am I going to have to go in there and bring the baby out myself? I want to meet her!"

In a better, fairer world, Stefani would have felt a rush of love for her friend. Not because Iaz was actually enthusiastic to meet Ella—Stefani knew Iaz's feelings about children too well for that—but because Iaz had worked so hard to manufacture the enthusiasm she knew Stefani would want her to feel.

But this wasn't a good or fair world.

Iaz did not miss the new shine in Stefani's eyes. "Steffi, what's wrong? What did I say?"

"I don't think meeting her would be such a good idea right now."

Iaz took a seat in her usual easy chair, worn and threadbare. Stefani only kept the ratty thing around because Iaz preferred it. "Tell me what's happened," she said. For the first time since she arrived, all Iaz's focus seemed directed at something other than whatever was haunting her eyes.

Stefani burst into tears at the intense worry of that regard.

"The birth was easy, the standard Caesarean," Stefani said once she'd calmed down enough to speak. It was hard to explain what she'd done. The risk of ostracism from her one real friend outside of work was only part of her anxiety. Prison or exile were very real possibilities. And she'd lose Ella. But this was *Iaz*. If there was anyone left alive on this world she would trust with this story, it was her. So, voice shaking, Stefani explained.

When she'd finished, she braced herself. The burden, carried alone since that wonderful, horrible night, had ground Stefani down in all the days since. Speaking it aloud lifted the burden from her, but with this newfound sense of freedom came the altogether less pleasant sense that anything could happen.

"Gods below, Steffi," Iaz said. "What's happening to her? Is she all right? Why couldn't the autodoc make sense of it?"

No condemnation. No censure. Just concern over her daughter's well-being. Stefani could have wept again, this time with relief. But there was little to be relieved about.

"As near as I can tell," she said, "her body is in a constant state of Mutagen Prime acceleration, which her immune system in turn keeps in check. I've never seen it before, not even in the historical records, though those are so spotty pre-Loss, that's not saying much. Could have happened two dozen times in the past hundred years for all I know."

"Seems to me she got very lucky in her choice of mom," Iaz said. "I'd trust you to figure it out over anyone."

"That's not what you should be saying," Stefani insisted. Grateful though she was, she couldn't leave it alone. She had to drive the point home, make absolutely certain Iaz understood the magnitude of Stefani's crime. "You're a magistrate, a former police chief. I broke the law in as profound a way as you can in this city. I should be locked up."

"That's why I like you, Steffi," Iaz said with a crooked smile. "You'd make such a terrible lawyer."

"And my baby should be in the hands of Gene Sequencing," Stefani pressed.

At mention of the organization, Iaz's entire demeanor changed. A scowl darkened her face. A sneer bordering a snarl bared her teeth. "If your choice was between your own care and Gene Sequencing, you did the right thing," Iaz said. "I don't care what the law says."

Stefani was taken aback. Hating Gene Sequencing with such passion had always been *her* thing, a toxic mix of long-stifled research and, if she were being totally honest, wounded pride over her rejected application years ago. Stefani had never seen such loathing for it in her friend.

Her intuition stirred. "Iaz, what's happened?"

This time it was Iaz's turn to focus wet eyes on her friend. Her lip lost its snarl, quivering instead. "Damon," she began, then had to collect herself, grimacing in pain. "Damon's dead, Steffi. He killed himself. The night of the election."

"That ... can't be," Stefani said, mind blank with shock. "I'd have heard." Stefani checked the obituaries every day. Between Mutagen Prime and the revenants beyond the walls, Coldgarden was a dangerous city. The ubiquitous joke was that no one would live in Coldgarden if they had literally any other choice.

"I couldn't let that happen, Steffi," Iaz said, and something awful and alien lay behind her eyes now, something Stefani had never seen. This wasn't some weird attempt at humor. Iaz was deadly serious.

Stefani surged forward and embraced Iaz, remembering only too late her friend was not one for physical affection.

But Iaz grabbed hold of Stefani as if she was the last rope up to a planetary evacuation that would never come. Stefani hugged back every bit as hard, and the two friends stood in each other's arms, each mourning their shared pain, loss, and fear.

At last, the full weight of what Iaz had said struck home, and

Stefani pulled away reluctantly, gripping Iaz by the shoulders and looking her square in the eyes.

"What do you mean you couldn't let that happen? Iaz, how did you cover up a death in this city?"

Iaz tried to put glib confidence into her words, but she looked hunted. "People die unrecorded and unremarked all the time in this city," she said. "In the streets. In the tunnels. Occasionally even outside the walls. I have a friend back at the precinct who owed me a favor. Damon didn't have any family, and we were his only friends. So I made sure he went unrecorded and unremarked on."

Stefani put her hand to her mouth in shock. "But Iaz, why? Surely ... surely not for the election?"

"No," Iaz said, and the naked ferocity of the word perversely calmed Stefani. "It's because of what I found in his room when he died. Steffi, I said he'd hanged himself, but I honestly can't be sure."

"Was there a note?"

"Of a sort. He'd painted a message on the wall. Or someone had. I think it was him, though, because it was a repeat of something odd he'd said to me the night before, after we dropped you off."

Gods below, that was the last time I saw him alive. I'll never see him again. The full weight of it threatened to hit Stefani then, but she beat it back into submission. "What did he say?"

"It's complicated." Iaz explained the message and the comment it repeated, and by the end, Stefani could not help but regard her with some concern.

"Iaz, you realize how unlikely that sounds, don't you?" *Please say you do.*

"There was a gun too, Steffi."

"A *gun?* Where on Earth did he—"

"I don't know," Iaz said. "The ID had been tampered with to make it untraceable. But it was arranged. Stood up on the butt of the grip, with the barrel propped against my face in the picture I'd given him."

"I—what?" Stefani didn't know where to begin.

"It was like a threat, Steffi. Like someone had killed him and left the gun there for me to get the message. Whoever was in there left the door open, like it was inviting me in."

It was too much to process.

"So, what are you saying, exactly? Someone killed him, but staged it to look like a suicide with a note painted on the wall, but also left you a warning in the form of this gun? How does any of that make sense?"

"I don't know what I think, Steffi. But can you at least agree I was right not to draw a lot of attention to his death? And before you answer, remember where he'd been the day before."

And Stefani did remember, of course. She'd made something of a scene about it at the bar. "Gene Sequencing."

"Treatment for his depression," Iaz said flatly. "Which had been under control and yet was suddenly concerning enough to bump him from his trusted doctor straight to a GS stooge's office. Someone named Kyne Libretta."

Stefani opened her mouth, not sure what she was going to say, closed it, then opened it again. "I'll admit that there's a lot that needs to be answered there." She regarded Iaz's stare. "And that I don't blame you for not trusting the traditional parties that would look for answers."

Credit to Iaz, she knew exactly when to deploy the ace up her sleeve. "Which brings me to the other reason I came," Iaz said, and at least she had the grace to look apologetic. "Sorry. But I have a very curious meeting scheduled for tomorrow. At my office in Watchfire Hall. A meeting I want you to attend also."

"What?" Stefani said, brought up short. "Iaz, no. I'm not going to be any good to you in a political meeting."

"This isn't any kind of meeting I would normally have, Steffi," Iaz said. "I was contacted by Rieve Revolos. Now I'm only vaguely familiar with that name—"

"*Rieve Revolos* contacted you?" Stefani asked, dumbfounded.

"—But I see it means something to you, at least," Iaz said, looking smug.

"Talk about infamous," Stefani said, whistling through her teeth. "She's the most notorious data-jockey outside of Gene Sequencing. Meaning the most notorious one we mortals are allowed to know about. She's a total recluse, but rumor says she's worked for most of the magistrates at one point or another, digging up secrets about one another."

There was a sudden shine in Iaz's eyes that had nothing to do with tears and that Stefani didn't like at all.

"Is there any service she could offer us that you can think of? Because it seems to me that both of us need information that only Gene Sequencing is likely to possess."

"What? No, Iaz. There's a reason she can't stick with one employer for very long. Somehow or other, she always pisses them off and they cut her loose. Her reputation is so bad, Magistrate Graysteel won't even touch her. She's never worked for Illuminance."

"Well based on the message she sent me yesterday," Iaz said, "she seems to think she can help us. And based on that message and what you just told me, I'm not sure we can afford to just brush her off."

Stefani's blood chilled to jelly. "Maybe you'd better read me that message."

Iaz was already bringing it up on her handheld.

"'To the esteemed Iazmaena Delgassi, Magistrate of Greater Watchfire, it has come to my attention that you and your friend, Dr. Stefani Palmieri of Illuminance's Mutagen Prime Grand Project, may have urgent need of my skillset. I would like very much to meet with both of you, because I feel quite strongly that we can help one another.' And then she provides the day and time," Iaz said, "which is the meeting I mentioned tomorrow. I didn't want to say yes without talking to you and figuring out what any of this could have to do with you, but now that you've told me about Ella, I think I know. Can it really be a coincidence that a woman with a reputation as a master of uncovering secrets would ask to speak to the pair of us?"

Stefani could not tell if Iaz was more nervous or hopeful. It was not a conflict she felt at all herself. What she mainly felt was a strong, instinctual urge to run, take Ella and hide somewhere they could never be found. Because she agreed with Iaz. This woman knew something. It was too much of a coincidence otherwise.

"It doesn't read like a threat," Iaz said placatingly.

"And yet you still think it might be," Stefani countered.

"Of course," Iaz said. "But, Steffi, what if she really could help? I have a few of my own leads I still plan to exhaust with regard to Damon and what GS had to do with his death, but what if we could slip the info straight from the source?"

"It's dangerous," Stefani said. "Insanely dangerous."

Iaz didn't say anything, merely gave Stefani a look. It was a look Stefani knew well in the face of her childhood friend. A look that said, without words, *and we haven't already crossed that threshold?*

"All right, Iaz," Stefani said, her voice hoarse. "Tell me when to be there."

CHAPTER 11

THE FOLLOWING day passed in a haze of nerves and excitement for Iaz. Six o'clock was the appointed time for the meeting. After normal working hours, when the building would be much emptier than during the workday. Not so late that it would appear suspicious if anyone was paying attention.

Or maybe Rieve Revolos hadn't thought in those terms at all. Steffi hadn't provided as much concrete information about the woman or her habits as Iaz had hoped.

By the time her last official meeting approached its appointed cut-off time with no sign of wrapping up, Iaz was entirely checked out. She could only hope the union representative of the vertical hydroponics district of Bounty Ward didn't notice. Forty agonizing minutes later, Johe showed out the overeager young man, who looked ready to talk Iaz's ear off for another hour.

When Johe returned, and with only fifteen minutes until six, Iaz opened her mouth to tell him to go home and enjoy his evening, only to freeze at the sight of who entered the office behind him.

"The archon is here to see you, Magistrate Delgassi," Johe said. He mouthed, *I'm sorry, he just barged in,* silently when he was certain his back was to the archon.

Iaz shut her mouth with an audible click, trying not to glance at the digital time readout on her wall. She knew what time it was. It was too fucking late for the archon to be dropping by with her maybe-illicit meeting a quarter-hour away.

"Please sit down, Excellency," Iaz said, the very picture of gracious decorum. "To what do I owe this unexpected pleasure?"

Teodori took the seat so offered, nearly masking his distaste at the office's and the building's and likely the whole ward's level of disrepair.

We can't all be suspiciously wealthy, Archon.

"Magistrate Delgassi," Teodori said by way of greeting. Then he paused, glancing pointedly at Johe.

"Go home and enjoy your evening, Johe," Iaz said, smiling a brittle smile.

"Yes, ma'am. I'll see you tomorrow," Johe said. He lingered just a moment too long before exiting, closing the door behind him.

"Very attentive lad," the archon said, turning his full attention to Iaz at last.

"A bit overly protective," Iaz said. "But there are worse sins."

"Just a guess," Teodori said, "but he was the author of that little press release that so neatly tied my hands?"

Iaz allowed herself a genuine moment of obvious exasperation, though she disliked mirroring the man's feelings in any way. "Yes. He didn't care for Undel's condescension toward me during the meeting, and he felt the record should be set publicly straight."

"Word of advice," Teodori said. "Cut him loose. Now, not later. A true believer like that is unlikely to be discouraged by slaps on the wrist. Eventually, he'll do you real harm. And by you, I of course mean me."

"What can I do for you, Archon Teodori?" *Get him straight to the point.* Iaz could feel the seconds ticking by. She had no idea if the archon knew Rieve Revolos on sight, but it wasn't a risk she was willing to take.

"I want to clear some of the air between us, Magistrate Delgassi."

56

If her dismissal of his suggestion had offended him, the man gave no sign.

"I'm not going to apologize for what happened to Undel." Iaz guessed the first thing she could think of that might bear a resemblance to his point. "The man was an incompetent, and if he'd listened to me—"

"Listened to the youngest ever magistrate, less than a week into her first term of office? Come now. Be fair. Even a brilliant politician would take a little time to consider such a suggestion, and Undel was never brilliant."

"But Undel is not what I'm referring to, Magistrate Delgassi. I wanted to be sure you understood the root of my opposition to your victory and your presence on this council."

"It wouldn't have anything to do with maintaining a majority voting bloc, would it?" Iaz knew she should stop, that the fastest way to be rid of the man was to agree with him, to show humility and bow before his wisdom and experience.

He was a handsome man, with a sculpted face, strong jaw, and aquiline nose. His iron-gray hair had a natural waviness. It was the face of a consummate politician, and no doubt it worked wonders for him. Yet every time Iaz looked at him, all she could see was Damon's swollen, slack face turning slowly at the end of a creaking rope.

Teodori smiled as though her answer was not only what he was expecting, but what he was hoping for. "Gods below, Delgassi, you can't afford to be so *predictable*. You saw how neatly I reversed that Undel situation. You think a voting bloc is something I lose sleep over?" He laughed at what must have been a comical expression on her face. "Oh, delightful," he said. "It seems that I won my bet with myself."

"What," Iaz began, still trying to process the information, "do you mean?"

"I will admit I did worry about your election to Indred's post. I worried you would let our past issues cloud your judgement, maybe even drive you to be insubordinate. Beyond the mouthiness, I mean," he said, waving a dismissive hand.

"But I'm beginning to think that you aren't insubordinate so much as cripplingly ignorant. It's quite all right. The latter is always preferable to the former. And some knowledge isn't meant to be known." His steel gray eyes glittered malignantly.

"Alternatively," the archon continued, "some knowledge should be revealed in its due time. I think you should know why I washed you out of the lancers all those years ago."

Iaz did not trust herself to speak.

"All good lancers must contain the seeds of true leadership," he said. "It's a basic sign of intelligence. The ones that don't possess it die quickly. A dead lancer is a failed lancer. And as it turns out, there are only two types of people fit to lead: those smart enough to know their limits and those tough enough not to have any."

He paused, as though savoring the words to come and the tension that hung thick and humming between them.

"I washed you out because I could see right away that you were neither."

Iaz flinched physically at the casual cruelty of his words.

"So in truth," the archon finished, each word ringing like the blow of a hammer, "I did you a favor. I looked at you and saw a dead lancer, a *failure*, in your future along that path you had chosen. And I chose to spare your life. Let me do so again and restate to you a message of extreme import: ignorance is always preferable to insubordination."

His face was an unreadable mask. His slight smile could have meant anything at all.

Iaz had feared she would have to find a way to force him out of her office early lest he run into people he shouldn't. Yet with more than five minutes to spare, Archon Teodori rose from his chair, nodded in acknowledgement, and walked out of her office; leaving Iaz wordless and desperate for a drink in his wake.

CHAPTER 12

TO MARRI'S EYE, Watchfire Hall looked out of place with its surroundings. It was a very old-fashioned building made of real stone, not something mixed and fabbed and layered like the rest of the city. Unlike grander buildings in the older parts, no columns fronted its face, but a modest dome capped the roof. There was a block at the corner larger than the rest. It read 2070 in deeply carved and weathered numerals, but Marri was unsure of what that meant precisely. But the details of the building's past and its construction didn't matter. What mattered was the woman inside it.

Delgassi.

The building was guarded, as she'd feared it would be. A pair of lancers stood at attention, one to either side of the large double doors leading into the lobby. Despite Marri's disguise, this did make her job of sneaking in a little bit harder. Fortunately, no one had noticed her yet. Marri would not be a little kid much longer, but as long as she was, she had a child's aura of "not dangerous." Before she'd begun plundering Underguts, that aura had helped Marri pick a lot of pockets.

However, sneaking into guarded bosses' buildings broke every rule she had. But somehow, she had to find a way to plead her case to this woman who held their fate in her fist. If Delgassi was going to replace Undel, she had to understand why that man had never allowed the tunnels to be sealed off.

Marri watched with envy as a short, dowdy woman walked right up to the door, showed the guards her credentials, and was ushered easily inside. Most of the people Marri had seen had been leaving, not entering, including a man she thought was the biggest of bosses, the archon, several minutes before. It was getting on toward evening, so people were probably going home.

Right now, the best plan Marri had going was to wait for Delgassi to leave the building and approach her then, in the street. The question was how many guards would she have, and could Marri get any words out before she got clobbered by an overzealous lancer? It was a bad plan, but she'd laid awake most of the previous night, wracking her brain for something better, and gotten nowhere.

By the time she saw the shadow falling over her, it was nearly too late to run. Marri got started anyway, and only the tone of the woman's voice made her pause.

"Are you all right?"

"Fine," Marri said, still not entirely sure why she'd stopped running. She couldn't bring herself to make eye contact, her gaze instead darting toward potential escape routes as she remained steadfastly out of arm's reach. She defaulted to her prepared lie. "I'm supposed to pick up a package from Magistrate Delgassi and deliver it across the city, but the guards wouldn't let me in."

"You're a courier?" the woman asked, eyebrow raised. That told Marri her lie had been seen through. But the woman seemed intent on humoring her. "Well, we can't have that package late. I'm heading into the building for a meeting myself. Why don't I say you're with me and then you shouldn't have a problem getting in?"

Familiar suspicion and foreign hope warred within Marri. She was getting what she wanted but too easily. She rose up on the balls of her feet, a hair's breadth from bolting.

"Were you a courier for Magistrate Undel too?" the woman

asked. Her voice was gentle, as though she were handling a fragile, precious thing. The use of Undel's name startled Marri out of her flight, and she struggled to keep her sudden storm of emotion from showing.

"No," she found herself saying. "But we prayed to him sometimes."

"You ... prayed to him?"

"Forget I said that," Marri said, feeling stupid and angry at the tears she had to scrub away with quick brutality. Something occurred to her then, an explanation for why she suddenly couldn't trust her tongue, and her mouth ran away with her thoughts yet again. "You remind me of someone, and for a second I ..." At last, she reigned herself in. "Forget it."

"What's your name?" the woman asked.

Marri regarded the woman for a long time, the woman that so reminded her of her mother. "Marri," she said at last. She meant it as a challenge, a dare.

"Well, Marri, my name is Stefani. I happen to be a little late for my meeting with the magistrate right now. Why don't you come in with me, and you can wait in the lobby, and I'll make sure after our meeting is over that you have a chance to speak with her."

"You'd really do that?" Marri said, still suspicious, but wanting to believe so badly.

"Promise," Stefani said, smiling.

Stefani meant it to be comforting, Marri was sure. But a horrible resignation settled upon her, like the warm, sickly weight of nausea. It was the certainty that this would go as wrong as everything else had. But she had to play it out, because she had no other choice.

"All right," Marri said with a sigh.

CHAPTER 13

TEODORI HAD GIVEN Iaz five minutes before her next appointment. It might have been enough for the drink she badly needed, but Rieve Revolos arrived early.

There was no Johe to show her in, but Iaz's first impression of the woman was she didn't wait to be shown in anywhere she felt she had a right to be.

Short and unflatteringly outfitted, Revolos swept into the office as if she owned the place, scanned it floor to ceiling with scowling eyes, then deposited herself in the guest chair.

"Have a seat," Iaz said dryly.

"Mmm," Rieve Revolos grunted. She swept the room again with her eyes. "This place is too easy to bug. We'll have to find you something better." She pulled a device out of her pocket and examined it briefly. "Nothing yet, but it won't be long now. Particularly if you're getting visits from the archon already."

"I'm Iazmaena Delgassi," Iaz said. Refusing to be swept away by the woman's storm surge, she doggedly stuck out her hand, leaving it in space until Revolos took it and gave it a single pump. "Magistrate of Greater Watchfire. How are you?"

Revolos blinked once as she retracted her hand. "You need to start taking my visits more seriously."

"I think it remains to be seen if there's going to be more than one," Iaz said.

The other woman rolled her eyes. "Where's Palmieri? I told you this concerns her too."

"Well," Iaz said, not bothering to conceal her annoyance as it shifted to her friend, "she said she would be here."

"I don't want to have to explain myself twice," Revolos said. She rose and turned, ready to go. "Maybe I'll call again once the pair of you have gotten your act together."

Iaz felt a surprising flutter of panic at the transparent threat. "Steffi will be here. It's tough to expect a new mother to stick to a rigid schedule."

"I suppose so," Revolos said grudgingly, pausing in her departure. "Especially in her case."

Panic had faded, replaced by a coldness that startled Iaz even more. "What's that supposed to mean?"

Revolos regarded her levelly. "Well, either she's told you, so you already know, or she hasn't, so you'll find out if she ever arrives."

"Assuming the 'she' you are talking about is me, I've arrived," Steffi said, blowing in as fast as Revolos had. "And I'd love to know why my ears are burning." She very pointedly shut the door, glancing out through the narrowing crack as though checking to see if anyone was listening in. It closed with the same squeal it always did, another reminder of the ramshackle nature of everything in Watchfire, even its seat of government.

"I'm not so sure you would," Iaz said darkly.

"Oh, you very much would," Rieve Revolos said. "Better to hear it from me now than from Gene Sequencing later."

"Hear what?" Steffi asked, and Iaz heard her inner chill echoed in the other woman's voice.

"Look at you both," Revolos said. "Wound up so tight. That's good, because your lives are a pair of ticking time bombs."

Iaz exchanged a glance with Steffi and was alarmed by what she saw there. By the way Steffi was looking back at Iaz, she felt the same way.

Revolos apparently tired of waiting for them to admit their sins. She pointed a laconic finger at Iaz. "Covering up the 'suicide' of your boyfriend," she said, and before Iaz could react, she shifted the finger to Steffi. "Covering up the abnormal Mutagen Prime readings of your baby."

Steffi's hand clenched around something in her coat pocket, and with a spike of alarm, Iaz wondered what the other woman had brought to this meeting, what contingency she was considering.

"Okay," Iaz said, hands raised placatingly as much for Steffi as for Rieve. "You're going to need to tell us where you got that information."

"Hate to tell you," Rieve said, "but the information is out there for anyone who bothers to look. You're just fortunate I'm the only one who has so far. But that won't last forever. Unless I help you, of course."

"Unless you help us," Iaz said flatly. "And I'm guessing that means you'd want something in return." Her mind spun, trying to find how to balance the equation of getting in trouble over Damon versus getting in trouble over whatever Rieve wished of them.

"I'm not the charitable type, it's true," Rieve said by way of reply. "But what I ask isn't too onerous. I just need some equipment to crack encryption. On this," she said, removing a carefully wrapped object from her coat pocket with greater reverence than she had shown anything else thus far.

She pulled back the corners of the microfiber cloth, delicately uncovering the object. What lay in the palm of her hand was a small, thin box about the size and shape of a deck of cards. It was matte black and made of an old-style plastic not seen much anymore.

"What is it?" Steffi asked, sounding curious despite herself.

"A data drive," Rieve said, real awe in her voice. "Extremely old."

"You mean ..." Steffi began.

"Yes. Pre-Loss."

"Where on Earth did you find it?"

"The tunnels," Rieve said. "There are still very old things down there if you know where to look. Layers below where any of the scavengers venture." This latter was said with profound disdain. "But I've never found anything like this. The encryption has a timestamp that confirms it is pre-Loss, and a drive like this could hold exabytes of storage."

"If it's that old," Iaz said, "surely our technology can decrypt it."

"Surely," Rieve said. "But I need the equipment to make that happen."

"I thought you did this sort of work all the time," Iaz said, filled with sudden suspicion. "You're telling me you don't have this sort of equipment lying around your apartment?"

"Private citizens aren't permitted to have that sort of equipment lying around," Rieve said. "I did have it at home, yes, but it was carted off at the termination of my latest contract. With Undel," she added pointedly with a look at Iaz.

"Well, if you were contracted with him," Iaz said, "it should be easy enough to reinitialize it now that I'm in charge. If, that is, you can actually help us in the way you claim."

But Rieve was shaking her head.

"It wasn't a *legitimate* contract," she said with another eye roll. "I can get the equipment myself, and it will come with the kind of powerful pattern-matching software this requires. What I need are funds, and maybe some official-looking signatures and top cover."

"And in exchange for all this?" Iaz prompted.

"I protect you both from discovery. And," she added with a lifted eyebrow, "I help you extract the answers you both want from Gene Sequencing." She finished with fists on hips, clearly convinced she had delivered the *coup de grace*.

"And I suppose if we don't help you," Steffi said, voice thick with emotion, "you'll make sure we're caught?"

"I certainly won't *try*, but if it comes down to selling your secrets or starving to death on the streets ..." She shrugged. "What would you do?" She pitched the question to Iaz, the former Watchfire orphan, who'd spent actual time living on the street. "Look," Rieve said, suddenly awkward, "I'm not intending this to be extortion. I can help you. You can help me. You're already breaking the law, both of you. All I want to know is a little information about the past."

Iaz didn't believe that last part for a second, but short of killing the woman, she didn't see a good way of silencing her that wouldn't result in inquiries. And she was fresh out of favors for disposing of bodies. She also didn't like the way her own thoughts were trending or the look on Steffi's face.

"Prove you are who you say you are. Rieve Revolos is a recluse," she said to a startled Iaz, as if trying to justify the demand. "I have no idea what she looks like any more than you do."

Rieve rolled her eyes in that way she had, then pulled out her handheld and triggered its holo projector. Her ID holo leaped into the air, alternating green, blue, and violet in color. It displayed a rotating three-dimensional representation of her head along with the necessary watermarks, constantly shifting geometries that stood as proof against forgery.

Steffi studied the ID holo for several intense seconds, then turned her burning stare on Iaz. "She's Rieve Revolos. And if anybody can do what she claims, she can. I think we have to help her."

Iaz was surprised at the relief she felt. She wouldn't have to learn what she—or Steffi—was capable of. Despite this sense of relief, she shook at a sudden chill, as though a brief draft had passed through the office.

"All right," she said, turning back to Rieve. "You have a deal. What is this equipment and where do you need it delivered?"

"Not at my apartment," Rieve said with a sharp shake of her head. "And certainly not here," she said, glancing around. Her gaze froze as it fell on the door. Iaz followed it. Steffi gasped.

A young girl stood inside the door. The closed door. The door that had never once opened or closed silently in all the time Iaz had been there. She was just shy of her teenage years, tawny skinned with a bird's nest of hair and lean in a way that made her look more hungry than gawky. Her heated gaze was leveled at Iaz.

"I know a place," she said.

"Marri," Steffi said, all her prior emotion fizzling in amused puzzlement, "how did you get in here?"

Iaz turned to her. "You know this girl?"

"Well, we just met," Steffi said, wincing at how defensive she sounded.

"How much did she hear?" Rieve said in a low hiss.

"Enough to know you need a place to hide," Marri said. "I'm really good at hiding." She raised one eyebrow as if to ask, *Do I really need to spell it out for you?*

"All right, enough," Iaz said.

"How much did she—"

"I said enough, Rieve," Iaz said, deploying her cop voice and rolling over the little woman with sheer authority. Rieve's cheek twitched once, and she didn't take her eyes off Marri but went silent. "Now," Iaz said, turning back to Steffi. "Who is this girl, and how did she get in here?"

"Well," Steffi said with a familiar twinkle in her eye, "her name is Marri, and you just heard me ask her the same thing."

Iaz felt her cheek twitch in the exact same way as Rieve's had. Steffi never could help tweaking Iaz when she was annoyed.

"I can speak for myself," Marri said, jutting out her chin defiantly. Her burning eyes were for Iaz alone, and they held the magistrate's gaze. "I have little mice who depend on me, and then you kicked out Undel and closed the tunnels, and now we can't trade for food!" Her hands were balled into fists at the end of too-thin arms. She was literally shaking with anger.

"Mice?" Steffi asked, bewildered.

"She means gutter mice," Iaz said, her annoyance melting away into sudden sympathy. "Not far off from the kind of life I almost ended up in."

Marri looked horrified by this notion.

"You'd raid the tunnels for scrap and sell it or trade it," Iaz said, squatting down so that she had to look up into Marri's face. "And now you can't because of the attack."

"Because of *you!*" the girl hissed.

The accusation from this child that might have been Iaz bit deep. "I suppose that's true, when it comes down to it. I'm glad you came to see me, Marri. I'll make sure none of your little mice go hungry."

"I don't want handouts," Marri said fiercely. "Handouts can be taken away anytime. I want to trade. You open the tunnels, and I show you the hiding place you need." She looked as pained by this last statement as Iaz had felt at the girl's accusation.

"I can't open the tunnels, Marri," Iaz said firmly. "We can't let the revenants have an easy way into the city. Even if I did, your mice wouldn't be safe down there. They'd be the first to get eaten up."

Steffi frowned, and Iaz could visualize her thought process perfectly, how this wasn't appropriate imagery to use when talking to a child. But for the first time, Marri looked pensive instead of angry.

"You're going to have to open them back up, at least a little," she said, sounding as if she was musing aloud.

"Oh really? Why is that?"

But Iaz's curiosity was apparently too much. The girl looked suddenly guarded again. "The hiding place is in the tunnels," she said with extreme reluctance. "So you can't avoid them forever."

Iaz surprised herself by feeling disappointed. What, after all, had she expected a homeless child barely getting by to hand her? "I think we can do better than a hiding place in the tunnels," Iaz said, straightening back up.

"You can't," Marri said. "It was going to be our hideout once we'd gotten enough to build it up. You can make it so nobody can get to it but from the surface directly! It's big enough for all the equipment you were talking about." Rieve's eyes narrowed dangerously at this, but Marri took no notice. "No one will find you there. You can do whatever you want, whether or not it's ... legal." She nearly trailed off without finishing, perhaps finally realizing just what she was admitting.

Steffi was trying to catch Iaz's eye, but Iaz held Marri's gaze. "Tell me, Marri, just how did you open that door without making any noise? It's the loudest door I've ever heard."

Marri shrugged. "Just slow, I guess."

"How old are you?"

"Twelve."

"Twelve. And you're living on the streets with a bunch of other children. How many?"

Marri again looked suspicious, but she answered. "Fifteen."

"Fifteen," Iaz said, stifling a growing sense of wonder. "What's the most you've ever had?"

"Fifteen," Marri said, looking confused herself now.

"But how many have you lost to the orphanage minders?" The minders scoured the city's slums, looking for uncared for children to put a roof over their heads.

"None," Marri said, her look pure contempt. "They don't even know we exist." Her face went a little pale.

Before today, Iaz realized. *This is her one enormous gamble to secure access to the tunnels again. She's risking her freedom.* It spoke plaintively to her desperation, and Iaz's heart went out to her. Even now, years later, she could recall the gnawing desperation that never strayed far.

"Are all the children your age?"

"No. I'm the oldest."

"How long have you been an orphan?"

Marri shrugged. "Don't really remember."

"What did you do before the other children came along?"

That guarded look again, but an angry, defiant one wiped it away. If she was going down, she was going down swinging. Iaz felt a swell of affection for the girl. *As brave as I was at that age.*

"I stole," she said.

"And how many times were you caught?" Iaz pressed.

Again, that utter contempt. "I was never even seen."

"Please!" Rieve scoffed. "We have no way of verifying any of this."

"The fact that she's standing here, much less that she got into the room without us noticing her, is at least some proof," Iaz said.

Rieve looked like she wanted to say more but didn't, for which Iaz was profoundly grateful. If they were going to be forced to work with this woman, the less she spoke, the better.

Iaz turned back to Marri. "I can't open the tunnels to you. Not permanently. But if you show us your hiding place and promise not to tell anyone else about it, I'll find you work that will earn you the supplies you need."

"Iaz," Steffi said, scandalized. "You're talking about putting children to work."

Iaz threw Steffi an annoyed *I'll explain this to you later* look but did not respond. In truth, she'd explained to Steffi before that only an orphan could possibly understand what being an orphan really meant in this city. It was as gentle a way as possible of pointing out Steffi's own life of privilege.

"What kind of work?" Marri asked.

"Finding some information," Iaz said. "Some information people might not want to be found." Then she took Marri by the shoulders, bent forward, and whispered an address to Marri. "It's my apartment. Come by in an hour, and I'll explain." She needed time with the girl where Steffi couldn't mother the whole relationship into nonexistence. Marri looked at Iaz with a sudden consideration and slowly nodded.

Beside them, Steffi frowned.

"I think that's enough excitement for one day," Iaz said, straightening abruptly. She gathered each of her three guests up in her gaze, one by one, making sure her expression brooked no argument. "I'll be in touch."

CHAPTER 14

IAZ all but fell through the door to her apartment, desperate for that long-deferred drink while she had a moment to herself. "What a long *fucking* day," she breathed out in a gust, speaking to her ghosts. The meeting with the archon would have been enough on its own, but to follow it up with another meeting where every participant—invited or otherwise—had been intent on annoying, scolding, or challenging her.

And I'm not done yet.

Despite this knowledge, Iaz poured herself a tall glass from a bottle she scarcely glanced at and couldn't have read in the dark even if she had. Some sort of whiskey, anyway.

Rieve's bombshells had been exactly as bad as Iaz had feared, which meant ulcer-worthy. The thread of hope the woman dangled wasn't nearly enough to restore even a ghost of comfort, and she suspected Steffi felt the same. At least she would if she could be pulled away from scolding Iaz over her temporary—temporary!—solution for Marri and her mice.

Steffi didn't understand, which wasn't her fault. The orphanage system had worked out in Iaz's favor, but there were plenty whom it hadn't helped at all. She understood how Marri felt and, more importantly, how she would behave if Iaz mishandled this. As for the girl's hiding place, it sounded like, at worst, a potential weak point in their Underguts fortifications worth knowing about.

Iaz took a seat, willing herself to achieve some level of calm, trying to force the anxiety away. It shouldn't be long now. Not if the girl was half as clever as she seemed.

Drink in hand already half-gone, she walked over to her home terminal and brought up her messages. As expected, nothing new from Dr. Kasmus. Damon's former doctor had apparently not had second thoughts about Iaz's requests for his patient information.

It was not the refusal itself that had been surprising, though. A non-relation attempting to acquire medical records, even with the next-of-kin designation Damon had granted Iaz, was never going to be simple in this city. But that hadn't been the objection. At least, not longer than Iaz's first attempt.

Gaze losing focus for a few moments as the drink hit, Iaz keyed a replay of the last message from the good doctor.

"Magistrate Delgassi, I wish you would understand what kind of a position these messages put me in, you a high-ranking official and all. You already know all I can tell you. I'm not any happier that his case was acquired by Gene Sequencing than you are, or than he is. I can't tell you how worried I am about his well-being that you are the one contacting me instead of him!"

As ever, Iaz couldn't suppress a wince at this.

"Now, please," Kasmus went on, her face on the screen haggard, her eyes wide, "please do not contact me about this again. But do have Damon contact me when he's willing. I understand he's angry, but please help him understand that I had no choice. I can't help you, but if he asks me, I can at least make some official inquiries."

The message ended there. No point trying to fake contact from Damon somehow. The woman's guard would be up.

"Who was that?" Marri asked from behind Iaz.

Despite expecting this very thing, Iaz jumped, nearly sloshing the remains of her drink over the side of the glass.

"You left the e-lock off but locked the normal lock," Marri said by way of apology. "So I thought it was a test." She shrugged.

"It was," Iaz said hoarsely. "But gods below, girl, you're quiet." Electronic locks, biometrically sealed, were on another level, but clearly Marri was quite adept at picking physical ones.

"Why did you tell me to come here?" Marri asked.

"So we could talk in private," Iaz said. "Some things are easier to talk about without Steffi. Definitely without Rieve."

"I like Steffi," Marri said. She frowned. "I don't like Rieve."

"I gather no one does," Iaz said.

She had to handle this carefully. The girl had probably revealed more than she'd meant to in her gambit earlier, but she'd studiously avoided disclosing where the children were staying thus far. If Iaz even hinted that she meant to dump the lot of them into the orphanage system, that would be the last she'd see of Marri.

The orphanages were the end goal, of course. But it had to be taken slowly, and their progress in the system would be something Iaz would monitor carefully to make sure they didn't fall through any cracks. In fact, the more she thought about it, the more a whole initiative seemed to form in her mind. She was the former orphan now turned magistrate. Who better to tackle the inadequacies of that system than her?

"I wanted to talk about our deal," Iaz said. "The one you proposed earlier. The location of your secret spot for—"

"For opening the tunnels back up," Marri said, as if by interjecting with her wish quickly enough, she could make it so.

Iaz shook her head. "Not possible. But we can pay you for the information. Money or vouchers for the shelters, whichever you'd prefer."

"You said you had more work after," Marri said.

It occurred to Iaz they were having this conversation in pitch dark aside from the wan light of her terminal interface. She palmed the nearest lamp on, giving the apartment an inadequate glow, but it was something.

"I do. Can I get you anything to drink?" Iaz asked, gesturing with her glass. "Not this, obviously," she added hastily. "Something to eat?"

Marri shook her head slowly.

"You can sit down at least."

Marri scanned the room methodically, then shook her head again. Iaz's cop intuition understood. *Nothing close enough to the exit. She doesn't want to be trapped here.*

"You said you had more work," Marri said again. Something about the way she said it made Iaz think she was counting the number of times she had to prompt. If the number got too high ...

"How good would you be at following someone so they did not realize they were being followed?"

Marri gestured at the screen, where the frozen image of Dr. Kasmus still lingered, her eyes pinched with worry. "Her?"

"Yes," Iaz said reluctantly, suddenly feeling as though she were turning something loose on Kasmus. "I'm going to call her and tell her something that she's not going to like, and I have a feeling after she hears this, she's either going to call someone or rush off to meet them in person."

"And you want me to follow her if she leaves?"

"Yes."

"What if she doesn't?"

"Then it won't be your problem, but I'll still consider it work you did for me."

"And after that?"

"If you do well, I'll have other work," Iaz said. She had no idea what that would be, but she would figure something out.

Marri's eyes narrowed once again. Her suspicion didn't surprise Iaz. It would have been more surprising if she'd been trusting. Even the girl agreeing to Iaz's invitation had been noteworthy. *Truly desperate. I can't take advantage of that.*

But isn't that exactly what I'm doing?

"All right," Marri said at last. "When?"

"Tomorrow," Iaz said, hoping fervently she could rope in Rieve's help by then as well. This would be a test of both of her new allies' willingness to stick their necks out a bit on something that shouldn't be terribly dire. "Seven o'clock. You have a way to keep track of the time?"

Marri rolled her eyes, then began an intense study of Kasmus's face on the screen. Memorizing it, Iaz realized. "Where will she be, this woman?"

Alone at last, all she'd wanted all day.

The bottle diminished at a rate she ought to have considered alarming, but Iaz couldn't bring herself to care. A numbing of emotion was precisely the reason she kept returning to the thing, a little less steady each time. She didn't drink straight from the bottle because demarcating it by individual glasses would allow her to control her portions.

At least that was what she told herself.

Damon appeared as he often did, an imagined wraith on the matching couch opposite hers, as though he could not bear to share space with her.

"You're finally doing it," he said. "I thought you'd forgotten me."

In the beginning of these exchanges, she'd tried arguing. She'd protested that the safety of the city's living people had to take priority. Once she'd said it wasn't like he was going anywhere, and the guilt of that statement had made her drink until she blacked out. This time, she said nothing.

Already the apparition's throat was darkening, its eyes beginning to bulge. But, perhaps in protest to her unwillingness to engage, the horrid changes didn't stop there. As a glaze of death settled over its eyes, the entire head began to shrivel, as though boneless and being dried into jerky. It waved around like a stuck-out tongue before sinking away and vanishing into a formless darkness pooled at its base.

Iaz nearly threw up every bit of liquor in her stomach. *I need to eat something.* She didn't, though.

It was a while longer, and several more of those carefully measured glasses, before the Ali apparition made its scheduled visit, emerging from her former bedroom at the end of the short hallway. Before Damon, Ali was the guiltiest she'd ever felt. A ward police chief who couldn't even protect her own roommate.

By this time, Iaz's self-control had slipped. "I miss you," she said in a guilty whisper. Even more than Damon, Ali had always been able to make Iaz smile. She'd been a friend who could absorb Iaz's every complaint, from age-old ones about her hatred of Teodori to whatever grim story *du jour* she brought home from the precinct.

The apparition did not possess the power to talk, sadly. This Ali said nothing, simply stood there, staring at Iaz through her curtain of crimson hair that so many men, and not a few women, had found irresistible. Her stillness was utter, and Iaz found herself unable to look away.

At some point in the midst of this faceoff, Iaz passed out from exhaustion and drink.

CHAPTER 15

"I STILL DON'T SEE why this is necessary," Rieve said testily over the earbud comm unit she'd given Iaz. "I'm going to get you the access you need. You don't need to bother with this Kasmus woman."

Maybe. But I don't want to just turn that process over to a black box like you, Iaz responded in her head. This was indeed a test, and Iaz was learning that Rieve liked to have control of things she was involved in. Not a surprise, not even a flaw necessarily, but useful to know.

"Humor me," Iaz said.

Which was funny because she was the one doing the humoring, forced into wearing essentially a second handheld. This one was, Rieve claimed, proof against any electronic intrusion so long as Iaz ensured no one else could put hands on it. The imposition annoyed Iaz, but she was beginning to see just how much of a politician's life was spent humoring people.

She was humoring Marri too. The girl had straight-up refused to carry any form of handheld, likely assuming she could be tracked. Hopefully, she was in place. She'd said she would be. It was nearly time.

"Are we ready?" Iaz asked again.

"Yes!" Rieve snapped. "But don't expect miracles with so little notice. This tap is sloppy, which means I can't leave it long or the systems will detect it and trace it back to me. So whatever she has to say better happen quickly."

"Stand by," Iaz said.

Neurotically, she checked again to ensure everyone, even Johe, had gone. It wasn't that she didn't trust Johe, but she worried that his over-eagerness might lead him to do something rash, the way he had with the Undel press release. It galled her that the archon might have gotten to her with his warning.

Returning to her desk, Iaz dialed Kasmus from her terminal line. She hoped to surprise the woman at her dinner, knock her off-balance. It rang twice before Kasmus answered, looking equal parts worried and annoyed, her tightly curled bun of graying hair in disarray as though she'd run to answer.

"Magistrate, please," she said, desperate and weary. "This is well past the point of being inappropriate. I understand you have strong feelings in this matter, but I can't help you. I would very much prefer to speak to Damon on this matter. Is he with you now?"

"You're never speaking to him again if I have my say," Iaz said. She allowed real menace into her voice for the first time during these calls, and Kasmus heard it, flinching back from the screen in surprise. "Not after what you did, handing him over to those ghouls like that."

Her heart thudded in her chest, but for the first time that day, Iaz no longer felt the sludgy effects of the hangover she'd so thoroughly earned. Implicitly threatening a woman apparently had a cleansing effect on her system.

"Magistrate, I've told you repeatedly I did not refer Damon to Gene Sequencing by choice." Her voice cracked a little, as though unwilling to speak the words Iaz had driven her to speak. "I would *never* refer a patient to Gene Sequencing by choice. You must believe me!"

"I don't need to believe anything, doctor," Iaz said acidly. Then she went for the jugular, because the longer this went on, the harder it would be to maintain the façade. "Now, I'm going to ask you one final time. What did Gene Sequencing do to Damon to make him this way?"

"I ... what? What way? This is the first you've mentioned his condition, despite me asking every ti—"

"Paranoid!" Iaz roared. She hadn't meant to say that, hadn't meant to provide any information at all. But more of the truth kept spilling out. "Delusional!" She only just stopped herself from adding the rest. *Suicidal! Potentially homicidal! Rein it in, before you wreck everything.*

"No, that doesn't sound at all like his profile." Iaz watched Kasmus wrestle with her morals versus the edict she labored under. She watched a decision get made. "I need to see him. Let me speak with him, Iazmaena. Now." The good doctor's voice was iron.

"I've already told you that's not happening," Iaz said. "Tell me what they've done to him. Final warning."

"I *can't*, because I don't know!"

"Well then," Iaz said, "I'd advise you tread very carefully going forward."

Dr. Kasmus's eyes widened again, but Iaz did not give her the chance to reply.

"Don't attempt to relay this conversation to Gene Sequencing. I may be just a magistrate, but I am not without resources, doctor, and I will be keeping a very close eye on your communications."

Without waiting for a reply, Iaz killed the connection. Immediately, Rieve's voice was in her ear.

"This will get you nothing and is a foolish risk besides."

"Because she doesn't know anything?" It was Iaz's honest take on the situation, but the woman was her only lead into the hermetically sealed vault of Gene Sequencing beyond the name of Damon's doctor there, Kyne Libretta, that appeared on no search she was capable of running. Likely Damon hadn't even been supposed to reveal the name to Iaz. If it was even a real name.

"Of course she knows something! But she's smart enough not to keep it in any of her records that are connected to a network, which means she's smart enough to know who the real threat to her is, a threat you just unnecessarily risked antagonizing."

But Iaz was still caught on the earlier part of that statement. "Have you been through her files already?"

"Obviously," Rieve said with a snort. "I was trying to find out what she knew beforehand to spare us this idiocy."

"Careful," Iaz said. "Remember whom you're talking to."

"Who *I'm* talking to? I offered you a better path than this."

"One I'm not convinced you can deliver on," Iaz said. She wanted to stop but couldn't. It was so hard now to master her temper. "It occurs to me that if you were really capable of defeating Gene Sequencing's security, you'd probably be working there, not scraping the bottom of Watchfire's barrel. But if you hold up your end of the bargain tonight, you'll get your chance." As an attempt at an olive branch, Iaz had heard better. Rieve apparently agreed.

"Oh, I'll keep my end," Rieve said. "You'll get your information, and it won't be like this."

"Just tell me if Kasmus contacts anyone."

"She won't be contacting anyone for a while," Rieve said.

"What? What do you mean?"

"I mean she's already left her offices," Rieve said. "Security cameras confirm. Without her handheld, which is still pinging in her office. She must have believed you about monitoring her communications. Wherever she's headed, she's likely headed there for an old-fashioned sort of conversation." Iaz could hear the other woman sneer. "I suppose it's up to the gutter rat now."

CHAPTER 16

MARRI WATCHED as the brain doctor, hunched and harried-looking, exited her ramshackle office building. She was already scanning around her as she did so, wide-eyed and frightened. Whatever the magistrate had said, it had put a scare in the woman. Made things more difficult but not impossible.

Even frightened people didn't see children as a threat.

Marri matched her pace to the doctor's, moving in and out of clumps of people as they presented themselves, all in ways that seemed as though the natural flow of human traffic forced her to. It was like slipping back into an old, well-fitting shoe. Though she was a lot taller now than she had been the last time she'd been following likely marks, so she kept catching herself getting too close with her longer stride.

The doctor worked in Inkwell and moved toward the city center, though she steered well clear of any of the border crossings to the other wards. That was good. Marri knew ways to avoid border crossings, but there was always a chance they'd have closed up one of the paths she hadn't tried in a while.

A few times Marri had to duck out of sight when the doctor got particularly paranoid, but as afraid as the woman was, she wasn't actually watching very carefully. At last, they arrived at a featureless building of old, crumbling brick with no sign or other labels to tell what was inside. There was only a blank door with no knob or handle or access panel to break up the pattern of bricks, its gray paint peeling from door and frame both.

Marri had kept a mental map of their route here so she could explain where they'd gone, but she worried that wasn't going to be good enough to earn the mice their next round of food. As she heard the doctor knock timidly on the door, Marri decided she needed to get closer and see who answered.

The only problem was any good vantage point would be in full view of whoever answered the door. *I'm not going to recognize whoever answers anyway.* Maybe listening was more important than seeing. Marri crept as close as possible to the corner of the alley, a view of the scene tantalizingly close.

The door opened.

"What are you doing here?" The voice was male, harsh in a quiet, angry way. "What's the emergency?"

"It's the magistrate. Iazmaena Delgassi," the doctor said, sounding miserable. "She keeps insisting on getting more information about—"

"What did you tell her?"

"What? Nothing! What could I tell her?"

"Then this wasn't an emergency. What are you doing here?"

"She's a powerful woman making threats! She said she was going to monitor my communications. What am I supposed to do about that?"

"She's bluffing. Continue not telling her anything. Don't contact us again. Most especially, don't come here."

"So you're just leaving me to fend for myself?"

There was a soft curse. Marri couldn't stand the suspense any longer. She had to risk getting a look at this man. As slowly as she could, she peeked past the alley's edge with a single eye.

The man wore a dapper suit. That was the first thing Marri

noticed, how glossy and expensive it looked. Tall and long-limbed, with broad shoulders, he was the kind of man she would never have tried to rob in the past. Some people were so rich or so physically scary they wouldn't hesitate to get violent if they caught you. This man seemed like both. He was glancing down as if in thought. As he brought his head up to respond, Marri was already slipping back into hiding.

"All right. I'll bring your concerns up the chain. I'll be in touch, but you are to continue to say nothing."

The door shut before the doctor could respond. Her shoulders sagged, but Marri didn't see what she was so upset about. Sure, the dapper man she'd asked for help had been mean and scary, but he'd listened in the end. Things could have gone much worse.

But that was not Marri's concern. She'd done what Magistrate Delgassi had asked of her, and it was time to disappear before she was noticed.

CHAPTER 17

STANDING at the bottom of a spiral staircase in the center of a roughly octagonal space five times the size of her apartment, Stefani was having second thoughts about what she was agreeing to do.

The garish lighting of their handheld spotlights added to the effect, throwing harsh shadows across the collapsed walls of the space and the irregular tunnels of Underguts beyond. Stefani had never set foot in Underguts in her life. Iaz and Lance Commander Yonnel certainly seemed fine with it, but Stefani couldn't forget this was where revenants came from when they came at all.

Rieve Revolos looked like she'd swallowed a toad, which went some way toward helping Stefani's mood. She kept directing bug-eyed stares at Marri, whose own face vacillated between satisfied and miserable. Stefani assumed this meant Rieve was also satisfied.

"Can the walls be reinforced?" Iaz asked Karl Yonnel.

"Rebuilt, you mean?" Karl asked, the picture of equanimity. Stefani found his unflappability calming in this place. "Certainly, if a group of children planned to do it, I think we can manage." This earned him a scowl from Marri, but he wasn't facing her to see it.

"You don't have any concerns about building in a place like this?"

Stefani asked, unable to help herself. This earned *her* a scowl from Iaz.

"Concerns?" Karl replied. "I have infinite concerns about building a lab inside Underguts. But it is true that we could almost certainly reinforce a small space like this to the point where it would be safe, particularly if the only way in is from above. I'll need to get a look at the surrounding area before we can make the determination that your questionably legal lab can be constructed here."

Stefani looked at Iaz sharply, catching her eye and asking an unspoken question in regard to Lance Commander Yonnel.

"It's all right, Steffi," Iaz said, looking much too eager for Stefani's liking. "I've briefed him on the situation." Though her expression said she hadn't told him everything. Stefani's secret would be safe. "If I can't trust my new lance commander, I'm not going to last long in this job."

"The way I see it," the lance commander said, "what does or doesn't happen in a lab which may or may not exist is above my pay grade. As long as you aren't keeping revenants as pets, my concern is for your safety. Besides, the magistrate has promised to demote me back to my old rank if I keep her secrets long enough," the older man said, gruffly but with a twinkle in his eyes and a grin from under his salt and pepper mustache.

It made Stefani smile despite her bundle of nerves.

"I'm afraid the lance commander is proving a great deal more gullible than I thought when I first promoted him," Iaz said without a trace of irony.

"Whatever it takes to lose your confidence, ma'am."

Iaz's eye-roll would have been worthy of Rieve.

"You're free to follow me as I explore," Karl said, "but please stay behind me until I verify there is no hostile presence."

Methodically, he paced the outline of the ruined space, shining his lamp into every darkened nook. Despite his words, the others waited at the bottom of the ladder down which they'd arrived.

"Well," the lancer said at last, "the chamber itself looks sound enough. As you said, magistrate, we'll need rebuilding and reinforcement of all walls."

"Whatever you think is best, Lance Commander," Iaz said magnanimously. "I want this facility both operational and secure. Whatever it takes to do those things, do it."

"First," Karl said, "I'll want to confer with the good doctor and Ms. Revolos here, as to how much space they expect to take up. I wouldn't want to encroach too much upon their floor space with my security precautions."

Again that twinkle in his eye. Stefani found herself enjoying that twinkle. *Get hold of yourself*, she thought, scandalized. *He's old enough to be your father.* Well, perhaps not *that* old.

"I'm sure we can come to an agreement that will satisfy both of our needs." *Gods below, could that have sounded any more suggestive?*

Iaz glanced at her with an arched eyebrow the lance commander could not see. Then she stepped in to the rescue. "I've taken the liberty of getting a list from both of them." She handed a small data drive to Karl. "You'll find it all here."

"I'm just an old soldier, ma'am," Karl said, taking the drive and plugging it into his handheld. "I'm not going to know the names of all these fancy—"

"Each is listed with the amount of floorspace it will take up, Lance Commander," Iaz said.

"That will do nicely, then," Karl said, smiling beneath his mustache.

Stefani wished she could feel as confident. She gestured Iaz over as Karl thumbed through the list then led her pointedly away from Rieve, who seemed keen to listen in. The impossible woman stubbornly followed until Iaz held up a warding hand.

"You really want to do this here?" Stefani asked Iaz once they had a modicum of privacy. "I have to admit, if I'd known this was what you meant when you convinced me to sign up for ..."

"Stefani," Iaz said, and Stefani didn't miss the use of her full name. It wasn't a weapon Iaz deployed often. "You know how important what we are doing is. You know that the worst possible thing would be for this to be found out before we are done. As aggravating as Rieve is, if she's as much a genius with networks as you claim, she can find a way into Gene Sequencing's systems, which should help both of us get the answers we need. This place is the price for her help, true. But you also need a place where you can study what's happening to Ella on your own without being discovered."

"I know why I'm here," Stefani said. "I just ..." She found she had to fight back tears all of a sudden. "I never expected to have to do this kind of thing."

"I know," Iaz said, her gaze downcast. "It's crazy the things we'll do for the ones we love."

And Stefani was reminded forcefully in that moment the person *she* loved could still be saved. Iaz was having to settle for justice.

Or revenge.

"All right," Stefani said. "If this is what it's going to take, I'll do it."

Iaz took Stefani's hands in her own, which in itself was a rare physical gesture. Her eyes shone. "Thank you for trusting me."

Stefani smiled back as bravely as she could, only to feel eyes on her. She shifted her gaze to find Rieve approaching once more. Stefani gritted her teeth.

"I'd better go confirm with Karl that he understands my notes," she said. "I think someone else wants a word with you."

CHAPTER 18

"IS THERE AN ISSUE?" Iaz asked when Rieve had taken Stefani's place. Even her brief time spent with the woman told Iaz she was always going to be difficult, but now she seemed positively sullen. *And here I thought Marri was the child.* Mindful of this, Iaz spoke again, trying to modulate her tone. "I'd have thought you'd be happy about us lucking into this space. It should have room for everything you need, plus all of Steffi's equipment."

The latter would take up far more room in truth. Rieve's requests were comparatively minor in terms of floor space requirements.

"It's perfect," Rieve said, her words sounding like teeth being pulled. "But I'm concerned how much faith you are showing in our ... youngest member." That last carried entire worlds of emotion, far more than Iaz had the energy to parse. But the general idea was crystal clear. *Marri shouldn't be involved in this.*

It was a sentiment Iaz understood, but her hands were tied. She couldn't abandon Marri and her unseen charges before ensuring they found proper homes. And if Marri could prove useful while Iaz was helping them, what was the harm in taking some benefit from the setup?

"You let me worry about her," Iaz said. Perhaps she should have explained herself more, but Marri's struggle mirrored Iaz's own too closely to speak of easily.

"At least stop her from trying to gather any more intelligence," Rieve said. Then she launched into her familiar refrain. "Yesterday was sloppy and risky. And what did it get you?"

Iaz was mindful of Marri not far away, lifting away a rusted plate of metal, likely looking for stray salvage even now. She replied in a low voice. "She proved she can follow orders and follow someone undetected."

"What *useful intel* did you get?"

"As to that, not much," Iaz admitted, lowering her voice further still.

"Exactly," Rieve said, not lowering her voice at all. "Which is why you need to leave that to me from now on." And unexpectedly, she reached into her pocket and pulled out a small data drive similar to the one Iaz had just handed Karl. "Since I apparently need to prove this to you, here. I scraped it up last night from a ... certain organization. I can't be sure how long the vulnerability will last, particularly now that I've been prodding it, but I think you'll find the information interesting."

Iaz took the drive, trying not to display too much eagerness. It took all her willpower to keep from plugging it in right there. Suddenly she needed a drink very badly.

"Thank you," she said to Rieve. "I'll give it my full attention."

Seemingly satisfied, Rieve nodded gruffly and moved off. Marri was standing right behind where she'd been. Fearing they'd been overheard, Iaz began mentally preparing ways to soften the impact of what she'd said. But Marri began speaking at once.

"What else do you need me to do? I'm ready."

"You've done enough right now," Iaz said automatically. All she wanted to do was have a moment to herself to examine that drive, but she had a strong sense she couldn't leave Marri to her own devices for too long or she'd disappear. "I have a busy few days coming up, but come see me in a week, and I'll have more for you."

By then, she planned to have the bones of her orphan initiative drawn up. Perhaps Marri could factor into that in some way that wouldn't offend her pride or arouse her suspicions.

Marri blinked then nodded. She wandered off to listen to Stefani and Karl, the former talking animatedly about equipment space requirements.

Left to her own devices at last, Iaz plugged the drive into her handheld and began to read the single file that appeared there. A grimace formed on her face that she could not smooth away as her stomach roiled.

Above it all was a thudding anger like the unrepentant beat of a malign heart.

CHAPTER 19

THEY PASSED beyond the edge of the tree line just as the clouds moved in to obscure the moon. It was just as the skies had spoken.

The city loomed, glowing, bristling upward from the dark cocoon encircling it. The wall. No cover on approach. But the sky gave darkness, the moon hid. Freed of the forest, they could cover distance with great speed. The group shifted their aspects toward that end. Segmented, scuttling pads for navigating dense growth became longer, loping limbs. Transformed, they moved as one, speeding across the swirling grasses toward their target.

Sounds arose as they moved, borne by wind. Swish of grass. Churn of water. But occasionally, very faint, high-pitched cries and laughter. These drove them, sharpened their focus, whet their hunger for memory. But they must not allow themselves to be distracted this night. They had a very specific purpose, even if they could not remember it yet.

The cool bath of darkness that marked the wall's shadow loomed enough that it cut off their view of the hotly glowing city. At last, they reared up short, the deceptively solid mass of the wall slithering before them. No climbing here. No climbing *anywhere*, except for special times, times which they did not fully understand. But that was all right. They were not here to climb. They were here to under-stand. Now they just had to remember how.

As one, they grew their brains. It cost them muscle and armor. Oxygen flowed into areas that had gone still as death while being preserved for later. Their minds engorged, raisins becoming grapes, a concept they began to understand again.

Only one portion of their original instructions had been held in the tiny living minds during their approach, a command meaning, roughly, *remember to grow brains at the wall*. Large brains consumed so much energy, something they understood at an instinctual level, and so physical strength and endurance came at great mental cost. But here, in the shadow of the objective, they were free to remember.

Dawning awareness also gave rise to more complex emotions, like hate. Hate sharpened the focus even better than memory. New limbs mutated, costing precious energy stores. Ultra-sharp manipulator forelimbs grew into being.

The wall flowed without seeming to. How many times had their kind tried to scale the wall in this state, only to find it responding to them as if it was alive? It grew mushy when they needed leverage, slick when they needed purchase. Their own morphing forms could compensate for a time, but rarely long enough to scale the full height of the wall, leading to many deadly falls in the early days.

The only way to scale the wall was when part of it went dead and dumb, becoming just a wall for a time. This happened, they knew, but they could not know when. Not yet.

They set to work, keenly aware with their sharpened intellects that they faced a limited amount of time until dawn, when the likeli-hood of detection rose greatly. They cut great rents in the wall with claws like razors, slices that the wall immediately began to heal over.

Once they had thought it possible to simply cut a hole in the wall and make it through that way, but even if it had not been able to repair itself, it was only the outer layer. Behind it lay another layer, another wall, flush against this one, a wall that was dumb, inert, and much too strong to tunnel through. It might have been climbable, this inner wall, if they could have removed the outer wall, but there was no way to remove enough.

Working as one, they sliced and pried, cutting additional gouges away from their objective, forcing the wall to waste energy healing injuries that didn't really matter. It was smart, but not as smart as they.

In this way they were able to peel a large chunk of the outer wall free. There was a quiet chitter of triumph as they rolled their prize nicely into a tube-shape.

Then they were gone as quickly as they'd arrived, leaving the gouged-open wall trying desperately to repair itself.

CHAPTER 20

"WHY WOULD THEY DO THIS?" Iaz furrowed her brow as she inspected the damage. "Why come so close and then simply make off with some wall?"

"They might have come intending to burrow through the wall rather than climb it, not realizing there was an impervious section behind the adaptive memory-matter. That's the obvious answer, ma'am, and the obvious answer is usually the best one." Karl looked troubled.

"But not this time," Iaz stated.

"No, ma'am. I don't think so."

On any other day, standing outside the wall would have left Iaz dizzy and giddy all at once. But now her mind buzzed with unspent anger, as it had since the previous day. The words of the file Rieve had given her rolled through her head, an endless boulder crushing every other thought.

It had been just a fragment of a larger file and read like a brief summary of someone's tasking to-do list, but it was informative enough to suggest a great deal more lay out there to find.

Blackburne op not producing results at current parameters. Time factor until election critical. Recommend pressure increase and more extreme operational boundaries—any means necessary. Awaiting archonal approval.

-K.L.

Iaz had seen formal missives from Gene Sequencing before, and this had all the watermarks. Even so, it was hard to believe.

Blackburne op. Pressure increase. Any means necessary. Archonal approval. Those initials, K.L. had to be Kyne Libretta, Damon's doctor at Gene Sequencing. And the timestamp had been just a few days before the election.

Iaz shook herself back to the present. *I'm outside the wall, and I need to focus.* She also needed a drink.

An inspection of wall damage by the magistrate of Watchfire was critical for appearances' sake, but Karl had insisted they wait until the sun was just past its peak, fully illuminating the side of the city and the wall, before venturing out.

Thanks to the bright sunlight, Iaz was able to see straight through the wall to the tiered hydroponic fruit and vegetable gardens making up its inner face. Sunlight encouraged the smart wall to render itself transparent for precisely that purpose.

"Why do you think the obvious answer is the wrong one?"

"Ma'am, we know from our monitoring, the revenants come to the wall frequently. They've been at this for years, and no matter what some might say, they aren't stupid. If they don't already know what's behind the memory-matter, I'll eat the business end of my lance."

"So maybe their goal was to see if a section of the wall could be removed?" Iaz looked at him expectantly.

"Maybe," he replied, sounding thoroughly unconvinced.

"Out with it, soldier!"

"If all they wanted was proof it could be done, why carry it off with them?"

"Some kind of trophy? Some kind of rite or a show of dominance? You said they were smart. We have no idea what their society is like, if there even is one."

"There's too much we don't know," he said, tacitly agreeing.

The edges of the wall's wound were already fuzzy as the memory-matter drew on its reserves of raw mass and solar energy to repair itself.

"How long until it's fixed?" Iaz asked.

"End of the day, probably," said Karl. "Plenty of sun to help it along."

"And is there anything else to learn here?" She wanted to be obsessing over the file, not out here for optics' sake. Plus, there was a long list of items for her actual job that needed her attention, particularly with Inkwell Day—and its promise of costing her an entire day's work—fast approaching on the calendar.

"Not that I can see, ma'am. We'll redouble our watches to see if we can catch them at it again. I'm a little surprised we didn't notice them in the act this time. But only a little."

"More sensor issues?" Iaz asked. At his nod, she went on. "Any headway on that?"

"None yet, ma'am. Difficult without specimens to run tests on."

Iaz blew out a frustrated sigh. "All right, then. As much as I enjoy adding to my list of nebulous future worries, unless you can tell me how this represents an urgent crisis, we're done here."

"Not an urgent crisis, ma'am, no. I just don't like it."

"I don't like it either, Lance Commander. But let's not like it from inside the wall."

"Yes, ma'am."

CHAPTER 21

STEFANI HATED every moment of setting up Ella's nook in the Underlab.

She tried telling herself it was a chance to see her daughter most of her waking hours, something she wouldn't have been able to do at her old position. That had been part of Stefani's excuse to a visibly unhappy Magistrate Graysteel as to why she was resigning to work for Iaz as her *science advisor*.

"You're going to miss doing real science," Graysteel had warned.

And Stefani very much feared she was right. As little real science as she'd done when heading up the Grand Project directly under Gene Sequencing's thumb, at least she'd had official sanction.

Down here, she'd spent most of her time making a place for Ella that could be hermetically sealed whenever someone else besides Stefani visited. The fact that her adult company would mostly be Rieve Revolos did not make things easier.

Stefani swore as she pinched her thumb in the process of installing the autodoc arm, but the work gloves she wore took the brunt of it. As badly as sweat was matting her hair and stinging her eyes, she was glad she'd left the memory-matter bubble installation for last. It could filter out everything larger than air, so it should be good enough to prevent any hypermutation spread if the worst should happen. Unless it was air itself that somehow did it. The fact that Stefani didn't know, despite it being her entire—former—job to find out, would never stop galling.

The arm installed, she rose, stretching to work blood back into her legs. She activated the arm with her handheld and put it through a startup test series, one she wouldn't have to monitor. Then she took a break by wandering across the barely finished lab, still sporting that new-lab smell. Everything looked shiny and new, everything that wasn't still in boxes that was. The octagonal space was fully walled-in now, the spiral stairway leading up to the surface hatch the only way in or out. It *felt* secure. Still, the idea of spending most of her waking hours here, splicing together scientific equipment she wasn't allowed access to so she could perform experiments she didn't know how to do, was a bleak one.

It will just be like that at the start. Once everything is operational, I'll feel better about it.

Her eyes drifted to the lance propped in a corner. A *just in case* gift from Karl. The pistol Iaz had found in Damon's apartment lay not far away, as though both Iaz and Karl were not as comfortable setting this lab up in Underguts as they let on.

Stefani liked the gun even less than the lance. At least the lance hadn't been involved in anything unsavory. Resolved, she wandered over and stuffed it deep into the back of a drawer she then locked.

"You look upset," Marri said.

Stefani whirled, startled. "Marri! You scared me."

"Sorry."

"What are you doing here?" That sounded either guilty or accusatory, so Stefani appended. "Is everything all right?"

"I have something I have to do, but I wanted to stop by here first. Just ... just to see what it looked like all finished." She couldn't smooth her face fast enough to hide her stricken expression as her eyes took in the totally transformed space.

This was going to be her safe place, Stefani reminded herself. "Well, stay as long as you like. I'd enjoy the company."

"No, I have to go," Marri said, turning back to the ladder leading up to the hatch. Stefani's heart sank a little, but she didn't press.

"At least go get yourself something good to eat at Inkwell Day," Stefani called after the girl's retreating form.

Alone again, Stefani turned back to check the autodoc test sequence. Barely ten percent complete. Sighing to herself, she examined the paltry list of samples she'd managed to smuggle out of her old office on her way out. Gene Sequencing had allowed her a pathetically small amount of pathetically inadequate revenant samples. Since she'd been a Grand Project of one, it had been child's play to alter the records so these would never be missed, however much guilt the action had wrung out of her. Still, each was a duplicate. She wouldn't steal anything from her eventual successor that couldn't be replaced.

Not that it would have mattered. The samples were all thumbnail-sized portions of revenant, each so thoroughly irradiated to prevent activating dormant hypermutation that the post-mortem process itself had halted. What remained had been freeze-dried and hermetically sealed for indefinite preservation. All in all, these bits of revenant, already killed once and destroyed twice beyond that, were unlikely to tell her anything she didn't already know.

Still, there were one or two gray-market pieces of equipment in the new lab she'd never have been permitted to have in the old. It couldn't hurt to see if anything new might be revealed when viewed by fresh electronic eyes.

CHAPTER 22

DESPITE GATHERING CLOUDS THREATENING RAIN, throngs of people crowded the Inkwell streets, laughing, selling, and celebrating. Even Marri had difficulty threading through them. There were booths and banners everywhere. It was a madhouse, the kind of place her younger self would have been drawn to like maggots to meat.

Marri didn't normally steal food these days, but these were uncertain times, and there were just so many people, all waving skewers of vat meats and awkwardly carrying too many miniature bags of candied fruits, that she couldn't resist. In short order, she'd gorged herself on a tangy skewer and a sweet skewer and stuffed a bag of fruit in each pocket to take back to the Mouse Hole.

But she couldn't lose focus. The Dapper Man had a much easier time with the crowds than she did. Twice as tall as she was and three times as broad, people tended to move aside whenever they caught sight of him. It was his suit as much as his size, Marri decided. It made him look too impressive and important to block.

Magistrate Delgassi had not asked Marri to follow this man. But she hadn't forbidden it either. Most importantly, she'd told Rieve that Marri had not provided any useful information after following the brain doctor, and she had yet to give Marri another task. Magistrate

Delgassi was a busy woman. Marri knew that if she didn't remain useful, she'd quickly be forgotten. And if she was forgotten, her mice couldn't eat.

Sometimes keeping her mice safe meant taking a little initiative.

It had been easy enough to find him again. The brain doctor hadn't called ahead to arrange a meeting, which meant the man had just been there already. Which meant he must spend a lot of time there. So Marri had just shown up and waited, reasoning he had to leave sometime.

She'd been right.

The longer the man went without buying anything or looking happy in any way, the more excited Marri got. He wasn't here for the celebration. He was up to something. He pushed toward a main pedestrian thoroughfare, finally encountering some resistance as he reached a point where police and lancers were shouting to clear the road.

Marri tensed in the way she always did when faced with any kind of armed authority figure, but they didn't sound angry or scared, just that they needed to clear space for something passing through. She took a risk and squeezed up close to the road herself, staying out of the man's eyeline but trying to get close enough to see what he was craning his neck to look for. It didn't take long.

A procession of people, men and women in suits surrounded by lancers, walked down the street, pausing frequently to shake the hands of the onlookers crowding for a glimpse. With a little gasp of surprise, Marri saw the archon, the biggest of big bosses, in that group. He was grinning broadly, stopping to shake nearly every extended hand he came across.

Then Marri felt an even bigger jolt as she caught sight of Magistrate Delgassi. She didn't look happy to be there at all, and Marri shifted sideways to be out of the woman's eyeline, at least for the moment. Suddenly her unasked-for following of the Dapper Man didn't seem like such a brilliant idea.

But she had no time to worry over being spotted, because as the group of bosses approached their spot in the crowd, the Dapper Man surged forward at the perfect moment to catch the archon's gaze. Marri had a perfectly timed glimpse below another person's upraised arm to see the archon's eyes widen in recognition, then he broke his current handshake and moved on toward the Dapper Man.

This was it. Magistrate Delgassi could see them meeting for herself, so if Marri wanted this adventure to be useful at all, she had to get close enough to hear what was said. She used her size to her advantage, squeezing and elbowing her ungentle way over to the two suited men with clasped hands.

"So good to see you out today, citizen," the archon was saying with a broad, toothy smile. Then he pulled the man closer by their shared grip. Marri forced her way up until she was squeezed against the Dapper Man's back, hoping he'd think it was because of the crowd.

"You come to me here?" The archon sounded angry, his words a hiss delivered through a smile. "Are you insane?"

Even this close, Marri could barely hear over calls of "Archon! Archon!"

"You said no comms until we knew the extent of the breach," the man replied, equally softly. "But Kasmus came to see me, complaining of continuing harassment from you-know-who."

"It's under control," the archon said. "And that's not your concern. Just deal with your target like I ordered you to. I want her taken care of!" Then he raised his voice. "Thank you for your support, sir. And thank you for coming to support the festivities here. It's so important to the ward and the city. It's people like you that make Coldgarden great!" Then he was moving on, and Marri was trying to slide away before the man realized there was no crowd behind him but her.

Too late, he spun on his heel, and though Marri kept clear of his eyeline, she watched his face furrow in confusion as he took in the empty pocket of space that had formed around him and tried to find the person who'd been pressed against his back.

Then one of the onlookers pointed at Marri.

Stupid, stupid, stupid risk! As the man's head turned, Marri hurled herself into the crowd, hoping he hadn't gotten a good look at her.

CHAPTER 23

CHELSEA TOWER in Inkwell showed the artistic influence of its residents in its décor. A rather plain structure consisting of two rectangular wings flanking a central square hub, each fifteen stories tall, the ward's civil servants had done their best to turn it into as much of an art museum as it was a seat of government. The result, paintings and sculptures sealed in transparent cubes with vidscreen displays adorning the walls, was cheerier than any building this old had a right to be.

Ward days were a regular part of the calendar, one per month with all twelve districts being covered over the course of the year. It was a means for the apparatus of government to get face time with the social and cultural leaders of each district, and for its citizens to show off their little slice of the city.

With Rieve's revelation drumming through her mind, it took all of Iaz's will not to rush Teodori the moment she saw him. Former lancer or not, he would not resist long before she beat some answers out of him.

But a heavily attended public celebration was neither the time nor the place. The degree to which her anger, which had morphed from uncertain to murderous, resisted this notion should have frightened her. But anger was its own cure for fright.

So she stood there, with an empty champagne flute and Johe at her elbow, allowing Inkwell Day to roll over her like a tide of deferred satisfaction. She tried to focus on the Underlab, as Steffi had taken to calling their new facility. Construction had been completed in record time, thanks to Karl and his lancers. It helped but only a little.

Noting the attendance of the event with dissatisfaction, Iaz leaned over to Johe and whispered into his ear, "Why am I the only magistrate here who isn't part of the archon's personal cabal?"

This close, it was impossible to miss his flush of embarrassment. "I'm so sorry, ma'am. The message said that attendance for magistrates was mandatory, but I'm beginning to understand that mandatory doesn't always literally mean mandatory."

In other words, she and Johe were the newest at the job, so they hadn't yet learned what events they could beg off successfully.

Johe seemed to read her mood, as he often did. "If you like, ma'am, I could come up with an excuse—"

"No." No matter how good his excuse wound up being, it would invite another dressing-down from Teodori, and Iaz was no longer sure what she'd do if she found herself alone with the archon in a closed room. His words about ignorance being better than insubordination now rang very differently in her ears. "Let's just consider this a lesson learned for next time and endure the day in as much stoic silence as we can manage."

"Yes, ma'am," Johe said, obviously relieved he wouldn't be receiving a dressing-down of his own.

There was no relief for Iaz, though. Even if she could escape this event, she could not escape her thoughts. There was only the ugly truth of what Rieve had shown her. In some way she didn't understand, she'd been targeted by the archon and Gene Sequencing.

And they'd been targeting her *through* Damon.

The tour began, and Iaz followed the group down the art-strewn side hall on autopilot, walking along, dutifully looking at each piece, but trying her best not to see any of them. If being in Inkwell brought up painful memories, seeing the style of art that was in fashion now— and that Damon had very much subscribed to himself—was altogether worse. Each piece, painted, sculpted, or crafted in holography, was a visual triumph depicting the transcendental agony of living in a city constantly besieged by form-shifting monsters.

More than once, Iaz found herself reconsidering Johe's offer. They didn't even need an excuse, only to linger behind and then slip away. Only the presence of their rear lancer guard deterred her. Someone was bound to notice them leaving.

That was when she saw it. The piece of art, oil on canvas, that couldn't be ignored. She knew the style too well. She even remembered him working on the piece.

She didn't know Damon had submitted it for display on Inkwell Day.

Most of Damon's recent pieces had disturbed her, but this one took it to another level. A formless black thing that was meant to be a revenant, oozing menace and death, occupied the entire right side of the canvas. On the left, a screaming human skull split open in a dozen places, and the tar-black paint, flowing from those fissures as well as the eyes and mouth, went on to form the revenant.

As though we're only imagining them. Conjuring them up into reality out of our worst nightmares. The shock of losing him, the pain, hit her as they had that night. Every bit as hard. Any scabbing over of the wound was ripped away in an instant. *He died painting things like this. He died miserable, and I did nothing to help him.*

Her eyes shifted to the archon, who had stopped to regard the painting. *Somehow, he took my chance to help Damon away from me.*

The archon's gaze drifted down to Damon's signature, perfectly legible. If there was any flash of recognition at the name, Iaz couldn't make it out in the man.

"I have to go," she said suddenly, automatically, to Johe. She turned and walked away without full awareness of doing it, her vision constricting down to a dark tunnel. She heard Johe try to follow only to be rebuffed by the two lancers that broke off their security detail.

"Please stay with the group, sir," the taller of the two said. "We'll escort her to the restroom and back."

The restroom. They thought she was going to the restroom. Although, now that she thought about it, the urge to throw up was quite strong. The restroom sounded like a fine idea. Iaz broke into a light jog, the lancers following suit to keep up as she rounded the corner back into the lobby.

The restroom alcove was in sight when the alarm klaxons began blaring.

CHAPTER 24

MARRI WAS NOT USED to being chased, but Dapper Man had, apparently, gotten enough of a look at her. So she ran full tilt, away from the main street, shooting the narrow gaps between people, bouncing off some, bowling over others. One man tried to grab her, maybe seeing the well-dressed man angrily chasing her and then recognizing her for the dirty thief she was.

"I didn't do anything!" she snarled, twisting free of the bystander's grasp. *Not to him anyway.* The man didn't listen. People never listened. Marri ran on.

"Get back here, rat!" the Dapper Man snarled behind her. But he was already breathing heavily. Big and strong as he looked, Marri bet he didn't run very often. Definitely not in an expensive suit.

If I can just get out of sight ...

She rounded a corner, hoping for another one before he could follow. But this street was larger and still crowded. Hard to disappear when anyone who saw her could point the way she'd gone. There was an alley, but a glance told her it was a dead end.

My dead end if he catches me.

She ducked around the larger groups, hoping her small size

would help her hide. She considered crying out for help, but no one would look at their respective clothes and think he was the bad guy.

She would give anything for a tunnel entrance, somewhere she could go to ground and hide. *Iazmaena,* she thought, the new prayer still strange in her mind. *Help me!*

Then Marri saw it, an answer to her prayer just beyond a crowd of laughing people. An old storm sewer entrance. Normally, those were too narrow for all but the smallest of her mice, but this one had been damaged, the composicrete warped as though it had buckled in the sun. She didn't have time to look whether he could see her. It didn't matter. She doubted he could fit even if he did, and she'd just disappear down the tunnels.

It would be like going home.

She hit the ground hard but kept her momentum, ignoring the bark of pain in her hip as she slid feet first into the sewer opening. Landing bent-kneed, Marri's hope withered as she found the way blocked. A circle of new metal with thick welds along the outer edge was in place where there should have been a tunnel.

Already sealed! Marri almost cursed Iazmaena then, but the way her prayer had been answered, she was afraid to. In a rising panic, she pounded the meat of her palm against the metal. It barely event vibrated, and she sagged her head against it in despair. No escape here. And if Dapper Man had seen her come down here, all he'd have to do was wait.

Something tapped hard on the other side of the metal plate. She could barely feel it. A series of taps followed, like someone signaling.

Or like the many bug-legs of a rev testing for weaknesses.

Suddenly all Marri wanted to do was to get out of the sewer.

She stood to her full height, expecting to see an angry pair of ice-blue eyes staring down at her just as jacketed arms reached down to snatch her. But the man wasn't there. She risked a peek out into the street, then flinched back as she saw him. But he wasn't looking at her. He was clearly looking *for* her though, scanning the street. Marri expected him to flag someone down at any moment, asking about the ragged girl who'd run by. Surely someone had seen her.

But he approached no one.

It was then Marri realized maybe this man was as wary of being noticed as she. Now the situation flipped in her mind. He didn't look angry so much as scared.

Scared of me. He doesn't want to be seen or followed. But I saw him. I followed him.

She waited until he gave up the search and started to move off down the street, looking agitated. Then, noises in the tunnels forgotten, Marri emerged from the storm sewer and began to follow him again.

CHAPTER 25

"SENSOR TRIPPED IN INKWELL, LANCE COMMANDER." The young lancer's voice was thready with nervous energy. She looked approximately twelve to Karl's weathered eyes, and based on his struggle to recognize her, this might be her very first duty shift. "Ground level."

"A daytime sighting," Karl muttered. "Was there any word in Watchfire?"

"No, sir, nothing on my boards. Unless I'm doing something wrong."

Suppressing a wince, Karl moved to stand over her shoulder. Likely she was just reading something wrong. Such speculation ceased as soon as he eyed her readout.

"No, Private, that is correct. A daytime sighting, and no word from Watchfire." Two oddities, both falling well into the *extremely unlikely* side of the scale of revenant incursions. "Sound the alert there please. Three block radius. Can you do that?"

"Yes, sir!"

Karl was already bringing up his wrist-mounted comm link, his direct line to dispatch, one eye cocked to her display to make sure she didn't screw it up in her excitement. "This is Lance Commander Yonnel. Get me Lance Captain Drozhke."

Drozhke was the section head of the Inkwell lancer detachment. It was unlikely she'd have many on site, but Watchfire was, by its very encircling nature, only a quick hop away from almost every district.

"Drozhke here. Did you call the alert, sir?"

"I did, Lance Captain. Automated sensors have registered a sighting, independently confirmed by sensors on a different network." Here Karl paused, swore softly under his breath at the second blinking light. "Make that *two* sightings, Drozhke. The second is still within the alert perimeter, but I'm going to widen it anyway. If you don't have people on site, get them there now. Center of the two sightings is ..." He consulted a map, then swore loudly. "It's right on top of the damned VIPs attending Inkwell Day. Get your people there now. Approach via ground, but we're going to need fliers in the air, too. A pair of them. One to deploy lancers, one empty for the VIPs. We've got to contain this now and escort the VIPs to safety."

"Copy, Lance Commander. Any idea how many we need to protect in that group?"

"Negative," Karl said, sourly. "They apparently declined to file an updated travel plan before taking off this morning. The archon will be there, maybe half the rest? They'll have normal protection detail but not much else. I'll raise the detail on comms and update them."

"Copy. Do you have a preferred containment formation?"

"Your discretion, but keep me apprised. Will update when I have a report on the situation locally from the guard detail."

"Copy, Lance Commander. We should be able to clean this up quickly; they won't be hard to spot in the daytime." The confidence of long experience rang in that voice, but also in never having really lost a fight.

"Don't give me assurances, Lance Captain," Karl said not unkindly. "Give me results."

"Yes, sir!"

"Out."

The comm link had no sooner gone dead than the number of automated sightings tripled to six, one falling outside the existing perimeter and two more skirting the edge. Swearing inwardly, Karl contacted dispatch again and demanded immediate connections to the section heads of neighboring wards.

"And get me the guard detail," he added.

CHAPTER 26

IAZ'S two escorts had her by the shoulders, holding her still while they consulted their local squad leader via shoulder-mounted comm units.

"We're moving in your direction," the tinny voice said over the speaker. "Lance Commander confirms all sightings are at ground level. We're doing a rooftop evac. Head there on the double."

"Copy that," the tall lancer said, then turned to Iaz. "Ma'am, if you'll come with us, I'll escort you to safety."

"I'm not going anywhere without my aide," Iaz said. "He's back there, and—"

"They're right behind us, ma'am," the lancer said with calm surety. Iaz wondered if she would have sounded that calm had their roles been reversed. "Right now, the best thing we can do is get far from the ground floor."

Screams echoed from the plaza outside. The plaza full of people and booths, celebrating the bounties of Inkwell.

"We need to help those people."

"Other squads are en route," the lancer said. "Please, ma'am, we need to move now. I'll carry you if I have to. Your safety is my duty."

"What's your name, Lieutenant?"

"Under-Lieutenant, ma'am. And it's Blides."

"Well, Under-Lieutenant Blides, I'll come with you, but if you threaten to carry me again, I'll make sure you regret it."

"Yes, Magistrate Delgassi," he said, with a grin.

His partner, Tiersi, rolled her eyes when she thought Iaz wasn't looking.

"This way," he said, and Iaz followed dutifully, though she couldn't help but throw glances over her shoulder repeatedly, looking for Johe and the others. They should have been right there. Perhaps the archon was putting up as much of a fight as Iaz had.

A mass of people rounded the corner then, ringed by lancers. Johe saw her and waved. Despite the backlighting from the bank of compglass doors leading out into the plaza, she could make out the relieved smile blossoming amid the fright on his face.

Then the light from the doors was cut off, and the revenants boiled in, tearing through stubborn compglass like it was rotted cloth. Each black carapace sported a different, brilliant undertone: ruby and sapphire, emerald and tourmaline. They rose like a surging tide, articulated gemstones of death.

"This way!" Lancer hands were on Iaz's upper arms again, dragging her toward the elevator banks.

"Elevators could be a bad idea," Tiersi said tightly.

"No way we outrun them up fifteen flights of stairs."

"No!" Iaz cried, seeing Johe spin in terror as the segment of lancers nearest the doors opened fire. The deep cracks of their lances reverberated through the space, making ten shots sound like a hundred. But echoes couldn't kill.

An arc of revenants dropped, but they were quickly replaced, those behind using their corpses as springboards from which to leap into the crowd. The lancers that drew first blood were the first to die themselves. More tried to file in and fire, but they were already outnumbered.

The last thing Iaz saw as she was manhandled through elevator doors already sliding shut was Teodori picking up a fallen lancer's weapon and Johe looking in the elevator's direction, his face perversely calm.

"Shit!" Tiersi pounded her gloved fist against the closed door as Blides used his ID chit to execute a priority override on the elevator's programming and punched the button for rooftop. "Shit! Shit! Shit! We just left them there."

"We have our orders," Blides said, but his face was pale and his eyes tight. He glanced at Iaz then quickly away, as if her presence shamed him somehow.

Their radios crackled in unison as the elevator rose. Iaz recognized the voice of the lancer guard's commander, Lance Lieutenant Kaishin. "Requesting command uplink! Where'd these fuckers come from? We need reinforcements, right now!" Several more booms erupted, mostly just static over the comms, and a heartbeat later, the elevator vibrated slightly in the same rhythm as the sound waves caught up.

Someone responded to the distress call, but it was overridden by a new, louder transmission before Iaz could make out any words.

"This is Drozhke. *Stormcrow* and *Stardust* on approach to evac zone. LZ appears clear. Status report on VIP evac, Kaishin. Over."

Whatever Kaishin said was lost in a flood of static.

"These old buildings are shit on reception," Blides said. "Begging your pardon, Magistrate. We put in for improvements, especially in the poor wards. It's bullshit that the tunnels have better comms than the surface."

"Repeat, Kaishin. Did not copy. Over."

This time there was no response. Blides and Tiersi shifted with obvious agitation. Iaz understood. All she could think about was Johe.

"They could be in the other elevator cars," Tiersi said.

"They could," Blides said, sounding more certain. Or perhaps he was a better actor.

The entire car shook then. The light flickered.

The car stopped moving. A sound of something scraping against metal rose up from below, growing closer.

"I told you!" Tiersi said. "We should have taken the—"

With a squeal, the elevator floor bent upward at her feet. Worn carpet split to reveal deformed metal beneath. Something was trying to break through.

"Stand by, *Stardust*," came Drozhke's voice again. "Sighting! Multiple rooftop sightings!"

The floor buckled again, tenting upward near where Iaz stood. This time the metal tore.

"Cover your ears!" Blides shouted, placed the tip of his lance at the gap, and fired.

Iaz mashed her palms over her ears just as the entire elevator rang. The shot widened the hole in the floor, through which claw tips sprouted.

"Door!" Blides ordered. "Door now!" He fired again, disintegrating the claws trying to pry the hole wider still. Tiersi moved toward the door but didn't make it half a step before the weakened metal at her feet split, and a black claw with an emerald sheen lanced upward and skewered her calf.

She howled, dropping her lance to the floor in a thump and collapsing beside it. Iaz moved away from the injury instinctively, knowing what was coming but unable to do anything but watch in horror.

"Do not approach, *Stardust*," Drozhke shouted. "LZ is *very* hot. All right, lancers, we have VIPs to evac and a roof full of revs. We're setting down and carving a path to the elevator banks. That's what lancers do! Pilot, clear me a beachhead!"

The revenant that had speared Tiersi's leg peeled the flooring back further, opening the elevator like a canned ration and climbing halfway inside on two pairs of its legs. Blides took aim, but the creature jerked at the last minute and lost only an already damaged foreleg instead of its life. It lashed out with another limb, but Blides danced out of range, trying to take aim without hitting Tiersi. The injured lancer's howls rose in pitch as she beat the elevator floor with her fists, and Iaz's brain locked onto a single word.

Hypermutation.

Out of that gaping wound, still pouring blood, bone fragments jutted and formed into large, curved spines that cut across one another. Torn muscle stretched and swelled, attached to the bones in random places and snapped them open and shut like scissor blades as Tiersi screamed in agony.

"We have to get out of here!" Iaz said to Blides.

But his eyes were glazed, as though he could see nothing but the revenant struggling to tear its way further into the elevator car despite its wound, which was beginning to wriggle along its edges too. Revenants suffered the same fates as their human victims. In place of its severed limb, this one had sprouted a pair of knob-ended bones lined with what looked like teeth, gleaming with unidentifiable fluid. Its carapace crumbled to dust at the point of the wound, as though the mutation expanded, consuming the chitin as it went.

"Hey!" Iaz said, gripping Blides by the shoulders, spinning him around to look at her. "I'm sorry," Iaz said, "but she's gone!"

"Don't leave me!" Tiersi screamed. Her voice sounded sluggish already, her body's energy reserves burning away in the haywire growth. The exception was her wounded leg. Iaz watched in dry-mouthed horror as the scissor-spines twisted unnaturally around, breaking her remaining leg bones in a series of pops as the spines clawed the elevator carpet in some mindless attempt to drag her body away. Tiersi could only shriek.

"You know she's gone, right?" Iaz asked, voice hoarse.

After several agonizing heartbeats, his face covered with sweat, Blides nodded.

"Door," Iaz said, "before it happens to us too."

Blides moved over and inserted his chit into the controls again. Iaz, with a calm she could not credit, toed the fallen Tiersi's lance close enough to grab. It had no blood on it—a miracle in its own right —and she picked it up, feeling the familiar top-heavy weight of its segmented stack of charges, none expended. Poor Tiersi, who had slipped into unconsciousness as her body killed her while trying to save her, had never even had the chance to fire.

The revenant, losing its own hypermutation fight now, turned its featureless head to Iaz when she leveled the lance at it. Its chitin split, beginning the formation of the toothed flower petals it used for a mouth, but all Iaz could see within, painted there by her mind's eye, was the face of Ali, whom these creatures had dragged off and eaten.

My friend, she thought. "Rot in every hell," she said, blotting out both faces with a pull of the trigger.

It was on the heels of the fresh ringing in her ears that the elevator doors creaked open halfway between the top floor and the roof, and Iaz and her remaining escort were faced with the unfolding horror at the top of Chelsea Tower.

CHAPTER 27

THROUGH THE OPEN DOOR, more like an eye-level window with the car stuck partway, Iaz beheld a wide swathe of carnage. A crescent of armored lancers held a tiny sliver of rooftop clear. They were trying to advance to give the evac flier a chance to land, but the revenants darted forward at irregular intervals and angles, juking in and out of rooftop cover that city ordinance shouldn't have permitted.

Occasionally, a revenant that got too close fell, but Iaz counted more than one lancer corpse already.

"Elevator door!" the comms squawked. "Someone's at the elevator door!"

"Identify yourself," Drozhke's voice demanded. "Over!"

Watching body language, Iaz pegged Drozhke as the lancer occupying the center of the arc. A leader in every sense.

"This is Under-Lieutenant Blides with Magistrate Delgassi. Lance Corporal Tiersi is wounded with terminal hypermutation. Believe all revenants down but elevator car is stuck between floors." Iaz could hear the emotion in his voice, but it held firm. "Over."

"Did you deliver mercy, Under-Lieutenant?" Drozhke asked.

"Not yet," Blides said, his voice finally shaking. But he didn't hesitate. Over Iaz's concerned gasp, he pulled a syringe from his belt, found a patch of bare skin at Tiersi's neck, jammed it in, and depressed the plunger. Her eyes popped open, then glazed over at once. Her legs, trying to walk in impossible ways, stilled.

A lead weight settled in Iaz's stomach. There had been no one to show Ali mercy when she'd been dragged away. She wondered if the revenants killed before they fed.

"Mercy given. Over," Blides said. He choked back a sob.

"Copy. I need you to get the magistrate out, Under-Lieutenant. We're holding this line, but we can't spare anyone to help you. Over."

"Copy," Blides said into the comm unit and seemed to steel himself. "Magistrate, I'm going to lift you out of the elevator now. I'll be right behind you, but don't wait for me. Move immediately and without pausing to the protected area."

Iaz wanted to laugh at the tiny portion of roof that he was calling "protected," but she was afraid it would sound mocking coming out of her mouth.

A trio of revenants rushed the line, right to left in Iaz's view. Two died, but the lancers didn't distribute their crossfire evenly enough. The furthest dodged two shots then grabbed a shrieking lancer and dragged him off at a right angle to its approach. Two of his fellows turned to try to save their friend, but in that moment, two more revenants emerged from cover to the right.

"Hold the line," Drozhke roared, and somehow, they did. The two revenants retreated to cover, their moment lost. But another attack would come.

"Now, Blides," Drozhke barked. "While there's an opening."

"Magistrate, please," he said. And Iaz heard his unspoken plea. *Don't let Tiersi have died for nothing.* Iaz pushed her recovered lance through the gap onto the roof and nodded to Blides. He knelt and made a cup of his hands for her to step into. Business attire was not the most dignified clothing to squeeze through an elevator door in, but with his help, she managed.

Once out in the open, everything seemed much louder and more exposed. Iaz ignored her guard detail's advice and turned to help haul him through as well, only to find him scowling as he pulled his own way up through the narrow slot of an opening.

"Go!" he shouted over another volley of lance discharges.

Iaz went, realizing then how very useless she was in all this. As a cop, she'd always commanded every situation she'd encountered. But human criminals and revenants were a universe apart.

Blides followed more slowly, as though looking for ways in which he could disrupt the next revenant charge. He moved to take cover behind what looked to be literal bags of trash someone had piled atop the roof, black and shiny wherever their crinkles caught the sun. Iaz resolved that if she survived this, she would find the person responsible for this building's revenant compliance and hang them by their toes from Canopy.

She lost herself in this minute fantasy of control, moving on autopilot right up until the refuse pile began to move.

There's one underneath, she thought in dawning horror. Then, as the movement clarified in her vision, she realized her mistake. *The pile is a revenant.*

The bags of trash lost their crinkles, became smooth with an amber sheen as they merged into a single shape. Not just the shape, but the very texture changed as the revenant took form a meter in front of Blides. And suddenly Iaz understood exactly how the creatures had gotten so deep into the city.

Camouflage. But of a type and nature they'd never seen before. Revenants changing forms to suit the situation was nothing new, but Iaz had never heard of anything like this.

If Blides was stunned by his chosen cover becoming his enemy, he did not let it show. He brought up his lance, smoothly lining up a killing shot. But the creature wasn't done changing. The last remnants of false trash bag became a leg that swept Blides's feet out from under him. Another newly formed leg lifted like a scythe of judgment, ready to pronounce sentence.

Iaz changed direction without conscious thought. The smooth, cool hardness of the lance's metal anchored her. "Hey!" she cried, but it was lost in the cacophony of competing screams.

Orders were barked and savage caws of triumph followed pointed cracks ripping the air. There were sounds of agony, too, and weeping. The bestial cries and scrabbling claws were just as loud. The line was collapsing.

The veil of fear adrenaline kept at bay pressed in close upon Iaz now, eager to smother her, but the world slowed as she brought up the lance, not bothering to set her feet.

She pulled the trigger just as the scythe limb began its terminal descent toward Blides.

It was a bad shot, but it severed the limb just as Blides rolled out of reach, trying to bring his own weapon to bear. Iaz fired first, planting her feet this time. Her shot found home in the screaming creature's featureless face.

Iaz didn't wait to be sure, lunging in and dragging Blides to his feet to get them clear of the biohazard area.

"Up, soldier!" It sounded farcical when she said it.

"Got to get to the line!" he responded.

"You're damn right you do!" Drozhke said over the comms, but Iaz could hear her words through the air a split second before they came over the speaker. "We've lost all contact with the ground team. We've heard nothing about any other VIPs, and we're cleared to evac. The rest of you, shoot anything else that moves!"

Johe, Iaz thought with a stab of despair. For her fellow magistrates, Teodori's creatures to a one, she felt little sympathy, and obviously Teodori himself stirred none. But all she could recall now was how Blides and Tiersi had prevented Johe from following her. He'd be all right now if she'd insisted on letting him come.

They ran as fast as they dared, wary lest any random object on the roof transformed into a revenant. A whine which had been distant grew closer. The flier, *Stardust*, was nearly at roof-level, skids an easy hop from the ledge.

My ride. But no sooner had the thought flitted across Iaz's awareness than half the structures the lancers had been using as a funnel to
the killing field began to transform, growing legs and spines and horrible, blank lozenge heads. Two of them approached from behind Iaz, but
she hadn't even had a chance to spin to face them when they were past.

The line collapsed entirely then, lancers falling backward or trip-
ping over one another in their haste to reposition. The revenants
ignored this entirely, leaping over the prone lancers, taking aim at the
flier itself.

All but one. That great indigo beast barreled toward Drozhke
while she was distracted, trying to restore order. But order never
had time to form. Drozhke realized her danger too late, raising her
lance, but the revenant managed to hook its foreclaws under the
edges of her armor, and Iaz watched with a sickening lurch as it
pulled.

Drozhke flew apart, ripped from thigh to shoulder, viscera
darting at the air like striking snakes. That quickly, the revenant
righted itself, slick in Drozhke's blood, now a direct biohazard in
addition to every other threat it posed.

Blides's hand pressed against Iaz's back, pushing her forward
toward the chaos. Iaz initially resisted, then Blides thrust his free arm
forward, lance leveled, and fired. The revenant that killed Drozhke
would never get a chance to eat her, at least.

The noise of the world receded into ringing ears as Iaz high-
stepped through the hazardous areas of the collapsed line, which had
disintegrated into fighting couplets. Her brain screamed at her to run,
but there was nowhere left to run *to*.

Two revenants had wrapped segmented claws around the skids of
the still-airborne *Stardust*, and it was banking left and right, trying to
shake them off. Its underslung turret had no firing arc. A third
revenant began its leap, but someone tagged it, fouling its jump such
that it went squealing over the edge. But as it fell, it skewered its
shooter on an outstretched limb, dragging the lancer over the edge
with it.

"*Stormcrow*, where are you?" Blides called into his comm unit. "We need immediate evac."

"Stand by," said someone, presumably the pilot of *Stormcrow*.

In this mad lull in the middle of chaos, Iaz swiveled her head until she found it. It looked to have lighted on the roof of a nearby building, possibly to provide fire support, but it was struggling to shake off revenants of its own.

Gods below. More than one building is under attack. It was the first time Iaz had really stopped and allowed herself a moment to take in the scope of this incursion. It was like nothing she'd heard of since the time of the first incursion and the Loss nearly a century before. That time, the city had nearly been overrun entirely.

"*That's got them!*" *Stormcrow's* pilot's whoop was triumphant as he performed a full barrel roll and two revenants lost their grip, plummeting to the unseen pavement below. The flier immediately made its way over to the Chelsea roof, but it was too late for *Stardust*.

Where *Stormcrow's* cry had been jubilant, *Stardust's* was one of panic and despair. Five revenants now clung to it, spearing spines and claws into its sensitive systems with no regard for their own safety, like sharks tearing apart a struggling whale. With trailing smoke, fire, and blaring screams across all frequencies, *Stardust* fell.

Most of the revenants' number had turned on the flier, leaving the remainder outnumbered. These died quickly to the few surviving lancers, who stumbled to their feet. Iaz counted five, then mentally dropped that to four as one, sporting a serious chest wound, began to shudder, slide to his knees, and clutch at the wound. The wound sprouted fleshy lobes that clutched back.

"Everyone stay back!" Blides said. Iaz had no idea who was in command now that Drozhke was down, but if it was not Blides, no one was complaining. They all obeyed, backing well away while leaving enough room for the flier to approach. "Lancer, can you hear me?" He called to the rapidly changing man.

A rough nod was the best the man can manage.

"It's time, Lancer," Blides said with solemn urging.

A moment's pause. Then another nod. The dying man dropped his lance then reached for a syringe identical to the one Blides had used. He jammed the syringe into his own neck with what looked to be the last of his strength. It took hold almost instantly, and he slumped over. The mutation continued unabated as the lobes sprouted hemispheres that looked like eyes, but it would soon burn itself out of energy to work with.

Stormcrow chose that moment to touch down.

"Is that Magistrate Delgassi?" the pilot squawked over comms.

"Yes," Blides responded, eyes not leaving the carnage of the roof.

"I've got Lance Commander Yonnel for her. Patching him through to your unit."

"Magistrate," Karl's voice sounded as haunted as Iaz felt. "Magistrate, you need to get off that roof right now and take the oath of office. Over."

"What are you talking about?" Iaz asked, before realizing that Karl could not hear her. Blides depressed the button to transmit. "What are you talking about?" Iaz asked, louder this time. Though somehow, she knew.

"We've lost contact with the rest of your party, Magistrate," Karl said. His voice grave. "Lancers, politicians, and staff. Our relief lancers can't get through to them, not now at least. Coldgarden law is clear. When—"

"When the archon is killed or otherwise unable to fulfill their duties in the midst of a revenant crisis," Iaz said, quoting from memory, "the Magistrate of Watchfire shall serve as acting archon until the crisis has passed, or until the duly elected archon resumes their duties." That lead weight that had been forming in her gut since the start of this mess at last dropped in an acidic splash.

My mess. It's my mess now.

CHAPTER 28

"MADAM ARCHON," Karl said over the headset Iaz had been handed once the flier was airborne. The air of the bay was wet with lingering decontamination spray, a necessary precaution to remove any trace of blood, human or revenant, from their bodies before sealing them up together.

"Status report, Lance Commander?" Iaz prompted, doing her best to hold herself together.

For his part, Karl sounded relieved that she hadn't fallen apart. Yet. "As you've seen, it's bad, ma'am," he said. "A massive incursion into Inkwell. Unprecedented in living memory. Potentially hundreds of revenants, an entire enclave if the reports are even half-accurate. No sightings in Watchfire along the Inkwell arc at ground level. Somehow the bastards got above and below completely undetected. Not sure how that's possible."

"I might be able to help with that," Iaz said. "The ones on the rooftop were using a near-perfect camouflage. Color, texture, body shape. Maybe I could have seen it if I'd known what to look for, but I wouldn't bet on it."

"Gods below," he said. "Why have we never seen this before? Although ..."

"This is no time to hold back, Lance Commander."

"Now I wonder if we have seen it," Karl said. "In the recent Underguts incursion. Maybe this is how they gave our sensors such fits." His voice was leaden. "Makes me wonder how many revenants really were in the tunnels that night. Like they were testing us."

"Still doesn't explain how this group got over the wall," Iaz said.

"My turn for theories," Karl said. "You remember that piece of wall they stole?"

"Yes," Iazmaena said, her dread rising.

"I'll have to check the specs to be sure, but my recollection is that any piece of the wall would behave the same way as the rest of the wall as a whole. Which means—"

"Which means," Iaz said, "they used a piece to learn the relaxation pattern and memorize when it would relax. Gods below."

"Just a supposition, ma'am, but yes."

"We'll have to come back to that," she said. "For now, they're in, and we have to get them out and save who we can. What are we doing about that?"

"Once the scope of the incursion and its proximity to the visiting officials became clear, I dispatched the entirety of Inkwell's assigned lancers to the site under the auspices of emergency powers."

"You don't need to cite regulations, Lance Commander," Iaz said.

"Yes, ma'am. I had Lance Captain Drozhke deploy her lancers in three waves to blunt the advance and extract VIPs. You are currently with the remains of the aerial detachment, so you don't need me to tell you the status."

"I do not," she breathed, each word a sigh, thankful that the surviving lancers could only hear her half of the conversation. "What about the second and third detachments?"

"Second came in at street level. While trying to force their way into Chelsea Tower, we suffered a mass casualty event when the *Stardust* went down."

"By all the hells. Survivors?" Iaz demanded, stricken.

"Hard to say at this point, ma'am. At least a few, as I'm getting sporadic reports there, though radio reception is poor. Reports of revenants carrying off people from the area."

"What people?" Iaz asked. Realizing how nonsensical a question it was, she clarified. "Are we talking about people from Chelsea Tower?"

"Again, it's hard to say. Some reports suggest that, yes. Lancers being carried off as well as civilians. But there are a lot of people out and about for Inkwell Day, ma'am. Thousands nearby when the attack began."

"Alive or dead?" *Johe.*

"I've heard reports of both, but, ma'am, you should know that anyone who starts out alive when carried off by a revenant doesn't stay that way for long."

"Yes, Lance Commander, of that I am painfully aware."

A moment of dead air followed as Karl no doubt recalled her recent personal history on the subject. "Sorry, ma'am."

"Please tell me we have good news on the third detachment."

"Yes and no. The third detachment was dispatched to find the tunnels the ground-level revenants entered through. This was before we realized they were attacking from both above and below. The seals we installed are locked down tight ... with one important exception."

"And can I assume that exception is a string of broken seals all the way out of the city?"

"That's the working, theory, ma'am. The lancers haven't back-tracked all the way yet. They're moving slow, making sure there aren't any ambushes. Ironically, we're in much better contact with them. Most of our communications enhancement grid is located in the tunnels—"

"Because that's where you presume the fighting will happen," Iaz said. "A lot of assumptions being proven wrong today. Such as the fact that the seals could hold them."

"If they can change shape as totally as you say, ma'am, there might be no barrier but the city wall itself they can't punch through.

And right now, I wouldn't take bets on the wall." His voice was bleakness itself.

"Can I safely assume we've had no *other* facility breaches?" She couldn't speak freely about the Underlab in this setting.

"Correct, ma'am," Karl said, clearly taking her meaning. "I've looked at that situation myself, and everything is secure and locked down. All personnel have been ordered to shelter in place."

"Good," she said, grateful for the small measure of relief his words brought her. "What about reinforcements from other districts?"

"I've ordered them to mobilize and organize. Sending in Inkwell's contingent piecemeal against so large a force may have cost us dearly." He left unspoken a question. His continued command of this operation was her decision.

"You have authority to use any and all lancer resources at your disposal, Lance Commander. Get out as many people as you can and get this crisis contained." Then Iaz took a breath to steel herself. "How likely are we to get this under control?"

His static-filled sigh conveyed more emotion than words ever could. But words were still called for. "I have hope this isn't outside our control yet, but, ma'am, it is spreading quickly, and we still don't know the full scope. Under the Emergency Powers, Continuation of Governance, and Martial Quarantine Acts, ma'am, I'm obligated to recommend that you invoke Martial Quarantine of Inkwell Ward."

Iaz flinched as if caught doing something illicit. Her eyes darted around the bay, briefly meeting each survivor's gaze. The pride of Coldgarden, utterly routed. Their eyes never left her, their new archon, and it was difficult for Iaz to avoid feeding on their mood of despondency.

Karl's words rang in her ear. Martial Quarantine.

She shivered as her brain dredged up just what that act, a true last resort, entailed.

"How close are we to losing the chance for containment in Inkwell?" A knot of something unpleasant in Iaz's stomach drew tighter and tighter with each word, with each moment closer she drew to the decision.

His answer came after an interminable pause during which she nearly repeated the question. "An hour, with luck. Maybe less. If it weren't for the camouflage, if I could be sure that my people wouldn't be walking into ambushes around every corner ..."

"And it's your recommendation that we bring up the cordon walls?" Iaz wanted to be very clear.

Another bone-weary sigh came across as static. "Ma'am, it's not in a lancer's nature to retreat, and I'm an old lancer. But this situation ... Maybe if we'd overwhelmed them at the start, we'd have this contained. But when the fight shifts to guerrilla tactics, with this new ability to disguise themselves, they've got all the advantages. We've already squandered more of the corps piecemeal than we should have. If we don't pull out now, we won't be able to mount an effective counterattack. So yes, ma'am, that is what I'm recommending."

A chill of death passed through Iaz. She tried to deny what it portended. *The people won't be trapped long. We just have to halt the revenants' forward advance, keep them bottled up.* The cordon walls didn't have the same weaknesses the outer wall demanded for crop-growing purposes. They'd be all but impossible to climb and watched constantly besides. Once they were confident the bulk of the creatures were contained, the remaining lancers could turn their attention to cleansing operations. Iaz had to believe that. How could she give the order otherwise?

"Start the timer," Iaz said, her voice not shaking at all. "Thirty minutes."

"That short, ma'am? You're certain? The regs call for an hour."

"You said an hour if we're lucky. We haven't been lucky yet today. All lancers on the last trains out or hoofing it."

"Yes, ma'am. Thirty minutes."

"Good," Iaz said, "now get me a general broadcast comm link."

Johe, I'm sorry.

CHAPTER 29

MARRI WAS the hunter once again, her prey in her sights. She'd never felt this way before. Her blood sang with the thrill and power of it. The Dapper Man was scared now, all his confidence from before gone. Marri watched him search his pockets, trying to figure out what she'd stolen. She hadn't stolen anything but finding nothing missing seemed to agitate him even more. *If not stealing, then what?* She could practically read the thoughts in his hunched posture, his quick steps. She'd been right there as he'd had his secret talk with the archon. What, he must wonder, if she'd been listening?

I was. I heard it all.

His head swiveled in search of her. Once or twice, he spun, but Marri never strayed far from groups, even if it meant letting him get further ahead.

They walked for some time that way. He wasn't heading back to his building. Maybe that was because he was afraid she was still following him. Maybe he had somewhere else to be.

Whatever you are up to, I will find out. And that secret would feed her mice for months.

Distant cracks and cries of delight told of fireworks being set off during the celebration. Normally, that would have been fun to see.

But Marri had a job to do. She was debating whether she could guess his path and cut ahead of him when the public loudspeakers crackled to life. Every person on both sides of the street froze, fixated on the speaker nearest them.

It was Iazmaena's voice, and it made Marri's blood run cold.

"Attention citizens of Coldgarden, this is Acting Archon Iazmaena Delgassi. A Class 5 Revenant Incursion is in progress within Inkwell Ward. Initial lancer response has been overwhelmed, and reinforcements have been called in to harden evacuation points. At this time, I am exerting emergency control over Inkwell as acting archon. All citizenry within that ward will proceed to border exits or mass transit points immediately. All passport scans, limitations, and restrictions are hereby rescinded for the duration of the crisis. Inkwell is to be completely evacuated. I repeat, please proceed immediately to the nearest point of ward egress, as marked on all registered hand-held devices and kiosk maps. Do not stop to collect valuables. Do not attempt to barricade your homes. Panic chamber security cannot be guaranteed in an attack of this severity. If you are already outside of Inkwell, you will not be permitted to reenter for any reason. This is your only warning."

Another voice, falsely electronic, spoke then. "Countdown to containment: thirty minutes." Then Iazmaena's recording played again.

"Attention citizens of Coldgarden ..."

Marri shook herself from her stupor, looking for Dapper Man. She caught a flash of coat sleeve as he rounded a corner, one headed the opposite way he'd been angling.

Back to the border. They were both going to the same place then. Marri consulted her mental map, but the only secret crossing she knew was much further away than just heading to the border directly, and Iazmaena had said they weren't checking passports. So she followed Dapper Man's lead.

But it wasn't so easy. Once-navigable crowds became a surging mass of people, all streaming along the shortest path of the border.

Friendly faces became panicked grimaces snarling at anyone who tried to cut ahead of them. It wasn't long before individual clumps of people hit a bottleneck and became a solid mass. Dapper Man hit it an instant before Marri.

Trying her best to thread herself through the ever-thickening mob of people, Marri despaired. The further in she pushed, the more impossible it became to move forward. Someone grabbed her by the upper arm and pulled her back. For an instant she fought like a cornered cat, certain it was the Dapper Man, but no, it was just some middle-aged man, round-shouldered and pudgy, his eyes wide with terror. He was just trying to get further ahead himself.

This wasn't going to work. She was too small to fight her way through but not small enough to slip between people. She spun, looking for areas where the crowd might be thinner. Then she caught sight of Dapper Man again. He was moving off, parallel to the crowd's movement. He was not alone. Several others had broken away and were moving that way too.

Toward the nearest tram station, she realized. The station was closer than the border. Sooner or later, more people were going to realize it. Marri took off, following not the Dapper Man so much as his idea.

But the more people who broke away, the more the rest of the crowd noticed and began to follow. Soon a scattered few became a loose horde, and the only difference between this one and the one Marri had just fled was that she was at the front of it.

She had never seen anything this bad. More of those crackling fireworks erupted in the distance, and only now did she realize they were lances being shot at revs. They grew more frequent with each step she took.

Shorter than the adults, Marri lost ground as the crowd surged toward the tram station's gates, flanked by lace-steel fencing that looked frail before so many people. In this level of emergency, those gates were left open, but there were still limits to how many could pass.

She watched it happen, watched the first group surge through that opening all at once, only to be forced to stop short at the platform's edge, resulting in a jam as everyone behind them piled upon one another. She marveled as Dapper Man, for all his size, was still forced back by numbers. He roared with fury, but his arms were pinned against his sides by the crush.

It would have been funny had Marri not understood that she had no hope of making it through herself. More and more people plugged the gap, and while some were getting through to the waiting tram beyond, far more were arriving to keep the jam growing. Marri found herself forced back too, losing ground, her small size dooming her.

Iazmaena's latest loop concluded, and the mechanical voice spoke. "Countdown to containment: nineteen minutes."

Ahead, Dapper Man finally gave up fighting and broke away from the crowd, heading off to the side again, moving at an angle that allowed him the space he needed. Marri waited for him to rush back in, arms freed and ready to bully his way through, but he kept moving away, once again as though he had a very specific place he intended to go.

Doggedly, Marri followed.

They left the crowd behind quickly, Marri losing all opportunity for cover. But being followed was apparently no longer his concern. Marri checked her mental map. It was a long way—too long on foot— to the next border crossing. And her secret shortcut was in the opposite direction.

Does he know another shortcut? More importantly, would it be one Marri could take as well?

Precious minutes passed, Marri following as quickly and as closely as she dared, afraid he would hear her steps and realize she was behind him. But his focus was all on the now-empty streets ahead. He slowed, eyes scanning the run-down buildings as if uncertain what he was looking for. Hope went sour in Marri. Was this all just a guess? They were very near the border now, so the ward wall, all composicrete and razor wire, was visible at the end of every street to their right. Buildings adjacent to the wall had no windows above its height.

Nowhere to jump from, in other words.

"Coundown to Martial Quarantine: ten minutes."

After a solid two more minutes of standing and looking, the side of his face lit with triumph. Following his gaze, she saw it. A solid-looking building of unadorned composicrete that didn't just run up to the wall, but seemed to pass *through* it. All the windows and doors at every level looked sealed so thoroughly that there was surely no path through.

But Dapper Man took off as though his life depended on it. Which, of course, it did.

As did Marri's.

"Countdown to Martial Quarantine: eight minutes."

Without a backward glance he approached the door, a flat expanse of metal with no hinge or seam Marri could see. But he waved something at the door, which slid open so rapidly Marri missed the motion during a blink.

Dapper Man disappeared into the darkness within, and Marri sprinted after him, knowing that if that door shut before she was past the threshold, she would die in Inkwell, food for some rev.

She didn't see it close, but she felt the wind of its passage behind her as she barely crossed in time, plunging her world into utter blackness. Even the gray light of a sky threatening rain was enough to render her eyes useless in this lightless building. Dapper Man could be just beyond, waiting for her. Certainly, he should be able to hear her labored breath.

"Countdown to Martial Quarantine: seven minutes." The voice was muffled by walls but still quite audible. As if on cue, the clouds broke in a peal of thunder and the rain began. Marri was grateful not to be caught out in it, hoping it would drown out any noises she could not keep herself from making.

She began reaching blindly for walls, something to orient her in this place as her eyes adjusted. She managed to find a wall to her left without stumbling and began moving along it toward the building's interior. Wherever Dapper Man was, she might have as little time to make it through the building's exit as she did the entrance.

"Where are the fucking lights?" his voice roared suddenly, much too close. Marri froze, tried to still her breathing and heartbeat both and clamped her jaw shut against a whimper. Had she really felt like a hunter a few minutes gone?

"This entire city is falling apart," he grumbled. There was a dangerous edge to his voice, the sound of a man who was close to breaking.

"Countdown to Martial Quarantine: five minutes."

"Shit!" he barked, then a light appeared, cold and blue-white, the LED from his handheld. He played it around him a bit, and Marri held very still, as though being motionless would keep her from being noticed if that beam passed across her.

Dapper Man moved off then, away from her, but the light was enough for her to follow and avoid major obstacles. The building appeared totally empty, as though its sole purpose was to provide an illicit path across the border for this man and whomever he worked with.

They came to another door, Dapper Man and his hidden pursuer, as sealed as the outer door had been. But unlike the outer door, Dapper Man's handheld did nothing to convince it to open.

"What are they doing to me?" he said, beginning as a snarl and ending in another roar. Marri would not survive being noticed by a man this desperate. Still, she crept closer. He had to open that door, and she had to get through it when he did.

"Coundown to Martial Quarantine: two minutes."

"Shit, shit, shit!" He managed to open up a panel, a piece of wall that rotated to reveal a keypad, by running his handheld off to the left of the door. Frantically, he began to enter passcodes, pressing the buttons so quickly that Marri wondered if he was just inputting random numbers.

Each time he completed a string, a buzzer sounded and the panel flashed red.

"No, no, no!" He started making mistakes, swearing and starting over, Marri silently rooting him on.

Again came Iazmaena's muffled voice. And after: "Coundown to Martial Quarantine: one minute."

He switched to pounding on the door with his hands. "Let me through! Let me through!" He tried to pry his fingers into the almost invisible seam at the door's edge. Marri wondered, increasingly desperate, if she should run up and help him.

When the amplified recording of Iazmaena Delgassi finally stopped, Dapper Man's raging sobs became the loudest thing in the world. But just for an instant. Then came the roar that was also an earthquake. The entire building shook. Marri lost her footing a second after Dapper Man did, barely stifling a cry as he howled in rage and despair. By the light of his handheld, Marri watched as cracks ran up the wall, spiderwebbing out over and over. Plaster split and fell away, revealing gleaming metal marred by vertical streaks. The stink of hot metal flooded the small antechamber.

The building continued to shake around them as the cracks turned the corner to the ceiling. Then chunks of composicrete began to rain down.

CHAPTER 30

STEFANI'S HAND shook as she thumbed off the lab's comm unit, Karl's warning—or was it the apocalyptic sound of the Inkwell cordon wall raising?—still ringing in her ears. Rattled by that sound and what it portended, she'd processed the lance commander's words only in snatches. *Major incursion. Stay put. Shelter in place.*

She made eye contact with Rieve, not sure what she was seeking from the other woman, but definitively not finding it there. If Rieve was shaken, she didn't show it, aside from even more twitchy energy than usual, maybe. Without a word, the data jockey turned back to her workstation, pulling her headphones into their customary position over her ears.

So the burden of comfort would fall to Ella. Waiting as the transparent memory-matter parted to admit Stefani amid a brief inhalation of negative pressure to keep the baby's air bubble in, Stefani's need to hold Ella in her arms in that moment was almost primal. But for all the comfort she took in the feel and smell of her daughter, the familiar percussion of guilt drummed through her also. *If I'm in danger here, so is she. And that's my fault.*

Stop it, she rebutted herself. *For once, we may be safer down here. The revenants are all up there.*

A dinging sound from her imaging equipment interrupted her vice-like hug of Ella. The analysis of the first of her ill-gotten samples had concluded. Placing a squirming Ella back in her crib, Stefani exited the bubble and stepped over to the imager, peering down intently into the high-definition screen.

It was magnification and resolution of a kind she'd never been allowed access to. Always before, if she'd needed something along those lines, she'd have to send her results to Gene Sequencing with an appeal for assistance, appeals that were perpetually ignored. A flutter of illicit thrill shuddered through her at this forbidden imagery, however mundane it would ultimately turn out to be. That was why she was doing this, she realized: simply because she'd never been allowed to before.

The sample in question was a shattered piece of revenant fore-claw chitin along with layers of softer tissue beneath. In truth, both portions were soft, a product of the radiation denaturing so much of its natural toughness. But the damage of the original shattering was still clearly visible.

In a grayscale image, jagged fracture lines like a spiderwebbed mirror crisscrossed with thicker, smoother, organic curves like topo-graphical lines on a map. The whole jumble should have held no meaning at all, and yet something tugged at Stefani's awareness, a nagging sense of familiarity. Some part of this was something she had seen before. And that intuition was enough to spur a quick thrill of excitement. If she had seen it before, it was likely in her studies of human samples, much easier to come by than revenant ones. And any similarity between human and revenant tissue could point the way toward positive identification of Mutagen Prime.

Because, different as they were, hypermutation afflicted them both. So anything they shared could be no coincidence.

"Rieve!" Stefani shouted, standing bolt upright from the imaging station. Shielded behind her headphones, the woman didn't respond. Seized by a spike of nervous irritation, Stefani strode over and pulled them roughly from the woman's head. An awful, thudding, screeching sound emerged tinnily from them. It was Rieve's preferred brand of garbage music. "You said your decryption software featured powerful pattern-matching algorithms."

"So?" said the woman. Despite her unenthusiastic tone, she jerked the headphones from Stefani's grasp with a scowl.

"Can it pattern match images?"

"Yep."

"And is it possible for it to decrypt your data while it's looking at something else at the same time?"

"Yes ...," Rieve said, suspicion evident in her voice now.

"I need to borrow—"

"Forget it. I'm using every bit of horsepower I have as it is."

"I'll let you listen to your horrible music without headphones," Stefani said begrudgingly.

Rieve spun her chair to look Stefani in the eye with a malevolent grin, and Stefani sighed internally.

"Only at levels that won't damage hearing," Stefani said.

"No deal," Rieve said. "You can wear earplugs if you don't like it. And before you complain about the *baby*," she said, forestalling just that, "the memory-matter can protect her little ears. So don't bother hiding behind her."

"Fine," Stefani said. "But I want the software ported over to a dedicated workstation so I don't have to keep bothering you."

"That sounds lovely to me," Rieve said. "But you aren't getting much cycle time, mind. It will take a while."

"So you'll set it up now?" Stefani asked hopefully.

The garbage music beginning to blare openly was the only response she got.

CHAPTER 31

MARRI AWOKE SHROUDED in utter darkness, choking on dust. There was no period of confusion. Maybe it was years of living on the street, but she instantly remembered where she was and what had happened to her. The only two surprises were that she wasn't dead outright and she wasn't pinned in place by debris.

She reached out tentative, probing hands, feeling at the blackness surrounding her. She couldn't even stretch her arms out to full length before her hands hit something, what felt like a piece of composicrete wall.

Marri was trapped in a cocoon of the building's rubble. She wondered how airtight it was. She wondered how long she'd been unconscious. The answers to both those questions could be related and very important. She fretted about internal bleeding and hyper-mutation, working herself up to a near panic until that cold voice whispered to her as it always did in her worst moments.

Nothing you can do about that.

Her mind stilled, she listened carefully before moving any further, straining to hear any sound that might indicate the Dapper Man had survived and was active outside her debris pile.

She heard nothing.

At last, knowing she couldn't hide here forever, Marri began probing at the debris with more force, looking for loose pieces that might not be holding the rest up, thankful for her thick gloves and coveralls to prevent cuts and scrapes. She worked methodically, searching every part of the pile in front of her then gradually working her way to the right. Her fear whispered to her constantly—*Trapped! Trapped!*—but she ruthlessly stamped it down. She did let herself cry, for she found she could do this without succumbing to panic. The tears stung her eyes, but she was in pitch darkness. She didn't need to see.

At last, she found a piece that gave way easily at her push. Marri was so startled by this fact she nearly fell onto her face at the lack of resistance. The hole left behind was small, but so was she. She felt carefully around the edges, making sure there was nothing that would tear her open even through the thick fabric draping her, then took a deep breath, forced it out to shrink herself, and squeezed through.

There was light beyond, a gray pool of it right in front of her. Enough that she knew it must still be daytime. She heard the sounds of rain outside. Freed from her prison of debris, Marri rose to her knees, squinting in the burst of late afternoon light before nearly falling over at a glimpse of something squirming just past the light's edge.

Recoiling away on instinct, she tried to bring her vision into focus. Her eyes complained painfully at the brightness. The moving thing resolved into a dark puddle of thick liquid with ... things growing out of it. Not wanting to see any details, she turned away in sudden understanding.

Blood. It's hypermutating blood. She double-checked, but her injuries were minor. No broken skin. That meant the blood must be the Dapper Man's. He'd survived the collapse, then, at least long enough to leave a puddle of blood as he'd left the building.

Or a rev showed up and dragged him off. Don't forget why all this happened in the first place.

Regardless, Marri moved away from the blood. Her efforts to avoid the writhing puddle nearly had her stepping into a second, smaller one near the edge of the rubble pile. Next to it lay a crushed handheld, apparently discarded.

He's badly injured. Not likely to last long. Maybe, just maybe, if she could catch up with him before he died, she could learn what he'd been doing before the revs showed up and salvage something from this whole disaster.

More importantly, maybe she could find out if there was any way past the ward's towering new walls.

⋈

Though she caught up to him easily, the Dapper Man was not in as bad a shape as Marri had imagined he would be. There was a serious wound on his side, judging by the number of cryobands he'd applied directly to the skin beneath the ragged hole in his once-fancy shirt. But he wasn't sprouting horrifying appendages or growing new eyes the way Marri had always heard this went.

Cryobands wouldn't actually cure the problem. They just slowed things down long enough to get an actual doctor to help. Though his steps were slowed by his wound, the Dapper Man looked too stubborn to die. He was going somewhere with a purpose, and that meant he thought he knew a way out. With only the two of them out in the open, Marri took extra care not to be seen, though the man still seemed too fixated on his course to notice he was again being followed.

Together, they stalked the border of Inkwell in the shadow of the immense wall that had sprung up between it and the rest of Coldgarden, severing streets, rail lines, and buildings alike. Taller even than the outer wall, it loomed black and imposing, a promise of permanence. Surely nothing that big could have come up out of the ground. Marri certainly couldn't imagine it ever coming down.

Gradually, Dapper Man's movements slowed, his wound finally

taking its toll. He stopped at a corner, swaying. For a moment, Marri thought he would collapse. Then, she was certain he'd found what he was looking for. Only instead of heading to the wall, he abruptly lurched to the right at a run, straight into an alley.

Quick as a flash, Marri was after him, closing the distance she'd left him and darting through the mouth of the alley as quietly and quickly as she could manage. She had no idea what kind of way back through could be down this alley, but if she lost him now ...

She saw it, then, across from a battered alley recycler, a stairwell leading down past street level to a door in the left-side building's foundation. The door was partially ajar. She pelted toward it, trying to figure out if the gap was large enough for her to slip through without risking opening it wider.

He was on her before she could cry out, hoisting her to face level against the wall of the building roughly. *Trick! A trick, and you fell for it, stupid, stupid, stupid mouse!* The hard edge of something sharp and cold came to rest against her neck.

"Cry out," the man said in a hissing whisper, "bring the revenants down on us, and I'll open your throat, you little gutter rat."

Marri's brain blubbered in panic. She kicked out as hard as she could, and he grunted as her foot found his groin, but he didn't loosen his grip. His nostrils flared. "You should be scared, you filthy thing, following me all the way to the end of the world. I have *you* to thank for being stuck here. If I hadn't chased you ..." Insane, animal rage contorted his face. "But I'm getting out of here." His eyes flashed to the stairwell. "Not you, though. You're way too committed to be a pickpocket. Didn't steal anything when you had the chance, did you? No, you work for *her*, don't you? Well, that's a problem, rat. That's a problem."

He was younger than she'd thought, and his face might have been handsome if not for the tightness of his jaw and the scary light in his too-wide eyes. Then the knife bit a little way into her throat, and she felt a warm bead of blood well and trickle, and there was no more time for thought.

"Well you found me, found where I was going, so good on you. But I'm sorry to say you won't live to report out to your boss. She's unclean, you know," Dapper Man said. "Tainted. Impure. We all are, and it's only me and mine that protect us from it. Your boss seems hell-bent on spoiling all we've built, so I think I'll strew your guts all over and see if she's smart enough to decipher the message."

Marri tried to twist away, tried to bite him, but his grip was too strong in both cases. *Iazmaena,* she prayed stupidly, pointlessly, *oh, Iazmaena, help me.* But Iazmaena was not a god any more than Undel had been. No god was going to rise up and save her.

She was going to die.

The darkness of the alley felt like a shroud, and pain exploded in Marri's back as the man hurled her down to the hard pavement. She found herself looking dazedly up at him from a puddle, pelting rain stinging her eyes as he stared down at her. His back was to the deeper parts of the alley, the sky's gray light illuminating his pale, insane face. Marri tried to stand up, only to feel his boot come down on her belly.

"If you hold still," he said, his words a manic promise, "I'll just cut your throat, quick and clean."

He leaned over, the softly gleaming blade of the knife bearing down upon her, and only then did the recycler move and change, rearing up behind him in sudden, spindly horror. The rev turned a featureless head upon them.

The once-dapper man whirled and faced the revenant, grimacing and clutching his wounded side at the sudden motion. When its black porcelain head cracked open into a jagged mouth that yawned open in four petals, Marri's mind went momentarily blank.

Her thoughts felt sludgy when they returned. *Move. He's not standing on you anymore.*

The revenant struck, its head lancing out impossibly far as its scorpion-tail neck unfolded, splitting off from where it lay flat against the bulk of its body, clinging only by its root. The combined shape of man and revenant hurtled over Marri and past the mouth of the alley, coming to a clattering, crashing halt in the street. In the gray light of the rain, a muted gold under-pattern was visible in the revenant's armored plates, waves of it slithering beneath as it moved.

The creature fused the length of its neck back down along its body, still gripping the man's squirming form as it began to swallow him whole. Something inside the creature's head stripped the clothing from him as he went down, the inedible cloth falling in bloody shreds at the revenant's feet. The knife tumbled to the street. The revenant's throat swelled, mottled skin peeking out from between the distended plates of its spine as the man went down. If he screamed, Marri couldn't hear it. She was torn between a savage triumph and a desire to vomit.

If anyone deserved it ... But the glory was fleeting. Fighting down the last of him, the revenant lurched back up to its full height, scuttling toward her. The creature had decided to eat the main course first, and now it was ready for dessert.

This terror tasted different than it had with a knife at her throat, primal in a way even a blade never could be. *Oh, Iazmaena, it's going to eat me! It's going to eat me!* Marri began a low, involuntary moan as the creature approached tentatively, as though giving her a respect and wariness it hadn't bothered with for the man. Quite without realizing it, Marri gave her moan words.

"Iazmaena, Iazmaena, Iazmaena, Iazmaenaiaz ..."

And the creature stopped short at this.

It held back, keeping its distance. It lifted its long neck free again, twisting its head to regard her almost quizzically. The head darted upward once, twice, three times. *Like a dog*, Marri thought. *Smelling the air.* With a heavy heart, she thought of all those times she'd told her mice that revenants couldn't smell worth a damn.

Several more moments of that eyeless regard followed. Then its head split anew into a four-petaled mouth, jagged and razor sharp. This time the jaw-petals didn't stop, but kept opening, wider and wider. Marri caught a glimpse of horrid inner teeth, irregular chips of jagged bone that had stripped away all of the man's inedible bits, and then her face was drawn to the center of the creature's flowering face, into which those chips of bone squirmed, coming together to fit like pieces of a puzzle.

Blood freezing, Marri realized what they were forming and she shrieked, long and loud and completely involuntary. A skull. It was a human skull. As if in response, the revenant sealed its carapace head back up, closing the horror back inside. Her conscious mind didn't register that it was in retreat but kept singing the song of her imminent death.

Then the creature was gone, and Marri was alone in the alley.

CHAPTER 32

KARL WATCHED THE BLOCK, compglass-reinforced lace-steel surrounded by a halo of ragged composicrete, fall through the rain, his mind imparting a cruel slow motion that the video feed in his Heart Hall office had nothing to do with. Below, the revenants waited. He'd seen this before. *I have to know,* he thought. *I can't risk the resources unless I'm sure.*

The mass hit the ground with a silent impact. The composicrete crumbled as it struck the slick paving. The lace-steel held better, but still warped dramatically, buckling around the boundary of its doors and opening gaps around that edge. Panic chambers. The good ones were so tough that it was easier to rip them free of the walls and toss them from the tops of buildings than it was to break into them.

So that was what the revenants did.

From the safety of the rain-soaked alleys, the many-hued shapes boiled, lunging for those new gaps, prying and clawing. It didn't matter, not anymore. The person or people that had been in that chamber would have died from the impact.

That helped little when Karl saw what the revenants pulled free of the ruined chamber. Those seamless heads opened and closed, tearing new jaws each time. The revenants seemed to shudder with pleasure as they savored their meal.

Karl had seen enough. He activated his direct line to Lancer Central. "This is Yonnel. Smash-and-grabs confirmed. Corner of Pointillist and Impression. Kill team authorized. Observe minimal risk to assets."

Minimal risk. It meant there likely weren't enough people there to be worth saving if it meant costing a squad of lancers. They were to approach in a flier and take out as many revs as they could before the creatures scattered as well as put rounds into any revenant-sized objects, keeping well out of leaping range. Assuming they could clear the area, the teams could then land to search other panic chambers from the same building complex.

This was all they could do, and how that galled. The revenants were clever, and the city's network connections to the Inkwell panic chamber were appallingly degraded. Inkwell was one of the oldest wards. Perhaps, once they recovered it, the archon—whatever new archon took over after the state of emergency was lifted—could set about changing that.

As if summoned by the thought, Iazmaena entered and stood at his shoulder, taking in the feed.

"Survivors?"

"We won't know until we can get in there," Karl said. "And we can't get in there until we can vouchsafe the area. But the revenants are smart, Madam Archon. They aren't just going to sit there and get vaporized, even if it means missing their meal. And there's the camouflage." He could already see them vanishing off the feed. Some scattered, others simply faded away, somehow disguising their heat signatures.

"Where are we on combating that?"

"Our people are trying to find methods," Karl said. "They said it would help to have samples to work with."

"Samples of dead revenants?" Iaz asked. "Tall order."

"Dr. Palmieri has a few partial samples, which she's careful to stress are wholly inadequate. She's working on something to address that, though." Which Karl was less than thrilled about. Recovering large chunks of a dead revenant, especially fresh enough to mean anything, would be extraordinarily risky.

"Makes you wonder if Gene Sequencing already has some of these answers," Iaz mused. It didn't sound like idle musing though.

"I couldn't tell you what Gene Sequencing has access to, ma'am," Karl said. "And I highly doubt they'd enlighten me."

"Yes," Iaz said vaguely. "Just remember you're no good to the city laid up with exhaustion, Lance Commander." As if she could talk. The dark circles under her eyes weren't some bold fashion choice.

"Since you're still here," Iaz said, "you can answer the same question from yesterday. Any word?"

"Same answer, I'm afraid," Karl said. "We have ample sightings, both eyewitness and electronic, of the revenants in Chelsea Tower carrying off human victims. But there was just too much chaos and not enough coverage. We've received no distress calls with the archon's call-sign attached, and we can't identify any of the victims that were carried off."

"So, we don't know if the archon's party is dead or not."

"No, we don't," Karl said, and he couldn't help but trail off. "But ..."

"But, begging your pardon, ma'am, I wouldn't hold my breath. None of the lancers we sent in to rescue them made it out, much less any of the honor guard minus one of the two with you. Plus, Chelsea Tower does, or did at least, have a highly secure VIP shelter with comms abilities. If they escaped the ambush there, that's the most likely place they'd have gone. And like I said"—he shrugged—"we've heard nothing."

"We're sure they still have power?"

"Yes, ma'am. A leaky old fusion core buried deep. It kicked on the moment the walls severed power to the ward. If anyone is alive to call, they aren't calling. But we'll keep listening."

Iaz nodded and closed her eyes briefly. It was barely more than a blink, yet Karl could sense the grief there. Not for the archon, he suspected—unless she just wanted out of this job—but for her aide.

"Lance Commander!" came a voice Karl didn't recognize over the comm. The voice was agitated in a way he seldom heard these days. Excited.

"Go ahead, son. Identify."

"Pilot Rednan, sir, *Lightbringer*. En route to the smash-and-grab, locked and loaded, sir!"

"Report, pilot," Karl said, holding his breath. This news could go either way.

"We just detected a transponder, active and pinging. It's faint, low power. We only detected it as we passed by. Sir, it's a mass transponder!" A panic chamber meant to hold many people.

Enough people to be worth risking a rescue.

"Affirmative, son," Karl said, looking at the coordinates being forwarded to his console. Close to the smash-and-grabs, but not that close.

"Sir, should we divert?"

"Negative, pilot, proceed," Karl said. With eyes and lancer guards quadrupled at every reasonable access point into Coldgarden, there were a finite number of revenants in the city. He couldn't pass up the chance to kill a clutch of them. "I'm dispatching another flier for a rescue. Nice work."

"Sir, yes, sir! Thank you, sir!"

Karl couldn't help but smile. "Good hunting, son." He killed the comm link, already patching back into Lancer Central to call up another flier. Outside, the rain was growing heavier. *Just about that season*, Karl thought, hoping the rain would not grow so heavy that the fliers couldn't operate. Hope. It was a feeling tantalizingly familiar yet sufficiently alien to be depressing.

"Sounds like some good news, at least," Iazmaena said. Karl suppressed a start. He'd almost forgotten she was there.

"Yes, ma'am. I'll send a report to your desk."

"That's fine," Iaz said, yawning. "But don't disturb me otherwise. Our little talk gave me a thought. I've got a call only an archon can make."

"Yes, ma'am."

CHAPTER 33

IAZ RETURNED to her new office. The archon's office. It was as grandiose as the man who had so recently occupied it, though of course the décor did not change much from person to person. High ceilings, white walls between thick beams of dark wood, matching wood floors that gleamed with wax around a deep-pile rug of crimson.

No telling how long it would remain hers, of course. All the more reason to act when she could. The revenants still remained in the city, but that would keep for a night. It wasn't as if she was out there with a lance herself, after all.

The door opened without so much as a knock. For a moment, Iaz thought it must be Karl with an update despite her request to be left alone. Then Rieve admitted herself, which made much more sense.

"Madam Archon," the woman said, inclining her head slightly as though meaning to offer a mock bow. "I see you are settling in nicely."

"Just settling in, yes," Iaz said pointedly. However useful Rieve was, she never grew less grating. As usual, the woman took no notice of the social cue.

"As long as you're here," Iaz said, acquiescing to Rieve's inevitability and determined to get something useful out of her, "you

154

can give me a report. Where does the Gene Sequencing effort stand?"

Rieve regarded her with confusion. "Are we still doing that? You're the archon now. You don't need my help. Gene Sequencing answers to you."

Iaz fought not to pinch the bridge of her nose, as that had been her entire plan before being interrupted. "I know you're used to working alone, Rieve, but surely you're aware that bureaucrats can slow-walk anything for a leader they don't like, particularly if that leader doesn't have the expertise to know better. And considering what you found about Kyne Libretta and me, safe to say they don't like me any more than Teodori did."

"You might be surprised," Rieve said. "They could have just been following orders whether or not they agreed with them." She gestured at Iaz's desktop terminal. "Only one way to find out."

"What would I do without you?" Iaz asked, trying to make it sound more fond than sarcastic. She keyed the terminal to life, activating the holographic keyboard and searched the array of icons she was still familiarizing herself with.

There it was, a glowing icon in the center of the screen, highlighted by holographic accents. GENE SEQUENCING—TAP TO OPEN COMMUNICATIONS.

Feeling a sense of trepidation, Iaz tapped.

The screen of commands was replaced by one with the Gene Sequencing logo, the stylized image of an unwinding double-helix of DNA with a third strand emerging from the background as though being spliced in.

Then the logo vanished, only to be replaced by the same one in antiseptic white and gold relief, attractively lit with LEDs. A man sat at the desk in front of it, staring out at Iaz, who was apparently being projected onto his far wall in whatever room this was. He had straight dark hair and sharp features and bore enough superficial resemblance to Damon that it put Iaz on edge. His expression carried the same air of being interrupted Iaz had no doubt shown with Rieve.

Rieve herself took up a chair in the far corner of Iaz's office and, though she could not see what Iaz saw from that angle, observed her patron with obvious interest.

"Madam Archon," the man said, nodding with the same mock deference Rieve had shown. "To what do I owe the pleasure?" It was clearly nothing of the sort.

"Forgive the lateness of this call," Iaz said, deciding that politeness cost nothing even though it felt like a lie in this case. "I'm still getting my bearings, as you might expect. But I'm afraid you have me at a disadvantage. I don't believe we've been introduced."

"Dr. Palo Hayasun," he said peremptorily. "I suppose you could say I was Archon Teodori's preferred point of contact. Apparently, some of his comm settings survived the transition to your stewardship."

Perfect. Iaz could not have asked for a better person to reach. He'd even admitted his utility to his previous master, making it harder to legitimately give her the runaround. The ember of hope within her glowed a little brighter. She knew she should lead with the more pressing issue, but she found she couldn't help herself.

"You sound like just the person I need to speak to, Dr. Hayasun. You see, I'm looking for records—all records, mind—of a particular patient of Gene Sequencing, and I—"

"I'm so sorry to interrupt, Madam Archon, but surely you're aware that patient records are strictly confidential, and not even you can—"

"I'm this patient's listed next of kin." If he was going to interrupt without actually being sorry, he could be interrupted in turn.

"Next of kin implies this patient is deceased or otherwise incapacitated," Hayasun said, pivoting smoothly. "I'm afraid that even with the designation, one of those two would have to apply—and my condolences if either does—in order for you to access their records without a verification from the patient themself. If you provide their name so that I can verify their status and your designation, I'll be happy to forward your request on to the records department." *So that you stop wasting my time* was implied.

He knows, Damon's voice whispered to her. And just like that Iaz could see him, sitting there in the corner opposite Rieve. *He knows you mean me. He knows what happened to me. And he knows you can't do anything about it without calling down trouble.*

Iaz wasn't sure if she should believe her hallucination, but she did. To reveal Damon as dead now with no record of such would invite very awkward questions. And though the power of the archon in Coldgarden was great, she found she didn't trust it to keep her immune to such questions.

"I recognize that I'm new to this role," she said evenly. To shout or berate would only make her look weak. "But my understanding is that Gene Sequencing answers to no one in Coldgarden. No one but the archon."

"It's a common misconception," Hayasun said, smiling sheepishly, embarrassed for her. He leaned in, as though imparting a secret. Iaz expected him to say something grandiose about how Gene Sequencing answered to no one, but he surprised her. "We answered to Archon Teodori, but the fact that he was archon was, well, not immaterial, exactly, but not sufficient. He was the right sort to listen to."

"And I'm not," Iaz said, trying to smooth the anger out of her face.

"If you were," Hayasun said, "you'd know it already. But you needn't worry. Gene Sequencing is more than capable of managing its own affairs until the right sort is back in that seat. Now, if you wish to appeal this turn of events, you are, of course, welcome to submit a complaint to the applicable department."

For a mad second, Iaz thought he was talking about appealing his refusal to accede to her authority. Then she realized he was talking about Damon's records. Anger flared at his condescension, and she almost gave in to it. She settled for gritting her teeth behind closed lips instead.

As if sensing her thoughts, Hayasun continued, "Of course, any such complaints are dealt with in the order in which they are received. Unfortunately, we can't allow rank or office to corrupt our processes." His smile was a smug little *fuck you* of exquisite precision. "I'm sending you the relevant links now. If that will be all?"

She should pivot now, should ask about any research they had that might enable the lancers to detect the revenants. But she knew, she just *knew*, that he would only rebuff her again. *I'm not the right sort to listen to.*

She ended the call.

"Arrogant little toad!" Iaz burst out, chiding herself for not at least waiting until Rieve was gone. But Rieve's importance had just reasserted itself yet again. "Sorry if you're tired of it, Rieve, but if that's the reception I'm going to get trying to get Damon's records, I'm going to need you to get back to digging."

Rieve frowned in a way that Iaz was coming to dislike intensely. "I guess I wasn't clear before. I'm afraid I've reached my limit at breaching their security measures. My last four attempts were rebuffed. They are, I must say, substantially more robust than I antici- pated when I made this deal, and they learned quickly after that first successful attempt. They nearly traced my most recent try to the point of origin." Her attempt at sounding sheepish came across more as boredom.

"This from the so-called master at breaking into networked systems?" Iaz said.

"It pains me to point this out, Madam Archon," Rieve said, "but you were right. There's a reason you found me scraping the bottom of Undel's barrel and not already working at Gene Sequencing. I may be good, but someone there is clearly better. If you want that informa- tion, I'm afraid you're going to have to get it through less subtle means."

"Meaning?"

Rieve shrugged. "Find a way to wield that power you have now. While you still do have it," she added pointedly. The echo of Iaz's earlier thoughts seemed to haunt the air between them.

After she'd left, Iaz sat fuming at Teodori's desk. Impossible to think of it as hers now, when her first attempt to flex her authority in a meaningful way had been so thoroughly backhanded. She knew from her time as a cop how useless attempting to insert investigators into Gene Sequencing would be, much less bring any of them up on charges. Given her actions with Damon, she'd be more likely to be brought up on charges herself. This only served to sharpen her anger further.

It was only after her gaze drifted back to the screen before her, to the file tree icon tucked away in a lower corner reading *Depot—PL*, that her anger began to abate. *PL* was a common designation for *pre-Loss*, the period before Mutagen Prime, before the Revenants, from which so very little in the way of records had survived. It was ironic Rieve had left before Iaz had noticed this. Perhaps if she found a way to be more helpful, Iaz might tell her what it contained.

Frowning, she tapped the icon and then spent the rest of the evening going over the cryptic list that emerged.

Outside, the rain's drumming continued to grow.

CHAPTER 34

KARL'S STORM uniform was leaking. This was nothing new, of course, and while it wasn't really the source of his agitation, it certain didn't help.

The door the archon had directed him to had been difficult to locate, even knowing exactly where to go. It lay in a part of the city he'd never seen before. That was something by itself. Karl wasn't an old man, strictly speaking, but he'd have said there was not an inch of this city he hadn't been through at least once.

But this claustrophobic square definitely qualified as new territory. The buildings comprising it looked to have sprung up like a surrounding thicket, allowing no daylight to squeeze through the spaces separating them. It was as isolated a location as Karl had ever seen topside.

Why it had to be him, and him alone, that made this trip deep into this forgotten quadrant of Heart Ward, Karl was still uncertain. Iazmaena was very sparing with her trust, which just made her a normal politician in his experience. But now didn't seem like the time to stretch her allies too thin.

Regardless, he hadn't come alone. Orders or not, standing regulations called for no lancer to travel solo, particularly during an incursion. Still, he tried to obey the spirit of her order. Lance corporals Trellis and Valerin were standing at the nearly invisible entrance to the square, keeping watch both inward and outward at a discreet distance.

Karl made his way across the square toward a low and unassuming building. Some of the oldest buildings in the city were brick, and this one was colored to look it. But as he approached, he could pick out the telltale sameness of the texture that spoke not of real earthenware but composite brick. No windows. All in all, it looked at a glance like a condemned building that wouldn't be worth trying to mess with or squat in.

An overwhelming sense of "why am I here?" stole over Karl. *Revenants still running loose in Inkwell, and she has me on a scavenger hunt!*

But that wasn't fair. With the office of the archon, Iazmaena had access to all kinds of information Karl couldn't dream of knowing. But surely this could have been left to a lower-ranking officer, not the one who was responsible for all the military recommendations during this time of crisis.

All this he thought right up until the moment he actually arrived at the door.

What he saw stenciled upon it sent his misgivings off in a whole different direction. Just four words, the first two in warning yellow, the second two in dire-warning red.

GENE SEQUENCING
NO ENTRY

It was not the sort of message one wanted to see on a door one had been ordered to open. Which looked to be academic, as the door had no opening mechanism he could see: no knob, no panel, no keypad.

He felt a sudden, intense sense of being watched. Unable to resist, Karl spun, scanning low and high in a full circle around him. His first impression of the square had not been wrong. He couldn't see a single sign of human habitation in any of the surrounding buildings. *In a city as crowded as this? Who managed that?* The answer, he suspected, was stenciled on the door.

Signaling to his distant escort with a gesture, Karl waved them to approach. They jogged over, sending up flumes of water each time their boots landed squarely in one of the many, growing puddles. All that water, relentless since the previous day, just reminded him of how rescue operations in Inkwell had ground to a halt. Flooding disrupted ground approaches even as the rain itself grounded fliers.

Later, he thought, much as it galled. *One task at a time.*

"Thoughts on getting this open?" Karl asked as the two men arrived. And then, because he knew the way lancer minds tended to work, "Thoughts which do not include firing a lance at it."

Iazmaena had not informed him what she believed to be in here, but he thought it likely she didn't want it shot. He knew she had no love for Gene Sequencing, but this was emphatically not their headquarters.

"Cutting torch?" Valerin offered.

"Breaching charges!" Trellis declared.

"I would very much like to be able to close the door again once it's open," Karl said with amused patience.

"We can put our own door on it after," Valerin said. "One we can open."

Which was both true and possible. Provided, of course, there wasn't some sort of trap in place to prevent tampering.

Karl sighed. There were any number of experts among the lancers that might have been able to help, but he had strained his order to the brink as it was. That left him limited options. He gestured the men back to their post and brought out his handheld, keying the unit to call down to the Underlab.

"Yes?" Stefani's voice said.

A casual greeting, but they'd all agreed not to use names no matter how secure Revolos swore the lines were. And perhaps that was for the best. Karl's training and manners all dictated that he call Stefani "Dr. Palmieri," but she continued to insist he use her first name, and he found he liked that she insisted. Perhaps liked a little too much.

"It's me," Karl said, hoping that his identity would be obvious as the lone male voice in their little conspiracy. "Can I get you and your partner up topside? I have a door that needs opening, and as embarrassing as this is to admit, it has me stumped."

Yes, he definitely enjoyed her amused giggle too much.

"I think we can manage that. Though door opening isn't exactly my area of expertise."

"I'm sorry to bother you with this," Karl said. "And you'll know just how sorry when you get a look at the weather, but this is something she wanted kept close." Again, he hoped his meaning was obvious.

Stefani wasn't listening though. Karl heard the muffled sounds of an argument.

"You *are* coming, Rieve Revolos," Stefani said, and Karl sighed amusedly. *So much for no names.* "You said yourself that your cracking algorithm doesn't need you to babysit it. If I can leave Ella in the care of the autodoc *again*, you can leave your computers for an hour. Karl needs our help."

Karl shook his head in fond exasperation.

"Send me the location," Stefani said a few seconds later. "We'll be there in twenty."

"Well, you say that," Karl responded, keying in the numbers.

⌖

An hour later, Stefani and Revolos arrived, and it was hard to tell who was in a worse mood. Karl's escort admitted them as he'd instructed and stayed back, also as instructed.

"You weren't joking," Stefani groused as she walked up. Her umbrella had done as poor a job keeping her dry as Karl's uniform had him. Revolos hadn't even bothered with umbrella or coat. She was absolutely sodden.

Stefani took one look at the door and turned to Karl. "I wasn't joking either. I'm not going to be any help to you. The only reason I came was to make sure she would show up." She gestured sharply at Revolos then fixed the little woman with a dagger-eyed stare. "And it's not as if my work is progressing with the scraps she's giving me and no new samples to test!"

"I appreciate the sacrifice," Karl said sincerely, brushing past the part of that which applied to him. "The archon wanted this kept as quiet as possible."

"Seems like that's what she wants all the time these days," Stefani muttered. Karl wasn't certain he'd been meant to hear, but it was interesting that Stefani felt the same way he was starting to.

"Leadership sits differently on every person," he said, equally quietly. "Give her time to get used to the weight of it."

Stefani flushed but nodded. Revolos, meanwhile, had made her way over to the door. Heedless of the rain, she pulled out a device Karl could not identify and passed it along the doorframe. After a few seconds, she grunted, and pressed a space to the left of the door, holding her fingertips there for a count of five by Karl's reckoning. That part of the wall slid away, revealing a rectangular panel with a keypad.

"You couldn't think to try that yourself?" she asked Karl, one eyebrow raised in a sort of disdainful triumph. Karl had ruined her afternoon, and she'd just proved it was due to his incompetence.

"We tried," he said, shrugging. "Just not for long enough, apparently. Not sure it would have mattered. I certainly don't know the code."

"And I do?" she bit back.

"Do you?" he said, unfazed.

"Possibly," she said after a grudging pause. She began punching in numbers at a rapid pace, each series of six being greeted by a buzzing negative. Each buzzing negative prompted a curse. But on the fifth attempt, a pleasant *ding* sounded instead.

The door pivoted open soundlessly.

"Lucky for us someone was lazy on security hygiene," she said. "It was one of the default codes for this brand of keypad. Even luckier that I got it on my last try."

"Maybe they relied more on being unable to even find this place," Stefani said, wringing out the obsidian cascade of her hair pointlessly.

Revolos shrugged. "Maybe. Or the Gene Sequencing label to scare people off."

"Still a surprising oversight," Karl said. He eyed the darkness beyond the door. "I know you ladies will want to get dry, but I think it would be best if I go in first." Just in case that manufacturer's code hadn't been the real code but had opened the door as a primer to some kind of trap. But he decided not to say that aloud. It sounded more than a little paranoid.

Hefting his lance, he crossed the threshold.

Instantly the darkness was banished by harsh, blued lighting, seemingly reacting to his presence.

Iazmaena had indicated this was some sort of warehouse, and she looked to be correct. Crates upon crates were piled floor-to-ceiling across a wide, low room with no furniture or walls to break up the space. The crates varied wildly in size, aspect, and material. Karl saw everything from lightweight composites to wood—actual wood! A thick layer of dust covered everything.

All the crates were labeled with stenciled paint. Most read simply *Bridge*, which meant nothing to him. Not all, though.

"Can we come in and get dry now?" Stefani called.

"Yes," Karl said, "though I'll ask you not to touch anything." He meant this mostly for Revolos, whom he assumed would view anything not nailed down as fair game for anyone who wanted it so long as that anyone was her.

It would probably be stupid to open up any of these crates

without first confirming with the archon what they contained, but Karl still found himself hefting the prybar he found in one corner and moving toward the nearest intact one. Instead of Bridge, it sported an alphanumeric code that meant equally nothing to him. The crate was wooden, as broad and low as the building in miniature.

Propping his lance carefully against a taller crate nearby, Karl fit the toothed end of the prybar beneath the crate's lid and levered down. The lid broke into pieces, the wood long ago gone to rot. Given how climate-controlled the space felt, that said something about its age.

Waving away the cloud of dust that rose, Karl peered down into the crate's interior. A gleaming, spherical object the diameter of his waist and covered in all kinds of warnings, including a glaring FOR MINING USE ONLY, shone metallically back up at him, untarnished despite the slow ruin of its crate.

"Perhaps you two can correct my assumption," Karl said, "but I find it very curious that a warehouse with Gene Sequencing labeling would contain crates of some kind of explosive device."

CHAPTER 35

AT THE BOTTOM of the alley stairs had been a basement. Beneath a stack of crates in the basement's corner had been a trap door sealed with a rusted padlock. Too rusted to lock anything, it had broken easily. Beneath the trap door had been a set of spiral stairs descending into an infinite dark broken semi-regularly by harsh, flickering lights.

Down Marri had gone, because down was the only direction she could go. She could neither climb the wall, nor go through it. Under it was the only way, and under it was clearly what had been intended by whomever built this stairway.

The only sounds were her feet, her breathing, and an ever-increasing amount of dripping. It was cold down here, so maybe that was why everything seemed so wet, but she was afraid it was the rain. She had no idea how hard it was raining, of course, but at least some of those drips were coming from directly overhead. If that basement was flooding, and water was running down here, she was afraid of what she'd find at the bottom. A narrow tube going straight down seemed like a bad place to be when a bunch of water leaked from above.

There has to be a bottom before you can worry about it being full of water.

She lost track of time quickly, but after a million or so hours, her legs protesting despite no end in sight, she wondered why this went *so far down*. Who would build stairs this deep? But despite gnawing hunger and parched thirst, some part of her brain could still think. *Because normally the walls are down here, stupid. If it's a tunnel to another ward, it has to go below where the walls would sit if they were still buried.*

This gave her some hope, because tall as they were, the walls ended eventually. That meant the stairs would too. This had been where Dapper Man was going. She was sure of it. He wouldn't have been going here if it hadn't been a way out.

At last, a ragged circle of gray and brown appeared, growing larger with each step. It glimmered with apparent motion, which gave Marri pause, but down remained her only option.

Her legs gave way when she reached the bottom, which wasn't great, because the glimmering motion was a few centimeters of water which sloshed as she fell into it, soaking her coveralls from the knee down along with her socks and gloves. Hard stone barked her knees. This part of the tunnel was carved out of rock.

She was already cold, and being wet made it worse. Still, it was water that was making her so much colder, and she was thirsty. She bent her head to slurp some up and spat it out at once. She wasn't thirsty enough for the bitter flavor of this water.

Not yet, anyway.

Dispirited, she looked back up. It was the same view as down had been, a tunnel up into blackness punctuated by flickering lights. She sputtered as a stream of water to the face made her choke. Staying here for too long was a bad idea.

There was only one way to go besides back up, and that was a rough hole carved into one side of the cave, half a meter or so above the floor. It looked small, a tight fit even for someone her size. It was also utterly black. There was not even a hint of light.

Marri stared at that hole for a long time, the sweat of her fear making her even colder. The tunnel was a little above the stone floor of this place, and the water had only just begun to trickle in. But how long until it flooded?

She had nowhere else to go.

Marri got back on her knees and crawled into that utter darkness.

The tunnel definitely wasn't as long as the stairs. At least, she didn't think it was. But dark as the stairs had been, this was complete blackness. She tried not to think of what might be lurking within. She tried to tell herself that all the scrabbling sounds she imagined hearing from behind her were just the trickles of slowly rising water.

Not that this was very comforting.

This place made her think of every time she heard an adult above exclaiming "gods below." It was a stupid phrase. No gods answered prayers. She taught her mice to pray to the boss of Underguts because it was people that could help you. Or kill you. Why pray to something that had no power to answer?

The prayer had worked on the revenant, after all, even if she didn't understand how. Still, Marri thought that if ever there were any gods below, they would be in a place like this, and they would be suitably terrible.

Far from drying, her clothing only grew wetter as what had been a tiny trickle along the tunnel's bottom became a small stream and then several centimeters of water. It was rising too fast.

Worse, the tunnel narrowed in places, forcing her to inch forward on her belly, but she got stuck only twice. The first time it was the water that kept everything slippery enough for her to squeeze past the choke point. The second time was tighter still.

Too small for a rev to follow, Marri thought over and over again. It was the only comfort she could take. She kept thinking about that human skull she'd seen, assembling itself out of the teeth the revenant scraped across its prey before it entered the throat. Almost as though it had been repurposed for that use.

No. Stop thinking about it. The revs can't get you here. And that revenant let you go.

She continued to wriggle, fighting panic, trying to work herself free, trying not to imagine teeth snapping shut over her ankles. *Oh, Iazmaena, help me!*

Then, all at once, she was out. Not *out* out, but in another chamber just like the first. For a crazy moment, she was sure she'd turned around in the tunnel and wound up where she'd started. The thought left her feeling panicky. *That's stupid. There was barely room to go forward. No way you turned around.* And the tunnel had been arrow-straight. This was just the other side.

Which meant it was time to climb. And quickly. The water here was past her knees, and so much was falling from above it might as well have been raining indoors.

If the trip down had been a million hours, the trip back up lasted a billion. At last, weak with hunger, thirst, and exhaustion, she found herself squatting in a too-cramped space between the top stair and a square panel of ceiling, a trap door like the one she'd used to get down on the other side.

It will be blocked, a little voice said. *It will be blocked, and you'll drown underground in the dark. Your mice will never know what became of you.*

But even tired as she was, that was stupid. Water was streaming down along the sides of the trap door. It clearly wasn't blocked. But it might be locked.

Marri's muscles were more water than the water. She gasped with exhaustion. She might only get one shot at this before the last of her strength was spent. *Have to hope the lock is as bad on this side.*

Lowering herself down to crouch, she wondered if she'd be able to straighten again. Then, bending her neck to protect her head, Marri pushed upward with a roar, leading with her shoulders.

There was a crack of wood and a *ping* of metal snapping, and wan daylight flooded in. For an instant that terror returned, that she'd somehow ended up back where she started, but she was clearly staring out into a different basement, and even the weariness of her limbs wasn't enough to contain her glee.

She pulled herself up as quickly as she could, got shakily to her feet, and made for the door on the far wall, feet splashing though the flooding space.

Spilling out into a rainy alley similar to—but different from—the first, Marri made for a major street. Wards were distinct, even where they bordered one another.

She was no longer in Inkwell. She was in Illuminance.

Made it. I made it.

She collapsed to her knees and, despite thinking she had no water left in her, began to cry.

CHAPTER 36

THE SOUND of rain on Heart Hall's lancet windows would have soothed Iaz in a past life. Now, mired in reports of worsening conditions in Inkwell as all that water built up with nowhere to go, it had the opposite effect.

This. This is why you don't rush major infrastructure upgrades. Because Underguts still served one valuable purpose beyond supplying orphan children. During the rainy season, it provided backup drainage of all that excess water, above and beyond what the cisterns, recyclers, and river could hold and process. Their efforts to seal Underguts, beginning with Inkwell, had impacted that flow. In her capacity as magistrate of Greater Watchfire, Iaz had seen preliminary analyses stating confidently that they were still within the safety margins.

But she was willing to bet those analyses, being preliminary, hadn't considered the effects of the cordon walls being raised.

Faced with spiraling thoughts of rising waters and no way to get to any remaining survivors, Iaz would have given almost anything for a distraction, however momentary.

The ringing of her handheld produced an almost delirious rush of happiness. Then she saw it was Rieve.

Iaz almost rejected the call. The woman had been pretty clear in their last conversation that she was unable to help any further with Gene Sequencing. Plus, she seemed like the sort of person who would only call when she wanted something. But in the end, a contented Rieve Revolos seemed less likely to hare off in random directions.

"Yes, Rieve? You need something?" Fortunately, the other woman never seemed to notice a tetchy tone.

"Good news," Rieve said over a piss-poor connection, and Iaz braced herself. The other woman's idea of what constituted good news could never be assumed. "We've struck gold in this warehouse you uncovered."

Irritation spiked in Iaz. "That building is strictly off-limits to anyone but Karl and myself at the moment." She would need to expand that circle of trust soon. Karl couldn't do everything. But not until she better understood what she was dealing with.

"Interestingly hypocritical of you, considering I'm the only reason he can even access it," Rieve said.

Iaz ground her teeth. Why had Karl roped the woman into this? He'd explained his reasoning well enough, but Iaz still would have opted for the cutting torch.

"Restricting access is the only way I can be certain nothing wanders off," she said. It was the wrong thing to say, and she knew it immediately.

"I'm not certain what you're insinuating," Rieve said, prickling up right on schedule, "but the pickpocket is the *other* short one in your little cabal."

This reference to Marri sparked a long-deferred worry in Iaz, but she deferred it again.

"You're right, of course, I apologize," Iaz said. Every conversation with the woman was a floor covered in glass shards. "Thank you for your help with getting access to the warehouse. But making sure we maintain the inventory is only part of the restriction. Considering we still don't know what's even in there, I'm telling you to steer clear for your own safety."

"And I'm telling you that you're lucky I don't obey your more idiotic orders, because otherwise I never would have found this computer terminal all tucked away in a little nook off the main warehouse floor."

All her frustrations and annoyance dropped away. "You found a Gene Sequencing computer terminal."

"I did, and from what I can tell, it's hardwired directly into their network."

"So this means ..."

"This means I might not have run out of options after all. To be clear, I still think the best way to get the answers you want is the direct way."

"You saw how my attempt went," Iaz said. She could wish Rieve *hadn't* seen that.

"I saw you ask. Archons don't ask, *Madam Archon*."

If only it were that simple.

"You're right, Rieve. This is very good news. As long as you are working that issue, you can come and go to the warehouse as you need. Just don't disturb anything else."

"I'll try my very best," Rieve said, her words dripping with put-upon sarcasm. She ended the call before Iaz could say anything more.

Fresh hope blossomed in Iaz, but that long-deferred worry quickly soured it. Marri. She'd heard nothing at all from the girl since being given the tour of the Underlab space. The girl had missed their follow-up appointment. She had no reason to believe Marri would have been in Inkwell that day as opposed to some other ward, but she couldn't shake the worry, either.

She's probably just gone to ground given all the changes.

Not sure what else to do, she resolved to reiterate her message to Watchfire Hall to be notified at once in case the girl came looking there and put it out of her mind once more.

CHAPTER 37

JOHE WORKED to maintain the same outer calm the archon displayed. And it was work. Two days of ceaseless, grating work in a substandard panic chamber, waiting for rescue. *Magistrate Delgassi will come for us. No, Archon Delgassi. She's the archon now.* Teodori had scarcely stopped griping about this fact long enough to breathe. Johe tried to let the repetition of this news hearten him. But the truth was, for Johe Istuil, Archon Delgassi might come too late.

"You're going," Teodori said, "because your archon *commands* it." His voice held that same calm but carried the thrumming promise of terrible anger.

"But why now?" Johe pleaded, hating how much it sounded like whining. "We have plenty of food and water. Another week at least! Why do you need someone to look around now?"

Teodori briefly looked as though he was going to choke, and even this stifled outrage was enough to make Johe want to quail.

The building groaned around them again.

"That's why now," Teodori said, gesturing around them at the sound. "I need to know what's going on out there, what's making the building creak around us. If I had lancers to send, I would send them. I don't. I have you. You are an aide without a magistrate to assist, and that makes you the most expendable person here. Now either suit up, or I'll have you shoved out the airlock without any protection."

None of this made sense to Johe. Yes, he was the least valuable person to risk. But though Teodori had been cagey as to what the hulking Magistrate Deecks had been working on since they'd taken shelter here, it wasn't hard to deduce he was attempting to fix the shelter's broken comm unit. And from what Johe had observed, he was nearly done at last.

Which made taking a risk like sending someone out to scout around at this juncture nonsensical as far as Johe could see. Still, the archon was clearly out of patience. Defeated, trying to tamp down the cresting dread within him, Johe rose to suit up.

The suits hung from racks in the wall. Johe spent a moment selecting the one that looked the least degraded by age. Serving as a fully sealed environment suit of a single piece, it would have been easier to put on with help, but beside one furtive, sympathetic look from Magistrate Trephis, Johe found no help when he scanned the survivors. Aside from himself, Teodori, Deecks, and Trephis, only Magistrate Bennefred and Magistrate Kaigern had made it out of that cauldron of revenants alive.

"Keep your eyes open," Teodori said to him a few minutes later as he swung the airlock door shut behind Johe, "and you might just survive." There was a strangely expectant light in his eyes.

It was strange being outside the panic chamber. The overly pleasant, computerized voice had warned Johe three separate times not to exit, that revenants were still present in the building. There had been a great deal of debate over the past three days about whether the sensors functioned properly after all these years. At the time, it had felt mostly academic, something to debate to keep them all from going crazy.

And now, here Johe was. Outside, at the archon's orders. The door loomed darkly behind him, still and dead beyond the small puff of dust its cycling had lifted into the air. His footprints joined those they had left collectively when they'd arrived. He found himself hoping fervently that revenants were not smart enough to decipher such signs.

Johe made for the darkened stairwell, stumbling a little as the massive building shuddered and groaned. The stairwell did not allow him access to the first floor. He had a vague recollection of the history lesson provided for Chelsea Tower on Inkwell Day. A security precaution, not allowing anyone access to the panic chamber directly from the lobby. Since the room was only meant to house VIPs in case of an incursion crisis, Johe supposed bitterly that they couldn't have any little people infringing on their right to survive.

An eerie silence reigned as he stepped out onto the second floor. At least, he thought so; it was difficult to tell over his own ragged breathing echoing within his haz suit. The material was thick and durable, but less flexible than he would have liked. Johe was painfully aware of how much of a speed advantage revenants held over humans in the best of circumstances. He would stand no chance at all if one spotted him now.

If you stand here all day worrying about it, they're bound to find you eventually. It was enough to keep him moving.

Again, the entire building groaned around him. Johe made for the nearest bank of floor-to-ceiling windows he could find, each the width of three of him. Through them, the source of the building's distress was obvious.

He stared out into a city utterly transformed as far as he could see. His building sat partially submerged beneath a new ocean, one island in an archipelago of neighboring structures. Panic, even vertigo, flared bright within him.

His confusion subsided gradually. The surface of the water churned in the driving rain. Rain. The autumn rains had been threatening even on Inkwell Day, but flooding should never have gotten this bad. The city's myriad drainage and storage systems were well-equipped to handle the rains. Half the city's water came from them.

With a sickening feeling, Johe slid his gaze up from the disorienting sight of streets that had become canals. The views from this window were not great, and the rain further limited visibility, but he could still make out a dark, monolithic shape far down the street where no shape had been before.

The cordons. The cordons had been raised. They'd sealed the ward off.

They were trapped in Inkwell.

His mind raced, trying to understand the implications. The cordon being raised meant that revenants were still in the wards. *Archon Delgassi is in charge.* The cordon plus the rains could explain why they hadn't yet been rescued. But given the rank of the people trapped with him and Archon Delgassi calling the shots, surely rescue was only a matter of time. They were in the same building they'd been attacked in, and as soon as Deecks got the comm equipment up and running—

Something moved in the window's reflection. Johe whirled. The revenant's emerald luster caught the gray light in rippling bands within its black armored plates. It crouched to leap, and Johe ran without thought.

He barreled through the swinging door of a woman's restroom cut into the aging black marble wall, realizing it was a dead end even as he was driven into it. But just as despair took him, he realized beyond the back wall lay a deeper darkness. An open panic chamber. A sanctuary, however hopeless, for the desperate. Behind him the revenant came crashing through the door, cramming its spindly body through. From the sounds, it took much of the frame and grimy tile along that wall with it.

Johe did not slow down as he reached out a gloved hand to slap the emergency door closed on the right wall. He impacted the rear wall of the tiny chamber at speed, bounced off dazedly, and slid dizzily to the floor, one leg jutting out behind him

He heard the sharp hiss of the door slicing shut, then an otherworldly screech of rage just as his leg first vanished in numbness then bloomed in fiery pain. Facing the wrong way to see what all the commotion was about, Johe tried to turn himself around, but the bloom became a bouquet and then an entire field of agony. He stopped moving when his vision went gray around the edges.

He twisted his head around painfully, trying to see around the edge of his mask. He caught only a partial glimpse of what lay behind him, but the revenant's neck had been caught by the door, just behind its head where it was still thick. It was mostly severed. That smooth, egg-like head, as big as Johe's torso, hung limp inside the chamber. The door had not been able to close fully, but based on his attempts to free his leg, it had caught him as well as his pursuer.

Johe sat very still for a few moments, willing the pain to subside and his mind to clear. A few moments became a few minutes, then a few tens of minutes. At last, he felt lucid enough to consider his situation. The revenant remained absolutely still, except around the edges where it seethed.

Hypermutation. It's probably dead then. Probably. The thought felt lucid for the first time since he hit the wall, even fighting through the pain. He couldn't stay like this forever. At best, he needed medical attention before he ended up like the revenant. At worst, another one would come along to investigate and find him easy prey.

Gingerly, fearing what even the slight motion would bring, Johe stretched out his left arm, trying to find the corresponding door release button, the exact opposite of its right-sided mirror image. It proved to be lower down than he expected, and he could only just reach it.

Probably dead. It's definitely probably dead.

He triggered the release.

Johe woke some indeterminate amount of time later from a rippling haze of agony to find the slowly altering corpse of the beast draped atop his injured leg, dribbling a foul ichor onto his suit. Panic seized him afresh, but he steadied himself. *The suit's not compromised. There would be an alarm if it was.* The same if he were bleeding. A fracture, probably, but not a compound one. Still, he had to get free.

Jerking his leg loose of the thing's massive weight draped another layer of red gauze across his vision. When he gingerly, oh so gingerly, reached to feel around the source of the pain through the suit's thick material, Johe had an instant's awareness of a long dimpling in the flesh of his leg where no dimpling should be before the pain rose up and swallowed him again.

He woke this time to find the revenant sprouting horrors at an increasingly alarming rate, things that looked unsettlingly like the bones of arms or extra ribs. A half-formed, spongy mass of unrecognizable organ protruded from the side of that egg-shaped head.

Hobbling up to one foot, gritting his teeth to maintain consciousness, Johe steeled himself to try and get past the beast.

CHAPTER 38

IN SOME WAYS, Iaz missed her ramshackle old office in Watchfire. Leaky and drafty though it was, the building could reliably be expected to empty out by dinner time. Heart Hall was much more difficult to empty out, no matter how she cajoled staff.

More and more, Iaz found that solitude suited her.

Today, though, she'd waited out the workaholics, and the grand old building was deserted. Her lancer bodyguard waited outside the main doors and around at the building's service entrance in back. That was far enough. Maybe that was stupid considering what was happening a ward away, but Iaz didn't care.

She kept waiting for this place to stop feeling hostile. It was her office. She was the archon. Every day made it less likely Teodori was still alive.

Oh Johe, I'm so sorry. The words had the feel of being rote now, their meaning lost with the numbing repetition. But they still rose unbidden.

A soft whirring from her desk startled her, the desk's comm screen rising from its inset, indicating a message. Iaz sighed in resignation, deciding she would answer it, whoever it was. She really couldn't afford to ignore calls anymore. Then the call information, what little there was, began scrolling across the screen in flashing red characters, and Iaz barely managed to fall into her chair instead of the floor.

The ID of the caller wasn't stated, but it was coming from inside Inkwell.

"Archon Teodori, sir," Iaz gasped, shock thankfully covering up the other, more complex emotions churning beneath. "We feared you were dead."

"So I gathered, given what seems to be a rather tepid search for us," he said dryly. There was no picture; the link was too old and too bad. But Iaz recognized the voice, flowery assurance and all. "If I remember my Coldgarden law correctly, shall I refer to you as *Archon* Delgassi?"

Easy now, she thought around the nauseating stew that sloshed in her stomach. *Don't let him bait you.* "I'm sure that isn't necessary, sir," she said with as much neutrality as she could muster.

"I don't suppose it would do any good to state that now I am back in communication, I can go back to issuing orders?"

A kind of insane glee gripped Iaz. It was so hard to suppress. "As you said, sir, you know the law." Total vertigo. Everything burdensome about the power she had fallen into now felt like spiteful triumph over the hateful man.

"Quite," he said, wearily.

Iaz's incoming message light blinked, shattering the feeling. *Oh, not now.* Of course it was Rieve, sending her a text message from the lab.

Who are you talking to? A prickle of anger. Not just the usual inappropriateness, but a more invasive kind of observation. The woman had no sense of boundaries! Iaz ignored the message and attempted to pick up the conversational thread.

"You said 'us' just now. Who is with you?"

"Four other magistrates made it here with me." That was it. No mention of other, lesser lives, as he'd no doubt see them. It might not mean anything. But Iaz had to know.

"My aide? Johe?" Hope constricted her chest like a vise.

There was a pause. "Your aide made it as well, you'll be happy to hear," he said as though not answering her, merely reciting a fact of mild, mutual interest.

Iaz refused to allow the tears welling in her eyes to come through in her words. She had to modulate her voice, command it down to something that spoke of control. So much weight had lifted off her at once she felt close to soaring, her words threatening to become squeaks. "That's wonderful, very, very wonderful to hear, sir. May I speak with him please?"

Another pause.

"Sadly no. He bravely volunteered to go on a scouting run to check out our immediate area. Once we got the comm working, we knew we'd need to provide you with adequate information to extract us. Being the lowest-ranked, he insisted on being the one to go."

The weight came crashing down again, her joy snuffed out so quickly it caused her physical pain, crushing her chest. And that pause hooked Iaz like a fish. A convenient absence, explained away by its inherent nobility. *He's lying.* Iaz didn't know how she knew, but she was certain. Johe wasn't with them. *He's trying to make sure I'm vested in his well-being.* As though she needed incentive to do the right thing.

A fresh message from Rieve popped up. *Holy shit, the archon?* It multiplied even as Iaz read. *He's seriously alive?*

The nerve of this violation derailed Iaz's train of thought for a moment.

Are you listening in on my conversations? She typed the message in response.

Luckily for you, Rieve responded. *I'm trying to protect you from yourself. Case in point. What the hell are you doing talking to him after what he's done?*

"Delgassi? Are you still there? Look, I'll make sure he calls to speak with you as soon as he gets back. You needn't worry."

"Of course, of course," Iaz said, hoping it didn't sound too distracted. "That sounds exactly like my Johe," she said carefully. Rieve's words resonated with Iaz's certainty that Teodori was lying. *If he is, I'll make sure he pays with all the rest. Somehow, I will.*

But how? She couldn't even compel Gene Sequencing to obey her despite having more power than she would ever again have, and Teodori being alive meant such power would rapidly come to an end.

"Tell me, sir," she said, as much to ground her thoughts as anything, "we've been pulsing panic chambers with very limited success, but you must be in a large, well-protected one. How is it we haven't made contact before now?"

"Because these systems are so old almost nothing works properly on the comm grid anymore. Rest assured it has moved quite high on my 'to do' list once we're extracted. Now, just when would that be?"

End. This. Call. Rieve was back to messaging.

I can't, Iaz replied. *He's the archon.*

No, Rieve sent. *You are.* It was like the woman was reading her thoughts.

"That's going to depend," Iaz replied, struggling to keep both conversations separate.

"Depend? Depend on what?"

"Sir, I don't think you understand just how many revenants attacked us. The numbers are unprecedented. The cordon is up on the ward. Inkwell is completely cut off. It was the only way to save the city."

That silenced him, but just for a moment.

"I ... see. I'm sure you did what you thought was best." He sounded torn, as though part of him believed what she said while another part relentlessly sought flaws in her reasoning. "What I don't see is how that hampers a rescue effort now that we've made contact."

"The autumn rains have started," she replied. "There's far too much water coming down for the fliers to get safely airborne, so an evacuation is going to have to wait."

"Send forces on the ground, then. Surely you can manage that much!"

"Impossible at the moment."

"I'm going to need you to stop saying 'no' to each of my very reasonable demands, Delgassi."

"Sir, with the cordon up, the new systems to seal off Underguts in Inkwell are working a little too well. The rains have thoroughly flooded the ward. Three meters at last count." Thoughts of Damon flooded up, and she briefly entertained a fantasy of all that water breaching the archon's shelter and crushing him in the cold and dark.

Get hold of yourself. Iaz glanced at the message window. There was nothing new from Rieve. Perhaps the woman had given up.

"Well," Teodori said wryly, "I suppose that explains all the groaning sounds the building's been making. At least we holed up in a proven structure."

"Where exactly are you, sir? Once we know, we can start forming some plans."

"We are in Chelsea Tower, where we were when this mess began. The basement level shelter for VIPs, but accessible only via a second-floor staircase. One of the oldest panic chambers in the city, I sincerely hope, based on the accommodations. But it is at least well-stocked with provisions. The alert systems continually warn us of revenant activity, though we've neither seen nor heard any ourselves."

Chelsea Tower. So at least some of the reports of high-level officials being carried off had been incorrect. A part of Iaz kicked herself for not immediately attempting a rescue, and damn the risk. Johe could be by her side right now if she had.

But it was a smaller part of herself than she'd expected.

"We'll have to do our own sweeps to confirm once the fliers can get airborne again."

"I'm going to require an explanation of how you let matters get so far out of hand, Delgassi. Why are there still revenants alive? Did rain ground the fliers that day? The streets couldn't be flooded all at once. Tell me what you have been doing to *stop* this disaster!"

She thought she could have killed him for the accusation in his tone alone.

"You were there, but you obviously don't understand, sir. We were overwhelmed immediately. After we cordoned off the district, the revenants immediately turned on the remaining civilians." Iaz would keep the tears from her voice. She would. She couldn't give this man the satisfaction of hearing any vulnerability. Having to explain herself was bad enough. But she also couldn't stop recounting the horrors of that day. "They butchered them."

Her spite leaked through around the welling tears, as if to say *it could still happen to you*. She couldn't help it. "We lost too many lancers before the cordon, before we understood just how bad the incursion was. We had no time to organize a sortie that wouldn't get even more lancers killed," she went on. "None of the fliers were in position to help. One had already gone down to revenant attack." *Fuck, I sound bitter.* She couldn't show weakness to this man.

"Start from the beginning," he said, his tone infuriatingly calm and reasonable, as though he was trying to *comfort* her. "How many are there in the city? Where did they come from?"

"We think there were around three to five hundred to start," she said. "And that we've killed no more than twenty percent."

"An entire *enclave*?" His voice was incredulous.

"So it would seem."

"How could so many get in?"

"Above and below, simultaneously. The working theory," she said, "is that they climbed the wall and once again came in via Foundation."

Another pause. "How," he finally asked, "are either of those things possible?"

There it was, an accusation he hadn't even bothered to veil. Revenants had done the impossible, so it must be Iazmaena Delgassi's fault.

"For the former, we have a working theory. You recall the damaged section of wall, not long before Inkwell Day? We believe they used that piece as a template to learn the wall's relaxation pattern so they could estimate when a portion of it would be safe to climb. For the latter, we've significantly underestimated their ability to change their forms. Which means our *very hastily installed* barriers may be more effective as bathtub plugs than they are at stopping revenants."

Let him take a taste of accusation for once.

"Even if what you say is true," the archon said, "the ones that came over the wall would have been detected in Watchfire. In *your* ward. So why weren't they?"

"Some new kind of camouflage ability. Both visual and infrared. It defeats our automated sensors handily and gives even live lancers fits. I saw it firsthand on Inkwell Day. It would be more than enough to get them deep into the ward before they were detected."

"Gods below, Delgassi! What have you been *doing* about this situation? You can't go back and un-let them in, that I understand. But *why* are these fucking creatures still infesting my city?"

Because of all the reasons I just told you. It was all so fucking typical, a powerful person used to getting everything he wanted, demanding that the way he wanted things to be must become reality, right fucking now. Iaz almost screamed.

Every second you are on this call, you give him weapons to hurt you further. It was Rieve. Her response was there, blinking to get Iaz's attention. *I traced the hardline he's using. Do you want to guess who he called just before you? Who he called just before calling the acting archon?*

Iaz stared at that message for a long time. Gene Sequencing. She was the acting archon, and Teodori had called Gene Sequencing first.

"Delgassi, I don't know what you are doing that is more important than answering me, but I swear—"

"Even prior to the rains, the revenants had mostly gone to ground," she began. Her voice was flat and affectless. "Given their camouflage, there's so much cover that we don't dare risk assets unless we are certain we have an overwhelming advantage. I initially ordered the focus to be on evacuations of positively identified groups of civilians. Before the rains grew in intensity, we would identify a likely area for a cluster of survivors, comm pulse it if we could, send in a flier with orders to take extreme caution and scout out for signs of human life, and hope. The rains have now made all of that impossible. If only we'd heard from you earlier ..." Iaz tried to keep the relish out of her voice on this last before continuing.

"And how many did you manage to pull out?" Teodori's voice was calmer now.

"Just under a thousand," Iaz responded her tone indecipherable even to her. It was a chillingly small number. "Even that cost us another two fliers, and almost a hundred more lancers. Counting the losses since, nearly a third of the corps has been lost." It still staggered her to wrap her brain around that. A *third* lost under her watch.

"Gods below," Teodori intoned, voice a whisper.

"Even without the flooding, I can't commit what's left of our forces to an ambush-laden killing field," Iaz went on. "Not when the possibility for further attacks from outside the city exists. And until we fully understand how they got over the wall and how to defeat their camouflage, there is that possibility. But now I know you're alive, we can begin a plan to extract you."

Over the next minute, she wound down the conversation, deflecting his concerns or promising she'd address them. But she was on autopilot. They signed off with Iaz promising Teodori she would resume contact soon.

She wasn't certain if any of it was true.

The instant the call ended, Rieve piped back up over messaging.

You need my help far more than I ever thought.

Iaz ignored this. *If he contacts Gene Sequencing again, can you tell me what he says?*

Not without direct access to at least one end of the conversation. But it's irrelevant. He won't be contacting Gene Sequencing, or anyone else, again. No one but you, that is.

Iaz stared fixedly at this message for a long time.

What are you talking about?

I locked him out of making calls. Piggybacked on the connection with your line. His comm unit is now a closed circuit with yours.

But why?

Because you need time without him scheming behind your back, Rieve typed. *Time to figure out whether you are going to use the power you've been given to get the answers you're owed, or not.*

Iaz didn't respond for a long time. It must have made Rieve antsy, because after a few minutes, she followed up.

Or should I undo the lock out?

Iaz let another minute elapse. There was a chance she could leverage answers out of a man who owed them to many people, not just her. A chance to learn why Damon's suicide note had implicated Teodori himself as the cause.

The entire city seemed to flex and stretch from its perch upon her shoulders as she keyed her final message of the evening.

No. Leave it in place for now.

CHAPTER 39

THE SOUND of the large panic chamber's airlock cycling sounded like a gunshot in Johe's fevered mind. His agony flared with his flinch, as though he'd actually been shot. His half-crawl, half-drag of his wounded leg back to a semblance of safety was only a hazy memory of anguish.

He fell through the open hatch back into the shelter as soon as the decontamination spray cycle concluded. A wail of agony ripped through him, echoing painfully in his suit. He caught a brief glimpse of a stunned and angry looking Teodori staring down at him.

"Check him!" Teodori barked, his voice muffled through the suit. "Pull him free of the lock!" Through a haze of pain and rising fever, Johe heard more than saw the others approach. Then the pain doubled and doubled again as hands grasped his wrists and dragged him across the orange-tiled floor. He strove to rise on instinct until piercing agony battered him back down.

"Far enough," Teodori called. "Someone check his leg, *without* touching it please. Let's not let this spread any further. Deecks, get ready to shove him right back out if he shows signs of hypermutation."

Panic seized Johe, a desperate sense of helplessness. "No!" The word was so sluggish he feared he hadn't been understood. "No, please, no!"

"Sorry, son," Teodori said, expressing the words if not the tones of sympathy. "But you—"

"Archon," another voice interrupted. *Trephis,* some lucid part of Johe's brain whispered. There were sharp tugs at Johe's suit, as though someone was cutting into it. "Everything looks normal. The suit wasn't compromised. The wound itself is a break, but it's not compound, and there's no sign of hypermutation present."

"Stay clear anyway," Teodori said.

"Without treatment—" Trephis began.

"If you want to risk yourself, go right ahead," Teodori snapped back.

"I believe I will, sir. Questions of ethics aside, I would think," she went on, "that having saved the magistrate of Greater Watchfire's aide might smooth over any further discussions you two have."

Discussion? "D—did Magistrate Del—"

"Don't try to talk." Trephis's voice was kindly. She was cutting away the rest of his suit out from under him, and just the feel of fresh air on his skin made Johe feel somewhat better.

"Boy," Teodori began sharply then moderated his tone. "Johe," he started again. "What happened to you?"

"Re—revenant," Johe said, fighting a fresh wave of pain. He felt a sharp tug on his thigh, then a wash of dreamy relaxation spread through him, numbing his leg. His teeth chattered as though they'd been awaiting just that signal. "Found me outside. I ran from it, tried t—to hide in a panic chamber. Slammed the door shut on it. And my leg. Door killed it. C—crawled back. Airlock d—disinfected suit."

"You're a very lucky young man," Teodori said, sounding sincere. "What else did you see?"

"Rain," Johe said. He felt suddenly as though he was falling into deep, warm water, perhaps the very water he'd witnessed. "Flood. Sea." Wonder filled him as darkness rolled over him.

CHAPTER 40

AFTER SLIDING BACK the fake alley recycler and exposing the hatch down to the Underlab, Stefani had to pause to steel herself. She was coming to dread these descents down into the dark, into a trap she felt she'd walked into herself.

But, in the end, Stefani had no choice. Sighing, she raised the hatch, stepped down onto the spiral stairwell, pulled the hatch shut behind her, and pressed the switch that would slide the recycler back in place above.

Only the thought of seeing Ella below kept her feet moving ever downward.

Promises of a way to help Ella had been what enticed her in, of course. But therein lay the trap, a puzzle with no solution.

Reaching the bottom, Stefani made a beeline for Ella's bubble. Retracting the bubble, Stefani picked up her baby, taking solace from the little bundle of warmth as she kissed Ella on her forehead. Only then did Stefani possess the strength to survey her futile domain. Rieve's workstation was dark, blessedly. That meant that in addition to a reprieve from Rieve's awful music, Stefani could bring Ella out of her little nook without risking anyone's safety but her own. The thought of Ella alone in her nook stabbed Stefani through with guilt, as it always did. Autocare equipment was commonplace even outside of illicit, subterranean labs, but it could not replace a mother. Stefani worried constantly this was what she was demanding it do.

The medical research equipment they'd acquired were all set up and, where necessary, repaired. The dedicated workstation Rieve had so begrudgingly ported her software to sat churning away, still processing its first imaging from the day the wall came up. Stefani had begun to wonder if the thing would ever finish processing. Rieve's software stubbornly refused to provide her with any kind of percent complete indicator.

Which was probably by design.

Lastly, there were what had been occupying most of her working hours, a pair of large test chambers which might, if she'd rigged them correctly, enable her to hold dead revenants safely in a quasi-stasis environment until she was ready to test them.

Testing them was, at root, the problem. Gene Sequencing, as the name implied, maintained a tight hold on any and all equipment intended for use in sequencing genes. They cited Mutagen Prime outbreak risk from such research as the reason, and Rieve had provided little to contradict that. That said, Rieve's data had been next to worthless so far. Portions of DNA sequences totally stripped of contextual information, or unrelated comments from reports without the corresponding DNA data, meant nothing to Stefani. What she needed was instructions on how to sequence DNA and how to build equipment that could do so since she couldn't procure any already built for that purpose, not even through gray market contacts that had provided them with much of their other equipment.

Stefani supposed she should be thankful that the Underlab had shown her how thoroughly she'd been wasting her life in "research" on Mutagen Prime. *Mutagen Prime* was a catch-all term for a ghost, and her work on it had always focused on trying to identify a causal element they were no closer to identifying after decades. Viral, bacterial, prion. It was something every human in Coldgarden was infected with, yet no causal agent could be located. Whatever it was must be transmitted on a vector totally beyond their understanding, something the revenants had brought with them, intentionally or not, when they'd arrived.

Now Stefani had at last been granted the latitude she needed to dig deeper, but without the means to do so, she was wasting her time.

The answer must lie buried in the DNA of people, but Stefani was having to reinvent the wheel from scratch in order to determine even how to start looking for it! She wished for colleagues, people as versed in the science as she, whom she could bounce ideas off of. Failing that, she wished Karl would at least call or visit more. The former was impossible, while the latter wouldn't really solve anything. It just would have been nice.

"How long are you going to stand there?"

Stefani nearly jumped out of her skin as Rieve's chair spun around, revealing Marri. Stefani gasped, pausing only long enough to put Ella back in her crib and seal the bubble before she rushed over and gathered Marri up out of the chair in a hug. Marri stiffened at the contact but did not actively resist.

"I was so worried when Iaz said she hadn't heard from you," Stefani said, setting Marri back down on the floor. "We were scared you'd been trapped in Inkwell."

"I was," Marri said simply. Her tone was mild, but she wouldn't meet Stefani's eye as she spoke.

"*What?* How are you here?"

Marri gave her a stubborn look, but it crumbled, and she sighed. "I was following one of the archon's people for Magistrate Delgassi. After the walls came up, he knew a secret way out. Too small for a revenant. He didn't make it, but I did."

Stefani barely heard anything past the first statement. *Iaz, how could you?* "She shouldn't have asked you to do that, Marri. I'm going to have words with—"

"No!" Marri shook her head violently. "She didn't ask me. I did it on my own, so that I could still be useful."

Stefani's anger shifted from Iaz to the cruelty of this city. *Iaz still*

shouldn't be indulging the girl's obsession with this exchange of work
for food. These children should be under adult supervision.

"None of my mice are going to an orphanage," Marri said mulishly, and Stefani flushed that she was so easy to read.

"What do you mean he didn't make it?" Stefani asked, keying belatedly on Marri's earlier comment.

Marri began pacing. "A revenant got him. Almost got me, too, but then ... it didn't. It let me go after it, after it showed me something." She picked up the portable radiation meter sitting atop Stefani's prototype stasis box and began to fiddle with it, brimming with nervous energy, reluctant to go on.

Stefani began to worry if the girl might be delirious, feverish. She placed the back of her palm against Marri's forehead, but it felt normal.

"I'm not sick!" Marri barked, jerking her head away. "And I'm not crazy. The revenant opened its mouth, and there was a human skull inside."

Stefani was horrified. "Oh, Marri, did you actually see it eat the man you were following?"

"No!" Marri shouted in frustration. "I mean, yes, but you don't understand. The skull was *part of it*. It was in pieces at the throat, like it had been broken and was being used as teeth, then the rev kind of forced the pieces back together to show me the whole skull." In her nervous fidgeting, she turned the meter in her hands, pressing buttons at random, and she clicked it on.

As it was facing her, the meter began clicking, picking up a reading.

Both stared at the device: Marri in confusion, Stefani in alarm.

"Let me see that," Stefani said, snatching the device away. Visions that Ella had been exposed to dangerous radiation flashed through her mind. The meter was for making certain nothing was happening inside the stasis box and was dialed down to incredibly sensitive levels.

She blew out a sigh of relief. The radiation levels were not dangerous. With a less sensitive meter, they wouldn't have shown up at all. Marri's contact must have been incidental. But that wasn't all. The meter recognized the signature it had detected.

"You're all right, Marri, don't worry. I apologize if I scared you." The girl just looked confused. "If I showed you a map, could you show me where in Inkwell you were?" Marri's look grew guarded. Stefani sighed. "I'm not trying to find your mice. I just want to know where you picked up a radiation signature the meter can read."

Still frowning, Marri approached as Stefani brought up a map of the city on her terminal. It was very high resolution and could be zoomed down to individual street level. Stefani allowed Marri to work it, and after a few minutes, the girl had oriented herself enough to show the path she had taken to incredible detail. Stefani marveled at the sharpness of her memory, but the path confused her, because it wasn't near any of the reactors responsible for this radiation signature.

"You're sure?" Stefani asked.

Marri nodded with affront.

Stefani had the map mark every reactor of this type still in the city, Inkwell or not. "Have you been near *any* of these in the last few days? Oh, gods below, Marri, I'm not trying to trick you into revealing your little hidey hole."

"No," Marri said, after examining the map for a few minutes more. "None of them." Stefani supposed she could be lying but didn't know what to do about that.

"Did you encounter anything else strange after the walls came up?"

"Aside from the revenant, you mean?"

The revenant. Revenants weren't radioactive. If Marri wasn't lying and the meter wasn't wrong, then it was possible the revenant had been in close proximity to one of the Inkwell reactors prior to its encounter with Marri. She wondered if that was significant.

"What did you say about the skull?" she asked, only then remembering.

"That is was part of the revenant. That's what I came to tell you. To tell someone, anyway. I couldn't find Magistrate Delgassi at her office. One of her guards shouted at me when he noticed me, but I ran away. I have something else I need to tell her. It's important. About the man I was following. I think he meant to kill her. I heard the archon say it, just before the walls came up. The man is dead now, but if there are others with the same order, Magistrate Delgassi is in danger."

Stefani's head spun. She still half-wondered if the girl were making things up to stay relevant, but Iaz had sworn that Marri had followed instructions so far to the letter. And the more they learned about Archon Teodori, including secret technological caches that had nothing to do with genetic research despite belonging to Gene Sequencing, the more she'd believe the man was capable of.

"All right," Stefani said. "It's late enough that I can take you to see her. No doubt she'll want to hear this from you directly. And to see that you're all right."

She sighed again. Ella would have to wait a bit longer for time with her.

CHAPTER 41

IAZ HAD JUST REACHED out to Rieve, looking for an update on the
Gene Sequencing probe, when Steffi charged into her office like a
bull, Marri trailing in her wake.

"Hold for a moment, Rieve," Iaz said, touching the earpiece to
mute it. This was likely not going to be pleasant.

Iaz said nothing as Marri told her story, not interrupting even
once to ask any of the dozens of questions she had, questions the girl
couldn't possibly answer. A man she'd followed on her own initiative
approaching the archon in the street while Iaz marched not twenty
meters behind. The brazenness of it had made the archon upset, if
Marri told it true. Iaz couldn't recall the man herself, but there had
been many such pauses to greet the crowd.

Steffi stood at the girl's shoulder the whole time, a protective
posture. She probably thought she was concealing her glare, but Iaz
had known the other woman too long for her to hide her feelings so
easily. *I didn't ask the girl to follow that man, Steffi.* Still, she apparently should have forbidden it.

"Did he mention my name?" she asked after Marri had wound
down. "Did either of them?"

"No," Marri admitted. "But it was like they were trying to talk in code. Nothing specific. It was a big crowd, and people could have listened." She shrugged. "I was listening, after all."

"Nothing explicit about killing?"

"No," Marri said again, clearly impatient. Her expression said, *I just explained this to you.*

"So we don't really know anything," Stefani said. She looked worried, though.

"Not with just this," Iaz said. "But with what Rieve has turned up already ..." Just then she remembered Rieve. She unmuted her earbud.

"Rieve, I'm going to have to call you back. I'm sorry."

An audible sigh and a click was all she got in response.

"Thank you for telling me all this, Marri," Iaz said. "But just to be clear, no more adventures unless I explicitly ask you to. Your mice will stay fed forever, you have my word. You could have died—"

"She very nearly did die," Steffi said, anger suffusing every word. "Three times, unless I misheard."

Far from ashamed, Marri just looked angry. "Shouldn't have said all that," she grumbled. "Wouldn't have said anything if not for the skull."

"One of you please explain to me about the skull," Iaz said.

Marri explained in more detail. When she finished, Iaz felt sick at how much danger the girl had put herself in on Iaz's behalf.

"I repeat," Iaz said, "you are to follow no one else. Is that clear?"

"I can help," Marri said.

"You've helped more than your share already," Iaz said. "I owe *you.*" This seemed to mollify the girl more than a simple refusal would have. "Remember, if something happens to you, no one knows where your mice are hidden. We couldn't help them."

She half-hoped this would prompt the girl to reveal her hideout, but Marri just nodded with slightly widened eyes, at last looking chastened.

"You can go now, Marri," Iaz said. She considered offering her an escort but knew the girl would only refuse. It was broad daylight, and she had certainly survived worse than the city was likely to dish out. "You did very well. Just don't ever do it again. Come see me in a few days. I'll leave instructions that you're to be let in."

The girl threw her an inscrutable look on her way out the door.

"What does it mean? This skull," Iaz asked Steffi after she was gone.

"Without seeing it myself, I couldn't say," Steffi said carefully. "I'm skeptical it happened this way at all, frankly."

Iaz understood, she had never once heard any story of a revenant showing mercy to a victim much less offering up a peep show. "Speculate wildly for me, then."

Steffi looked exasperated. "We know they can change their shape and texture. Maybe that relies partly on raw materials they have on hand. Perhaps they lack some metabolic processes we take for granted, and part of why they hunt and eat people is that they use parts of us to build themselves. I don't know, Iaz, maybe it had been sucking on someone's skull like a piece of hard candy and showed it to Marri to watch her scream."

"That wasn't it at all!" Marri's voice called through the closed door to the office, at which she'd clearly been listening. Iaz was going to have to get guards back there after all. "It spared me when it heard your name! It was trying to tell me something!"

"Goodbye, Marri!" Iaz called back. She walked over and e-locked the door for good measure then lowered her voice. "Let's assume for the sake of argument that all this really did happen and that she interpreted it correctly. What could a revenant be trying to tell her?"

"I have no idea," Steffi said. "We know almost nothing about them, really, thanks to the Loss. So many of that generation died of revenants or hypermutation, that we don't really even have the fallible record of passed-down stories to work with."

It flashed Iaz back to a similar conversation with Karl just outside the wall. "You're right," she said. "We know almost nothing." Her face hardened into grim lines. "I wonder if Gene Sequencing knows more?"

"Probably," Steffi said wearily. "But with Rieve on the job, it will be centuries before we do. Right now, I'm more interested in this radiation signature Marri picked up. If that came from the revenant, and at this point it's as likely a source as any, then I want to know why."

"What good is radiation on one random revenant?"

"That's just it," Steffi said. "If only one random revenant was near a building reactor, what are the odds Marri happened to run into that exact one?"

"You're suggesting there might be more."

"I'm wondering if there's something about those reactors that draws them." Stefani's eyes sparkled. "If so, that could be our way to find them and clear them out. But we'd need a way to prove it."

"Time for you to talk to Karl, I think," Iaz said.

CHAPTER 42

THE MEETING with Steffi plus an apologetic and ultimately pointless return call to Rieve left Iaz ready for a drink and sleep as she climbed the battered steps in her building. It was true that sleep and drink didn't go well together, but Iaz was resolute. She would find a way.

She reached her landing only to have her handheld buzz. Sighing despondently, she almost ignored it, but found she couldn't.

Rieve. Of course, Rieve.

On my way to your apartment. Have something you'll want to see.

That curious feeling, hope mixed with dread, spiked in Iaz again. It was, above all else, exhausting. But stopping Rieve was like standing against a revenant charge. Iaz didn't even bother responding, just rounded the corner, and her knees nearly buckled at what she beheld. Her door lay at the end of the hall, just as Damon's had on his hall.

And it was now ajar, just as his had been.

Iaz immediately drew her sidearm. She'd taken to wearing it again, concealed, after the revenant incursion. The familiar weight of it was a comfort where so little else was these days. Despite this, she stood rooted for several moments. Anxiety flayed her.

"Go," she whispered to herself. "It's not like it can be Damon again." It was enough to get started, and getting started was enough to keep going, though her heartbeat and breath ran wild. The hallway seemed to constrict as she advanced, lengthening even as her vision tunneled.

She heard an unmistakable thump from within.

Burglar. She told herself this, not believing it for a second. Marri's warning rang in her ears. She cursed herself for training her guards so thoroughly to leave her alone. There could be anything in there, human or otherwise, and she was the archon, even if no criminal would mistake this building for an archon's residence.

She shouldn't go in. She should call for police or lancer backup. Yet on she went.

The door was not just open but broken open. The bolt was still engaged and had taken part of the frame with it as it tore free. Not Marri, then. A part of Iaz wanted to fling the door the rest of the way open, burst in, and hope to catch whoever it was by surprise. But she was smarter than that and instead angled herself to sidestep in without touching the door. It opened onto a narrow entryway, so there were thankfully no corners to check.

The figure moved the instant she entered. It stood in the center of the room beyond, and its head turned to regard her. Human and male by the proportions.

Not a revenant at least. Which meant it was probably one of the archon's lackeys.

Then it took a single step forward into the wedge of orange light spilling in from the hall, and all thought stopped.

Dark, close-cropped hair. An angular, familiar face.

"D-amon?" Iaz lowered the gun without thought, which apparently was what he'd been waiting for. If he'd rushed her, to embrace her, to kill her, she'd have stood no chance of stopping him. Her heart ached for either of those things to be his goal. But the figure dropped something he'd been holding and ran the other way, heavy steps thumping as he slid open a window on the room's far side and ducked through.

Cursing, weeping, Iaz followed, but he was already out of sight. There was a fire escape a short hop away from the window ledge. If he was running down it, he was lost to the night.

"Hey," came a voice from behind her.

Iaz whirled, bringing the gun up to find Rieve staring at her with widened eyes. The little woman's hands shot up, one palm open, the other one clutching something.

"Not the welcome I expected," Rieve said, the words a little strangled.

"What are you holding?" Iaz demanded. She tried to calm her breathing before giving it up as impossible.

"D-data drive," Rieve said. "For you. Why are you pointing a gun at me?" She looked legitimately scared for the first time Iaz could remember. It was this fact that calmed her. *Gods below, what must I look like?*

She lowered the gun.

"I'm sorry," she said. "Someone broke into my apartment. A man."

"Who?" Rieve asked, voice hushed. "One of Teodori's?"

"That's what I assumed," Iaz said. "But it looked like ..." No. She couldn't answer that. This looked bad enough as it was.

"It looked like ...?"

"Nothing," Iaz said. "It was too dark to tell." She stooped to examine what the intruder had dropped. It was a digital frame featuring a favorite photo of her and Damon, the same one she'd recovered from his apartment. The screen had cracked during the fall. Suddenly deflated, she wandered over to her cabinets and poured herself a drink that barely stopped below the glass's lip. Not enough, but a start. She gestured with the glass, careful not to slosh. "What's on that?"

"I'm not sure I should show you in this state," Rieve said, some of that fear returning.

"You just startled me, Rieve," Iaz said. It was a lie, but she thought it sounded convincing at least.

"Get out your handheld," Rieve said. "I'll transfer it and leave you to read in peace."

I should threaten to kill her more often.

Iaz did as she was bid. Rieve reached from as far away as she could, as though Iaz was infectious. The file transferred, Rieve bobbed her head and scooted to the door.

"Are you going to be all right alone?" Her eyes flicked briefly to the half-empty glass then back to Iaz.

"Not my first trip around this block," Iaz said. The alcohol was doing enough work to make her not care much about admitting this. "And this," she said, hefting the sidearm, "will keep me safe from anything outside my head."

Rieve did not need further coaxing. She nodded again and left.

Iaz turned her blurring attention to the file. It was the same as before, an excised portion, like a summary bullet point, from a larger file.

Blackburne op failure. Catastrophic breach likely. Expedited termination order issued for target. All assets: execute at earliest opportunity.

-V.T.

The Damon operation had failed. As a result, the target was to be killed at the earliest opportunity. Given that he'd died the night of the election, it certainly seemed *expedited.* Iaz didn't know what catastrophic breach meant, unless it referred to the loss of Teodori's voting majority. But *target* didn't seem to work for Damon.

Me. I was the target of the Blackburne operation. This is referring to me.

Here it was. A kill order by one V.T., Vernon Teodori.

Marri had been right after all.

Suddenly, Iaz wondered if that had indeed been Damon's face she'd seen. Because there was another face she'd seen recently, one that had reminded her strongly of Damon.

Palo Hayasun, Teodori's preferred lackey at Gene Sequencing.

CHAPTER 43

THE RAIN outside Heart Hall was lighter today, but what kind of omen that might be, Iaz couldn't say. It was taking all her energy just to hold herself together for this, an in-person meeting with people other than her closest associates.

She imagined Hayasun, or other shadowy figures, always lurking just out of sight.

She wanted to understand. Needed to. Why had it been so crucial to kill her? How had Gene Sequencing tried to rope Damon into it so thoroughly that he'd either killed himself over it or been murdered when he resisted?

Yes, it took everything she had—everything—not to wallow within this toxic stew of paranoia and rage. More than once she had almost reached out to Teodori, whose continued silence somehow added to her anxiety, determined to reveal all she knew and bluff him into confessing. But if he was as cold an operator as he seemed, admitting what she knew would reveal her hand too soon.

So she continued to return silence with silence.

The final stragglers arrived for the meeting. Large as it was, there was not enough seating space or infrastructure to support such a meeting in Iaz's office. She had invited all the surviving magistrates.

Graysteel, Losche, Osira, Dumbarton, and Radnor had each blown off Inkwell Day and the performative nature of making an appearance there. Technically not even a quorum, but they were overlooking that little point of legality until new elections could be held after the crisis had passed.

None were known to be cronies of Teodori. But how much could Iaz trust such conventional wisdom any longer?

Steffi was last to arrive, which would have been uncharacteristic of her once. This earned a cool look from Magistrate Graysteel. Likely that was for her leaving the magistrate's service for Iaz's as much as for the tardiness.

Even Rieve was present, albeit remotely, because Rieve was Rieve and wasn't a fan of people. She listened through the customary earpiece Iaz wore in her left ear concealed beneath the fall of her hair.

Karl stood ramrod-straight at the business end of the conference table, a rectangular slab of real wood polished to a high cherry sheen marred only by the holoprojector at its center. He would be doing most of the talking today, at Iaz's behest. And if he was only slightly less agitated than she was, she'd be happy if she were hiding it half so well. Still, she sympathized. It was far easier dressing down a bunch of rowdy recruits in uniform than it was attempting to impose your will on politicians.

With Steffi seated, Iaz nodded at Karl.

Karl cleared his throat. "Thank you all for coming. Archon Delgassi asked me to host this meeting because of the set of circumstances that provide us with a unique opportunity, but also a pressing time window. So I won't belabor the introductions. I think we all know one another here."

He waved his hand and a holographic image appeared above the projector. It depicted a wire map of Inkwell, complete with cordon walls which the simulation immediately dissolved into scattered pixels of vanishing light to better aid visibility.

"Inkwell," Karl said unnecessarily. The holograms picked out three buildings in glimmering light brighter than the rest. City record searches had revealed these buildings shared several traits, larger and older than their neighbors being the most prominent, aside from the obvious.

"These three buildings," Karl said, "Chelsea Tower, Mirror Center, and Harps Plaza, currently have power courtesy of aging fusion reactors within their foundations. We've compiled credible sensor intel that at least some revenants cordoned in Inkwell show signs of exposure to radiation." Karl was being intentionally cagey on the source of this intel. Marri might not make the most compelling witness. "Based on this, we've conducted some sensor sweeps that track revenant movements toward these three structures. At least, more so than the average."

"Not a very ringing endorsement of data matching," Magistrate Graysteel said pointedly.

"No, but the correlation could be growing," Steffi said, picking up the thread now that Graysteel had redirected the conversation toward the scientific. "That's what the data seem to show. It's hard to parse, because we still can't reliably see past their camouflage when they are still. But we've gotten much better at spotting them on the move. All indicators are that more of them are gathering in these places, and that they are doing so with more urgency as time passes. The theory is that they are somehow drawn by the ionizing radiation leaked by the reactors. To what end, we don't know."

"You should have made something up." Rieve's voice in Iaz's ear startled her, but she thought she managed to hide the reaction. "Saying 'we don't know' always invites someone else to advance their garbage opinion."

Iaz couldn't respond, of course, which had to be Rieve's dream come true.

As if to purposefully make Rieve insufferable, Graysteel continued, "Given the seriousness of this situation, I think some degree of informed speculation is in order, no matter how distasteful I normally find it."

"Whatever their purpose," Karl jumped in, picking the thread back up before it could get away from them, "you can bet it's not in our best interest."

"I think we can all concur on that," Graysteel conceded.

"But is it possible that these are just buildings where survivors have congregated?" Magistrate Osira's open, guileless face belied a keen mind and dogged determination in everything that grabbed her focus.

"Osira," Rieve scoffed in Iaz's ear. "The things I could tell you *she's* been up to."

"Possible," Karl said. They'd discussed this line of argument beforehand. "But statistically unlikely. Plenty of other buildings in the ward still have emergency power as well, through more advanced battery systems that these three older structures lack. Consequently, there's no reason for us to believe that panic chambers with survivors remain only in these three buildings."

"I remind you that Chelsea Tower was the focal point of the initial attack," Iaz said. It was the first time she had spoken, and she found she could not keep all emotion from her voice. But the others viewed her with a kind of awe for being the attack's sole elected survivor, so she commanded their undivided attention. "It stands to reason that any survivors left in that building were rooted out long ago. "

She marveled at how well Teodori's panic chamber must be hidden to make this previous statement such an astonishing lie.

"Your voice is thready," Rieve said. "Try taking a few deep breaths to calm yourself down. But do it quietly. You don't want to look insane."

It was all Iaz could do not to tear the earpiece out and drop it in the water pitcher sitting in front of her. But thready or not, the other magistrates nodded at Iaz's words, swayed by her reasoning.

"Respectfully, esteemed Magistrates, Your Excellency, we have to assume they intend something with those reactors." Karl gave this statement the force of finality while wording it as though he was presenting this conclusion to Iaz for the first time. Of course, this was just another thing they'd discussed ahead of time.

Blessedly, another round of nods.

"But what does this buy us?" Magistrate Losche spoke this time, a blunt man with a reputation for saying whatever was on his mind, though in Iaz's experience, he didn't speak nearly enough for that to be true unless his mind was particularly sedate.

"Biggest idiot of the bunch," Rieve offered.

"Aside from the identification of a potential wider threat to the city, nothing by itself," Karl said. "But we're looking at a weather forecast over the next several days for significant gaps in the rain. It's a window of opportunity. A chance to get fliers into the air and focus their attack on where the bulk of the revenants will be. Tomorrow, specifically, with the day after as a backup if the better weather holds off."

"To what end?" Graysteel asked, spreading her arms, palms upraised in confusion. "We have no mass-casualty capable weaponry, nor would I want to use one near those reactors. Do you intend for the fliers to pick off revenants with their belly guns one or two at a time when all the revenants need to do to avoid being spotted is hold still?"

"I'll leave that to our esteemed Archon." Karl turned to Iaz.

"Remember," Rieve said. "Don't let them see you sweat."

"Respectfully, Magistrate Graysteel," Iaz said, "we do, in fact, have the ability to inflict mass casualties. A capability I only just learned about the other day." She stood, drawing the eyes of the room to her. She willed her knees not to shake. This began the second of her objectives today. "In combing through Archon Teodori's records, I noticed an odd entry. With Lance Commander Yonnel's help, we have located and gained access to a warehouse full of, at the risk of sounding melodramatic, mysterious technologies. All pre-Loss."

She gave it a moment for the hushed gasps of surprise.

"This tech and equipment," she went on, "were kept totally out of the public eye by my predecessor. Even the Grand Projects had no access to it."

"What?" Graysteel's face was suddenly a thunderhead as dark as her name. "What are you talking about?"

"Most of this technology appears to be pieces of a single, massive object that's been disassembled or possibly destroyed," Iaz said instead of being sidetracked. "Something labeled, 'Bridge.'"

"Are you sure it's wise to be telling them all this?" Rieve cautioned in her ear.

"But there are a few crates distinct from the rest," Iaz continued, "one of which is relevant to our discussion here." She turned to Graysteel. "Tell me, Magistrate, does the term 'matter-eater charge' mean anything at all to you?"

"No, Madam Archon, it does not." Graysteel was genuinely taken aback. She'd either never heard the term before or was a master actor. Stefani claimed she was very hands-on with her scientists and their Grand Projects, maintaining a high-level of knowledge in each focus area. "Perhaps you would care to enlighten me?"

"I'd appreciate your people's opinions on the schematics," Iaz said over Rieve's hiss in her ear. "But whatever they are, we have four of them. Here I feel I must pause and state that this cache of technology represents a degree of secrecy I'd not believed the previous administration capable of."

Judging by the faces of the magistrates before her, they were just as shocked as she claimed to be. Now for the part she *hadn't* discussed in advance with the others. It had been Rieve's idea though, and it was as good a notion as the woman had ever conjured up.

"And I'm extremely troubled by the notion that this warehouse is listed as belonging to Gene Sequencing, and that all my attempts to solicit further information in my official capacity as acting archon have been rebuffed."

This was a small lie. She had not, in fact, tried to ask them about *this* at all. Given how badly her queries into Damon had gone, she'd known not to risk tipping her hand. But the groundwork for matters after this operation had passed needed to be laid, and Rieve was right about one other thing.

Once that moment arrived, Iaz wouldn't have much time left in power.

And how exactly do you view that transition of power? Damon's voice mocked her. *With the ascension of a new leader ... or an old one?* Iaz banished the voice because it was a question she had no answer to.

"I would very much like to view these schematics myself," Graysteel said. "But surely you have some idea of what these devices are capable of?"

Iaz gestured back to Karl.

"Ma'am, I believe we do. The included specs recommend their use for mining, but I believe they can be weaponized simply enough. Now, I am the last person that would advocate turning some unknown destructive device against our own city." This was a preplanned line which Karl executed flawlessly, hopefully fore-stalling the same argument from one of the others. "But I believe that, even given the reactors, we can employ these weapons against concentrations of revenants safely. The buildings them-selves will be destroyed, the reactors with them. No collateral damage.

"The alternative," he continued, again answering an obvious question before it could be asked, "would be to continue our work to defeat their camouflage and dig them out like ticks, pardon the metaphor, one at a time. It would, frankly, be bloody, costly, and time-consuming."

"It's a bold claim. But surely this action won't rid us of all of them either," Losche protested. "You said yourself the projections of revenants heading toward these structures was far from one hundred percent."

"There will be some tick-digging this way too, sir, yes," Karl said, nodding. "But if we could wipe out sixty percent of the bastards, or even just fifty, it would make things a whole lot easier for my men and women when it's time to go in." Here he paused, looking down, as though overcome by emotion.

Iaz frowned. They had not rehearsed this.

"It would also be a huge morale boost," Karl continued, raising both his head and his voice, which shook a little. "And the lancer corps could use that desperately right now."

It was by far the most fervor he'd shown the entire meeting, maybe ever. His eyes positively blazed. Iaz did not miss Steffi's reaction to this sudden fire, either. The flush of her cheeks gave away her feelings even if she wouldn't admit them to herself. It made Iaz smirk, which was itself a respite, however fleeting.

At the moment, though, she needed to step in to aid the argument. Her pulse pounded in her ears. It was the transgressive feeling of having more information than she had shared with anyone in this room. *There's still time,* a part of her whispered. *There's still time to do this by the book.*

But not much more time, Damon whispered back. *You're seeing to that.*

Deep down, she feared how legitimate a trial the rightful archon of the city could be subjected to. How fast would evidence disappear when it came time for it to be arrayed against him? Any wholly independent judiciary had died with the rest of the world around Coldgarden.

"If these devices function as we believe," Iaz said, marveling at the stillness in her voice, "then they will safely demolish not just the buildings, but some amount of the Underguts space beneath them as well. This will open up the tunnels beneath the city to the surface, draining the floodwaters. We'll be able to move ground troops in, even if the rains resume."

"That sounds like an invitation to more revenants getting into the ward," Graysteel said, frowning.

"Esteemed colleagues," Iaz said. "Until we can reliably address their ability to climb the wall or see through their camouflage, they can already enter the city with impunity. Inkwell Day proved that.

Right now, we need to focus on removing the ones we know about, because that's what is in our power to do."

"But not for long," Karl said. "This window of opportunity is already opening, and soon enough, it will begin closing again."

"Magistrates," Iaz said, "by city law, in this state of emergency, I have unilateral power to address the threat. But I don't want to do something this drastic without your unanimous support. So that is what I am asking for. There are many questions that need answering in order to prevent another attack of this nature. But the immediate crisis is *these* revenants, not hypothetical future ones."

There was reluctance and worry in those five faces, but as they exchanged glances among themselves, resolve took root upon each.

One by one, they nodded.

"Provided I and my experts agree with your assessment of these devices," Graysteel added sharply.

"Thank you," Iaz said. She turned to Karl. "Lance Commander, see that she gets the schematics, and then get these creatures out of my city."

Something deep within her trembled in dread. A countdown of a different sort, one no one present knew about, had begun.

CHAPTER 44

THE VOICE SOUNDED like it bubbled free from boiling tar, yet it was still familiar to Johe.

"He's getting worse every day. He hasn't remembered where he is or what happened to him for two days now. The fever is cooking him alive."

Iazmaena? But no, her voice was clear and ringing and beautiful, and he had not heard it in a very long time. She was coming, though. She was coming to save them all. *It's what she does. It's who she is.*

Colors swam in his vision where there should have been darkness. Even with eyes pinched shut, the world was locked in a lazy spin around him. Had he been drinking? It felt like he'd overindulged.

Where am I?

"We're still in the panic chamber, Johe," came the mystery woman's voice, and something clammy and damp affixed itself to his forehead. Panic flooded him, a certainty that this new sensation was some horrible piece of revenant anatomy, a prelude to being devoured.

"Do you remember?" The voice came again, and the dampness

left him, warmer now. "You were injured scouting the area around our shelter. You've been feverish ever since returning."

He recognized the feeling of fever at once, as though it danced before him, incarnate, just waiting for him to open his eyes and see it. He recognized the voice, too. Kiranna Trephis, one of the other magistrates.

"Awake again, Mr. Istuil?" A much different voice. Johe needed no memory jog to recall it. *The archon.* "How long will it be for this time, I wonder?"

"Easy," Trephis said, an unaccustomed note of steel in her voice. Johe's mind ground back into motion, trying to remember what that might mean, why it surprised him to hear. "He's desperately ill."

"And the meds have all expired or run out, yes. I certainly hope none of the rest of us will be needing them. If you're unable to speak to verify that you are alive when the time comes, boy, you could at least do us the courtesy of dying so we can stuff your corpse out the airlock and save the rest of us."

Johe's head swam. What was the man going on about?

"That's enough!" Trephis all but shouted. "How can he verify he's alive when she won't even take your calls? Gods below, Vernon, what did you *do* to her?"

There was a flat, smacking sound, a startled cry, and then a thump of someone falling.

"Once we are out of here," the archon said slowly, dangerously, "there will be changes. Of that you can be certain. Many people will answer for many things. Sooner or later the rains will have to stop. And then she will be out of excuses. Gene Sequencing knows where we are, even if we've lost comms to them. They will come for us when Delgassi doesn't."

Even through Johe's fever haze, the implication of Teodori's words was clear. *He thinks she's leaving us down here on purpose.*

"I still think we should risk our own escape," came a third voice. *Deecks.* "Leave the boy and make our way back ourselves. Gene Sequencing's got to be watching for us."

"I'd almost risk it," Teodori said, "if the sensors weren't buzzing non-stop about revenants all around us. More than when we first arrived. No, we're stuck here, waiting for—"

"Archon, we're getting a signal," Deecks said. "Someone's finally calling you back."

The world swam anew, as though Johe's sudden desire to remain awake triggered a surge of his infection. *Magistrate Delgassi. Iazmaena. You see, she's coming for us. I want to talk to her, to tell her I'm all right.* Johe tried unsuccessfully to stifle a moan, his head sinking back down to his sweaty pillow.

"Keep him awake!" the archon barked. "If it's Delgassi, I need him awake and talking!"

Johe tried to obey the archon, tried to stay awake. But the knowledge that Magistrate Delgassi was coming for him soothed his fears too much, and his body betrayed him, dragging him back down into sleep.

CHAPTER 45

THERE HAD BEEN A TIME, and not that long ago, where Iazmaena Delgassi would never have considered smuggling liquor into her office at all, much less for the purpose of drinking on the job. Even as a cop, she'd had her limits. But on the evening of the planned Inkwell operation, an operation she needed to direct personally due to the magnitude of the authorizations required, she faced a quandary. She couldn't direct the operation from home, even if she'd felt safe enough there to do so. She also couldn't direct this operation without drinking.

So, there it was.

That particular line crossed, she quickly lost track of precisely how much she was drinking. It didn't matter, really. She knew what *enough* felt like, and she hadn't reached it yet. Her desk comm unit buzzed. She focused on the identifier. Karl. She keyed the line active.

"Madam Archon, you asked to be informed when we were ten minutes away from go-time. That moment has arrived." Karl was overseeing the loading of their kludged-together ordnance onto three of their precious fliers from a hangar location central to Heart. Putting three fliers and their crews at risk was enough to tie Iaz's stomach into knots all by itself, but the idea they might lose all their charges in a single attack or crash was even worse.

But it was the timer Karl had just begun—the final timer—that occupied all of Iaz's attention. She spoke deliberately but not too deliberately. It was important to mask the slurring of her words without making it obvious what she was doing.

"Thank you, Lance Commander. Carry on."

"Ma'am, if I may, I have another request. Not mine. I'm against it, but I promised her I would."

Despite everything, Iaz smirked. "What does Steffi want?"

"A sample, ma'am. After the charges go off, she wants the fliers to engage in a low pass to see if they can collect a fresh sample and put it into one of the stasis boxes she's finished."

"I don't understand," Iaz said. "How is she going to deliver a box before go-time?"

"They're here now, ma'am," Karl said. "As is Dr. Palmieri."

"And you think it's too risky."

"Yes, ma'am."

"Well, Lance Commander, for once we disagree." Iaz felt a sudden urge to backpedal, not fully trusting herself on this much drink. Not for innocent lives, at least. "Final call is on you, but I hereby order you to lean toward approving it if you think it's feasible."

She heard a sigh of someone who regretted keeping his promise. "Yes, ma'am."

"Thank you, Lance Commander, please keep me informed of any updates to the timeline or issues."

"Yes, ma'am. Yonnel out." The line clicked off again.

Time, Damon whispered.

Time. Had there ever been a time where he hadn't been constantly chattering in her head? But he was right. There could be no more putting it off. Iaz had a decision to make, and in order to make it, she needed more information.

She keyed the command to call Teodori's bunker ... only to receive a reject.

For a few moments, Iaz blinked in confusion. She tried again with the same result. A wondrous feeling of burgeoning relief rose up in her. Perhaps the revenants had found the bunker. Perhaps her enemies were dead, and she didn't even have to give the order to end them.

More likely, the comm line had just gone down. Iaz hovered there, poised upon the tip of indecision. If she just let things play out, she could move on in ignorance, never knowing if there were deaths on her hands or not.

On the other hand, she would never know for sure what information he knew. Or if she was rid of him.

She reached up to her earbud and connected to Rieve.

"Is it done yet?" Rieve asked without preamble. She'd asked to attend, but Iaz had shut herself in her office alone with her booze and locked every door. This wasn't a state she needed anyone seeing her in. No doubt Rieve had found some other way to monitor things anyway, and the question was merely meant to humor Iaz.

"No," Iaz replied. "What's happened to the shelter comm link? I thought you said I'd still be able to reach him."

There was a pause, and Iaz realized she hadn't said who. But Rieve piped up. "Yes, I see the problem. Remote breaker tripped somewhere. I can reset it from here, but ... is that really the best idea? You know now, even better than you did last time, how dangerous he is."

"If he doesn't answer my questions," Iaz said darkly, "he won't have much time left to be dangerous." She immediately felt nauseous and tried telling herself it was just the liquor.

"Right," Rieve said, clearly not convinced. "But what if he doesn't *need* much time? We still have no idea how he was trying to turn your boyfriend against you. What if even talking to him ... I don't know."

Iaz hadn't heard the woman sound so discomfited since she'd had

Iaz's gun leveled at her face. What was she implying? Some sort of post-hypnotic suggestion? It sounded ridiculous on its face, but then Iaz thought about Damon, about how little she seemed to understand what went on in this city despite being the most powerful person in it.

But no. She had to talk to Teodori. She had to give him a chance to confess to what he'd done.

"I'll take the risk," Iaz said. "Fix it."

"I really don't think—"

"Damn it, Rieve, fix it right the fuck now, or you can kiss your patronage from me goodbye." She regretted the words instantly but couldn't call them back. Rieve knew entirely too much to be threatened. Another thought that roiled Iaz's stomach.

"Fine," Rieve said, her voice clipped with anger. "But just remember you can't trust a word out of that snake's mouth. It's done." She clicked off. Or at least, that was what it sounded like. One could never be certain with Rieve.

Iaz punched in the call again. This time, it went through, ringing four times before the connection completed. At the moment it did, an icy, sickly calm spread through Iaz, coating every organ.

"Are you there, Archon?" she asked into the static.

Teodori hesitated a long time before answering,

"Delgassi," he said, all sneering disdain. "Finally troubling to return my calls, I see."

Iaz blinked in confusion, wondering just how long that breaker had been flipped. But her booze-soaked brain let the thought float away. *Focus! Don't let him redirect you.*

"If you've called me since we've last spoken, Teodori, I haven't seen it. We've had some comm troubles. I can't say I've missed talking to you, though." Her control slipped, and the last words came out slurred. Nothing for it but to press on. "But I do think it's time we talk again, Vernon. You see, I know what Gene Sequencing has been up to."

"Gods below, Delgassi, are you drunk? I suppose I shouldn't be surprised."

"Don't change the subject," Iaz said, low and dangerous. "I'm giving you this chance to come clean."

"Or what?" Teodori scoffed. "You'll continue leaving us in here to rot? Well, you have a high opinion of your power, Delgassi, but you can't control the weather. As soon as the rains let up, what Gene Sequencing will be up to is getting us out of here, with or without your help."

"The weather has let up," Iaz said. "Hence the call."

"Realized you're running out of time, eh?" Teodori said. "No wonder you've taken to drinking."

"Since you refuse to stop deflecting," Iaz said, "let me tempt you. It's a beautiful night. You should see the stars! I will have assets in the air over Inkwell in just a few minutes' time. We're going to deal with the revenants tonight. Tell me what I want to know, confess what you've done, and I can divert one of them to your location and extract you."

"I'm afraid I have no idea what you are talking about. I think you must be drunker even than you sound, and—"

"You know *exactly* what I'm talking about, you arrogant fucker! I know why Damon killed himself. I know it was because of something you did to him. He said something to me, right before he died. He implicated you. And I've been piecing together the evidence. Now *tell me what you did.* Tell me if you have any shred of hope for a future for you and your little gang. This is your last chance!"

There was a long pause. Then Teodori spoke.

"Bargaining with the lives of citizens, of *elected officials,* for your own personal gain? You've turned into quite the little tyrant, Delgassi."

Another fucking deflection. Iaz took a deep pull from the bottle and felt her resolve hardening even as her mind softened. She was about to kill the connection when Teodori went on. His voice was very cold, and very quiet.

"You will tell me, immediately, where you heard that nonsense. Who told you I'm responsible for your boyfriend's death?"

It was as close to a confession, Iaz realized, as she was ever likely to get. And it had exactly the opposite effect she'd expected. A fresh surge of rage washed over her, and as she saw another call coming in —Karl again, looking for final confirmation—she made her decision.

"From Gene Sequencing," she said with spiteful glee. Technically not a lie, given where Rieve had pulled it from. "I found a warehouse full of their toys too." Let him chew on that in his last moments.

"Listen to me carefully, Iazmaena," Teodori said. He sounded afraid now, and this unexpected delight was like a balm to her soul. "Your aide is here. He needs medical attention. You are being man—"

Iaz killed the line and connected Karl's call.

"Ready to go on your orders, ma'am. Give the order, and we'll pipe the feed to your monitor there."

"Do it," she said. "Good hunting." She killed this line as well, then dialed Rieve.

"Cut that comm line permanently," she said when the other woman connected. The savagery Iaz heard in her own voice warmed her like a campfire.

"Yes, ma'am." Rieve sounded just as satisfied.

Alone in her office, numbed by drink and blissfully untroubled by her demons, Iazmaena Delgassi drained the last of the bottle and raised a toast to Damon as she watched the buildings vanish in distorted globes of amethyst light.

⚮

Iaz started awake at her desk, the trill of an incoming call chasing away the alcohol-soaked nightmare that plagued her. She was still drunk—she knew that much at once. Unavailable was the only ID the comm unit offered, and for a few moments, Iaz wondered if she was still dreaming.

She considered trying to make herself presentable before giving up and accepting the call as audio only.

"Delgassi," she said, deciding not to risk fumbling on more words.

"Ms. Delgassi," said a tight, angry voice. "You've done a very grave thing tonight. And you've done it knowingly." It took Iaz's mind longer to place it than it would have if she was sober but place it she did.

Palo Hayasun. Gene Sequencing. It was a call she should have expected. Rieve had told her that Teodori had called Gene Sequencing first. They'd have known he was alive and where he was located. For the second time that night, a cold certainty descended upon Iaz, and a decision she'd been waffling on was made.

"That's Archon Delgassi to you, Hayasun," she said.

"Not for much longer," he replied. "Count on that."

The line went dead.

CHAPTER 46

ONLY SPIKED coffee held back the hangover well enough to keep Iaz functional for the next morning's after-action report in her office with Steffi and Karl. Iaz tried not to make it obvious she'd never returned home the previous night.

The call from Hayasun had already soured what should have been a jubilant mood.

What had been difficult to see in the dark was revealed by daylight. Iaz stared at three separate images of where buildings had once stood. Large, perfectly smooth craters had been gouged out where their foundations had been, opening up Underguts tunnels beneath in graceful, curving arcs.

Iaz couldn't tear her eyes away from the Chelsea Tower image. The blast, if blast it could be called, had gone deep enough to ensure the consumption of the reactor, which meant deep enough for the panic chamber. She'd confirmed this with Karl twice already but doubted she would ever fully believe it.

The charges had performed exactly as advertised, but it was one thing to hear it described and another to see the seemingly impossible right before your eyes.

"They weren't joking when they labeled them matter-eater

charges, were they?" Iaz asked, as much to focus her own thoughts as to make conversation. Her voiced rasped from a combination of drink and teary catharsis after the archon's death.

"That's what I said," Karl commented, turning to look at Steffi.

"The matter isn't really gone," Steffi said, and it had the sound of a long-running argument which half-amused and half-exasperated her. "That isn't how matter works. I just ... don't know where it is."

"Can't matter become energy?" Iaz asked. She was certain she remembered this from somewhere.

"Under certain extreme circumstances, yes," Steffi said patiently, "but since the city is still standing, that isn't what happened."

"I wish I knew where this technology came from," Karl groused. "I don't like the idea of a weapon that I don't understand."

Sudden dread seized Iaz, a terrible certainty. "If we don't know where the buildings went, how can we be sure the revenants aren't still out there somewhere?"

Yes, Damon said in her mind. *Because it's the revenants you're most worried about.* As though summoned back by Hayasun, Iaz's demons had not stayed away long.

"I've thought of that already," Karl said. "Here's the video."

All three images were replaced by paused video from the previous evening, when the buildings still stood. Karl advanced the video slowly, and Iaz caught the glint of something falling from above toward each structure as the charges were rolled free of the flier bays. The videos had been synched such that the explosions happened simultaneously, even though they hadn't in real life.

It began as an intense flash before resolving into an ellipsoid of violet light surrounding each building, intersecting with the ground. Darker bolts of purple lightning danced across their surfaces. Then, as one, they collapsed into points of light, and the buildings were just ... gone.

"If you run it back and go even slower," Karl said. "Watch carefully. It's hard to see in the dark."

It was even harder to see in her state, but Iaz endured the brilliant light again and watched closely. At last, she saw what Karl was indicating. The collapsing shell of light did not simply eat the structure whole but crumbled it along the edge and dragged the accumulating rubble along with it as it shrank to a point, when it all just vanished.

Iaz breathed a silent sigh of relief. Dead, then. Truly dead.

"Good eye, Lance Commander," Iaz said, her smile a genuine thing for once. "And Steffi's sample?"

"We recovered a good one! A head, even." Steffi was practically bouncing. "And the stasis box appears to have worked as hoped."

"The good doctor's luck knows no bounds," Karl said, and Iaz was pleased to see there was no sound of a grudge held over the prior disagreement.

"Excellent," Iaz said. "Go forth and do great science with it. But be safe." She turned to Karl. "What happens now?"

Karl frowned slightly. "Now we begin the hard part. Clearing out the rest, with a goal toward eventually reclaiming the district. You, ah, already approved that plan, ma'am. But I can show it to you again if you'd like another review."

"Yes, of course," Iaz said, suddenly recalling. "I'm sorry. I'm a bit scattered."

"Understandable," Karl said. "With your permission, I'll begin executing it."

"Yes, please," Iaz said hastily reviewing her memory of the plan's troop deployments. "But, Karl, I do need to make one amendment. The reserve lancers, I need one division held back for other duties."

"Of course, ma'am. If that's your order."

"It is."

A pause. She had not discussed this with him, and she always discussed lancer deployments with him before issuing orders. "And what will their mission be, so I can draft up a new plan for approval?"

It was the question he was supposed to ask, yet Iaz found herself annoyed all the same. It didn't matter, because she didn't need his approval.

"Alive or dead," she said, "Teodori was engaging in some very questionable behavior, and I'm convinced the warehouse is only part of it. Gene Sequencing allegedly answers to the archon yet is stonewalling all my demands for transparency." *Whatever they're up to, I have to get in front of it.* But how she phrased this was important. "Until I can secure Gene Sequencing's cooperation in determining for certain if they or Teodori are somehow involved in our current situation, I'm ordering that division of lancers to seal them off from the rest of the city."

"I ... see. You want me to lay siege to them." Karl's voice was carefully neutral.

Even Steffi wore a small frown. Steffi! About Gene Sequencing! It was hard not to feel a little betrayed.

Karl continued, "Ma'am, I don't mean to question, but surely suspected misbehavior by the previous archon is more a matter for the police than the military."

"Normally, I'd agree with you completely," Iaz said. "But the discovery of that warehouse changed matters. The matter-eater charges were just what they had laying around. Who knows what other weaponry they might have directly in their possession? If they've gone rogue in some way, I want to make sure we've got our best in position to counter them. However, I recognize that we aren't out of the crisis yet. If matters progress and you deem the division necessary to your operations, I will of course return it to normal duty status."

There was the briefest of pauses before Karl said, "Yes, ma'am. Of course. I do understand."

But as he and Steffi filed out, Iaz wondered if that was so.

CHAPTER 47

STEFANI REGARDED the computer image of the revenant head being rendered by her test chamber and made mental note that she owed Marri an apology. Even before making the computer assemble the fragments of bone, she could tell what shape they would form. There were too many telltale geometries, like an obvious portion of a human eye socket, to be anything else.

And they weren't just stuck in there haphazardly. They were integral to the head of the creature somehow. Stefani didn't want to follow that line of thinking, didn't want to leap to conclusions. But it was difficult not to.

Her terminal buzzed. With a flash of annoyance at the disruption, Stefani checked the ID. Karl. Her mood improved instantly. She opened the line, bobbing Ella on her knee, something she seemed to like.

"Well," she said, "to what do I owe the pleasure? I don't think I'm delinquent on any science-y answers to your questions, am I?"

"No," Karl said. "I have some downtime between sweeping Inkwell operations."

"And instead of getting valuable sleep, you're calling me." She tried to keep the grin in her voice from being too obvious.

"Seems I am," he said, and she could tell he was smiling too.

"So, how goes the great siege?"

"Not sure I'm permitted to discuss operational details."

"That well?"

Karl's laughter sounded like half a sigh, though maybe that was just the static. "Truth be told, I don't expect this to last long."

"It's been, what, two days?"

"Gene Sequencing isn't a fortress," Karl said ruefully. "They have no supplies. They'll crack soon."

"That's a good thing, though, right?" Stefani asked. "I got the sense you weren't a fan of the order. This means you'll get your reserve division back sooner."

"You are trying to get me in all kinds of trouble," Karl said. "Look, I wouldn't say this to anyone but a close friend of hers. The reserve lancer division isn't my concern. We shouldn't need them for clean-up operations. It's her I'm worried about. This sudden pivot toward Gene Sequencing when we haven't dealt with the revenants fully yet, it's ... well, I've said too much as it is."

Stefani regretted asking. Karl had been good about leaving her and Iaz their secrets, but now he was pressing at those secrets without realizing it. Stefani understood perfectly well why Iaz had pivoted to target Gene Sequencing, even if the move made her uncomfortable on some level.

It might be your only way out of this, a little voice whispered. *You should probably thank her for taking the risks you won't.* That didn't seem right, though. They hadn't started this with Iaz in control of the city, after all. With Rieve running interference, Gene Sequencing had no reason to come after them—at least, not until Iaz had provoked them by laying siege.

"I think I've made you uncomfortable," Karl said. "I apologize. Maybe I'm just too old to recognize when change needs to happen. I'll let you go."

Stefani was surprised at the strength of the panic she felt. "No, please, don't go. I—"

Her next words were cut off by an immense rumbling. The entire lab shook, and it was only quick reflexes on Stefani's part that kept several fragile items from tumbling off the desk. Clutched tight to Stefani's chest, Ella was bawling by the time the rumbling ceased.

The shock wore off by degrees. As it did, the whole experience seemed worryingly familiar to Stefani.

"Karl? Are you still there?"

"Yes," he said, voice tight. "Are you all right?"

"We're fine," Stefani said, wanting to reassure him quickly, because surely he would have other pressing duties now. Still, she had to know if her memory was right. "Karl, what was that?"

"The cordon," he said grimly. "The cordon around Inkwell just came down."

CHAPTER 48

IAZMAENA MET him at the cordon bunker, white-faced with fear or fury or both. Karl understood the emotion. On this point, at least, they were in lockstep once again.

Dimly lit, cramped, and somehow smelling of mildew despite being compositeel top to bottom, the bunker housed the controls for the cordon walls throughout the city. It was staffed around the clock by no fewer than three lancers ready to respond and raise cordon walls on a moment's notice.

It was also a crime scene.

The officer in charge, Lance Captain Ruhe, tried to turn them away from the bunker's outer chamber before getting a good look at whom she was addressing. Then she blanched and ushered up to the open door of the inner chamber but no farther.

"Biohazard," she said without being asked. "One of my men is dead in there. I'm waiting for a clean-up squad."

"What happened?" Iazmaena asked.

"I'm still trying to figure that out, ma'am," Ruhe said, eyes wide. Then her face contorted in rage. "Near as I can tell, one of my men killed the other and triggered the wall to come down. It was quick, silent. The victim, Lancer Lassis, is still in there. The survivor, killer, whatever, Lancer Joril, stomped out in a hurry."

"You didn't think to stop him?" Iaz asked.

"It wasn't that sort of hurry, ma'am," Ruhe said, misery incarnate. "It was the sort of hurry where you figure he ate something that disagreed with him, not that he just killed his fellow lancer. I ... I don't understand how this could happen, ma'am."

Grim-faced, Iazmaena sidestepped the stricken lance captain and walked up to the threshold. Karl followed, if only because he had to see. Lancer killing lancer. It didn't seem possible. If there had ever been a tighter-knit military unit in the history of humankind, he could not imagine it. Their mandate was, quite literally, the preservation of the species.

Lassis was there, his body sprawled over a console, a pool of drying blood caking it from matching wounds to either side of his neck. It was just beginning to seethe with signs of hypermutation, and the group kept their distance.

"Stabbed," Karl said pointlessly.

"Gene Sequencing," Iazmaena muttered.

Karl spun on her in alarm. He watched her face. It was like he could see something breaking there. Some final, vital thing.

"What?" he asked.

"How long until we can get the wall back up?" Iazmaena asked Ruhe, ignoring Karl's confusion.

"Weeks," Ruhe answered.

Iazmaena blinked. "What are you talking about, weeks?"

"Ma'am, raising the walls totally discharges the batteries. Lowering them takes minimal power, thanks to gravity. But even with the time that's elapsed since they went up, it will be weeks before we will have enough power banked to raise the walls again."

They regrouped in Iazmaena's office an hour later. Karl walked in and was immediately concerned at the frenzied look in the archon's eyes. He worried she'd been drinking again.

"I underestimated the degree to which they'd infiltrated other organizations around the city," Iazmaena said as soon as he'd shut the door. "Even the lancers! I should have seen."

"Respectfully, ma'am, what are you talking about?" Karl asked, though he already suspected.

Iazmaena turned an almost pitying stare upon her lance commander. "Doesn't it seem just too big a coincidence that the second we establish a siege around them, they act to try and divert our attention elsewhere? Lowering the walls allows the remaining revenants access to the rest of the city. At least the water had time to drain out through the damaged tunnels, or we'd be dealing with widespread flooding as well."

"And along those lines, ma'am, I'm going to need that division of lancers around Gene Sequencing back. We can't ignore the escalation of the revenant threat this represents. I'm going to need lancer squads sweeping the city around the clock, and I already don't have enough for that kind of effort."

"Gene Sequencing just launched an all-out attack on this city and its people," Iazmaena said incredulously, "and you want me to *remove* my leverage over them?"

"Respectfully, ma'am, the culprit is still at-large, and his motivations have yet to be established."

Iazmaena looked at him as though he were insane. Then came something much worse, as her eyes narrowed in suspicion, just for an instant.

"Your request is denied, Lance Commander," she said with an air of finality. "You are to work with what you have and deal with any revenants that have escaped."

"Ma'am, I—"

"Dismissed!"

CHAPTER 49

DESPITE THE WALLS coming down ahead of schedule and revenants loose in the city, Stefani was grateful, because the Underlab was blessedly quiet. Rieve was there, buried under headphones and uncommunicative. What she was doing, Stefani had no idea. After all, Rieve was still technically allowed to listen to her music at full blast if she wanted by the terms of their thrice damned agreement. The imaging software had *still* not concluded its analysis.

Reveling in the silence, Stefani keyed her latest completed animation to start back up. She watched as the sealed revenant head split open along four petals, saw the human-like skull within likewise split along previously invisible seams, each petal carrying a portion with it. Like an explosion in slow motion. The animation reversed, and the skull came back together as the petals sealed tight.

Between this instance and Marri's account, they now knew of this phenomenon in two revenants. The odds of it being the same revenant were absurdly low. That meant all revenants likely shared the feature.

Stefani had claimed to Iaz that perhaps this was a form of acquisitive tool use, the revenants making use of something they found. But a human skull hardly seemed the best template to fashion large, interior teeth at the base of the throat. And given the revenants' shape-changing abilities, why couldn't they just fashion what they needed? Their chitin was surely strong enough for the task if bone was somehow out of the question.

The thought had briefly crossed her mind that the skull use might be cultural. The way the creature had revealed this seemingly foreign object to Marri, almost like a threat display, a warning, went some way toward supporting that notion. They had no idea if the revenants had culture or society, but the fact that they kept surprising their human prey with their ingenuity suggested that underestimation of the revenants was a frequent human mistake.

But that option, too, now seemed unlikely. Stefani couldn't deny what her examination of the revenant head was showing her. Within the context of the whole head, the fragments of skull looked to have grown in place.

This took her mind down darker, more disturbing paths.

As if in response to this mental detour, Stefani started as she heard an electronic chime. She glanced around, confused, until she realized it came from her borrowed terminal, the one performing the imaging analysis on her inadequate revenant sample. Stefani felt a strange trepidation, as though the machine had been waiting for this precise moment to deliver some damning piece of information.

She was right to be afraid.

Rieve's borrowed algorithm had taken the image of the shattered piece of revenant chitin and surrounding tissue and reassembled it as closely as possible to what it would have looked like whole. It had then run its pattern-matching to attempt to identify the organic curves which Stefani had found so oddly familiar.

Fully reconstructed, Stefani did not even need the computer's identification to know what she was looking at. But it still provided the text, glowing in amber like condemnation.

PROBABLE IDENTIFICATION: HUMAN FINGERPRINT.

It was only then that Stefani realized how badly she hadn't wanted to believe what ought to have been obvious.

She called Iaz without delay.

Her friend sounded strange when she picked up. "What's up?"

Stefani had known Iaz for a long time, and something in the tone of those two words sounded like Iaz pretending to be herself. It threw Stefani off nearly as much as her news had. "I ... I have some really important news to ..."

"Steffi, what's wrong? You sound awful."

Speak for yourself, Stefani might have said. "This is a lot," she warned. "Both to hear and to believe."

"Everything is a lot," Iaz said wearily, and that sounded almost normal. "Just tell me."

Stefani steeled herself with a breath. "Iaz, I think they were people once. The revenants. I think they used to be human. Not these. But generations ago. I still have a lot to verify and even more to understand. It's just hard to accept. Some truths are hard to accept, you know?"

"How is that possible?" Iaz asked. She sounded fully focused for the first time.

"I'll need more time to figure that out," Stefani said. "But I knew you needed to hear this right away."

"Gene Sequencing," Iaz all but spat. "Somehow they're involved in this."

A chill closed around Stefani's heart. Iaz sounded feral, as though she'd become rabid in the space of a breath. It was not that Stefani of all people believed Gene Sequencing couldn't have known anything about this, but the speed with which Iaz's ferocity had asserted itself frightened her.

"Maybe we'll have answers soon," Stefani offered lamely. Abruptly, despite feeling so alone just minutes before, she found she wanted to end the call. "There's more I need to look at. Maybe I can find some of those answers on my end. I've got to go."

"So do I," Iaz said, sounding distracted once more.

"Take care," Stefani said. She meant it in the most emphatic of senses.

There was no response, so she hung up.

The sound of the Underlab hatch opening started Stefani from a daze. She was not expecting company, and she felt a sudden apprehension, as though the forbidden information she'd uncovered had invited down some kind of terrible retribution.

Then Stefani saw that her visitor was Karl, and all such maudlin thoughts fled her in a rush of warmth and internal sunlight. Despite everything, she smiled reflexively at seeing him.

"Hi," she said. She only had to force her brightness a little. "Is the city overrun yet?" She saw the pain on his face and knew at once it had been a poorly timed joke.

"We need to talk," he said, his eyes refusing to meet hers.

Stefani's anxiety ratcheted upward another two notches. Karl's eyes continued their roving, trying to see around the corner into Rieve's nook.

"She won't hear you," Stefani said. "She's been wearing her headphones for hours. Karl, what's going on?"

Stefani lost her patience after his third false start. "Tell. Me." She fixed her eyes to his, willing them to drill holes in his hesitation.

Karl's eyes looked so sad. "Something has to be done about Iazmaena," he said, the words barely more than a rasping whisper.

Stefani felt her own eyes pop wide in shock as she took in his meaning. "What are you talking about?" she said in her own whisper. But her own voice whispered to her. *You already know.*

"She's obsessed with Gene Sequencing, with the idea that they lowered the walls. An idea I find ... well, implausible is putting it charitably."

"She was ranting about them to me just now, actually," Stefani said, her heart sinking. She almost told him everything she discovered, but on top of what he was saying, it just seemed like too much to put out into the world again. "Who do you think lowered the walls?"

"I don't know, but that's not even the point. The point is that I need the lancers she has around Gene Sequencing to hunt for the revenants that must be all over the city by now. I asked for them, as she invited me to, and she refused. An hour later, I and every other lancer, received this over official channels."

He held out his handheld, and Stefani read it.

PRIORITY. ALL ORDERS REASSIGNING LANCER GENERAL DUTY STATIONS ARE TO BE CONFIRMED DIRECTLY WITH THE ARCHON'S OFFICE FOR THE DURATION OF THE SIEGE ORDER.

"Most of the corps regard her with awe," Karl said. "Even if I were to go to lancers I trust, I can't be certain what their response would be."

"Can you assault the building and take it? Then she'd have to give you what she needed."

"Too risky. We have too few lancers as it is. It's one thing to wait out a group that isn't equipped to outlast a siege. But Iazmaena was right during the meeting with the other magistrates. Gene Sequencing shouldn't have any heavy weapons, but given that warehouse we found, who knows what happens if we assault them outright?"

He stopped there, but Stefani thought she detected a hint of stubborn principle in there somewhere, a determination that lancers fought revenants, not humans. *Is there still so big a distinction?* More and more, she was coming to think no. But something he said caught her attention.

"The other magistrates," Stefani said. "If you went to them—"

"It's a state of emergency," Karl said, gently but firmly. "Now maybe more than ever. She doesn't answer to them. If I involve them, I ..." He trailed off, looking guilty.

"You risk their careers, too?" Stefani asked.

"I'm not talking about careers here," Karl said. "Stefani, I need you to listen. Your friend, our archon, is sick. She's allowing revenants free run of the city, while besieging a group of her own citizens in their lab based on a hunch? A personal vendetta? I'm no doctor, but it's become clear the *leader* of this city, the person in whom all the authority legally resides, is suffering from some sort of mental imbalance. Even if Gene Sequencing and Teodori and the entire council are guilty of some malfeasance, I can't ignore an unknown number of revenants running loose in humankind's last city! That has to come first. It has to!"

She's been my friend since we were children. I love her as much as anyone save my own child. "So what are you going to do?" Stefani asked. It was the closest she could get to admitting he was right, and she was afraid she already knew the answer. Stefani clutched Ella more closely to herself, only then realizing she'd forgotten to put the baby back in her bubble. Karl's presence made her lower her guard. She really ought to. It was the only safe thing, but Karl's grave expression left her needing the warmth and comfort of Ella's presence.

"She can't be allowed to continue as archon," he said. "We need to be saved from her, and she needs to be saved from herself. I'm honor-bound, duty-bound to intervene. I'm going to take Iazmaena into custody for everyone's good, including hers."

"You're going to *depose* her?" Stefani's voice cracked around fresh tears. Her mind began tugging at memories of her recent times with Iaz, looking for something, anything, she could have said to preempt this from happening.

"You know her best." His voice was pleading. "You've seen how she's become. The drinking. The paranoia. The seclusion. She can't be allowed to go on. You know she can't."

"How many lancers will you take?" Stefani heard herself asking.

"One," he said. "Me."

"Karl, no!"

"If I can't take one politician into custody safely," he said, forcing a smile, "I don't deserve to wear the uniform, anyway."

"What do you need from me?" Stefani asked. "Why involve me at all?" She tried not to sound resentful.

"That's just it. I need you to promise me to stay away and let me handle this," Karl said. "However this goes down, there will eventually be fallout. Legal or otherwise. You can't help but be involved with her at this point, but the more peripheral your involvement appears to be, the more insulated you'll be from consequences." He sounded as if he hoped this more than knowing it for sure.

"This feels like such a betrayal," Stefani said. She realized she was crying. Ella joined her, as if sensing her pain.

"She needs help," Karl said. "This is the only way we can give it to her. Graysteel or one of the others can take over after. I'm willing to face the consequences either way."

Stefani hesitated, then gave him a quick embrace with one arm, Ella on her hip, and a kiss on the cheek. He tipped his hat to her, and then was gone up the spiral staircase.

Rieve remained completely engrossed and hadn't noticed a thing.

I'm sorry, Iaz, Stefani thought. *Please, please come quietly.*

CHAPTER 50

AN EMPTY BOTTLE lay mockingly on its side upon her desk, obscenely open, transfixing her gaze. *No more.* Not until Gene Sequencing fell. Iaz had to keep her wits about her. Easier said than done. Her office was dark. She hadn't bothered with anything but her desk lamp.

The call with Steffi rang in Iaz's head, her revelations somehow seeming less important than what they portended. She worried she'd come across as too obsessed. No one had the information she had. Perhaps keeping all that information to herself had been a mistake, but it seemed impossible to bring anyone into her confidence now, lest it led back to what she had done. Necessary or not, she worried none of them, not even Steffi, would understand.

We're all close to the edge, Iaz reflected. *The trouble is, I'm the only one that knows where it is.* She'd stopped dreaming of Damon, and perversely, she missed it. She still saw him during her waking hours, of course. But those experiences were less pleasant. In her dreams, she sometimes forgot he was gone.

It didn't matter. If she and Steffi were near the brink, Gene Sequencing had to be even closer. In lowering the wall, they'd crossed a line they could never come back from. They'd already earned Iaz's hate, but now they'd endangered the entire city in their attempts to destroy her. It proved their desperation. Her victory was close.

Damn it all, why don't they just fucking surrender? I could order an assault. Abandon this siege foolishness and just be done with it. Such extremity would be justified, given the treachery with the wall. Many GS personnel would undoubtedly die if she did attack, but Coldgarden might not be safe with any of them alive.

She'd begun to worry about the remaining magistrates, though. Iaz had expected resistance by now, with the threat invisible and her actions so seemingly bizarre. She'd certainly braced herself for a move against her after the wall debacle. Yet they collectively offered no objections and mostly seemed content to see to the task of managing their own wards.

But what if that was just an act?

It was so hard to keep focused, to keep from suspecting everyone.

Footsteps dragged her attention from her thoughts. They thumped heavy and staccato, stomping a stilted rhythm as they approached her office. Iaz's standing orders for Heart Hall were clear. She was not to be disturbed without direct invitation. No exceptions, force authorized. Moreover, Iaz knew the sound of lancer boots, which these were not. Which could only mean her guards had been overcome.

So, they weren't content with the wall as distraction. Here was Gene Sequencing's latest attempt on her life. Iaz drew her sidearm, keeping it concealed beneath her desk but pointed at the door.

That door opened on a dark shape which became a handsome man as it stepped into the small pool of light, draped in a trench coat soaked in liquid too thick for mere rain. Splattered with something else.

"Who," she began imperiously, but then she gasped, all her righteous fury dissolving in mute fascination. The dark, close-cropped, spiky hair, the lean face, high cheekbones, and a strong yet narrow jaw. The eyes, dancing with delight and hidden pain both.

Damon.

It both was and wasn't him. Beneath the coat, the joints and angles of his body were off somehow. Alien. One moment she saw nothing but all the ways the face was not that of her love, and then the discrepancies were washed away and it *was* him, perfect and real.

This was not a hallucination. Those did not interact with objects like doors or drip gore on the carpet. This was Damon, standing before her. The gore repelled her, awakening the bone-deep fear of a resident of Coldgarden, yet even it was not enough to overcome the draw she felt from those features.

"How?" Her mind was a war zone, the side that understood what this couldn't be and what this must be both versus the side that saw only what it wanted so desperately.

Damon raised its hands in placation. It spoke, and though the words she heard were harsh and halting, her brain filled in, smoothed over, because they were words from his beautiful mouth. Her Damon.

And so "Want. To. Talk," became "I just want to talk."

"Why do you look like him?" she asked the revenant. What else could it be? Yet forcing out those words, admitting it, even to herself, were like fingernails on the slate of her mind. *Gods below, are you him? Oh please, what does this mean?*

"Ali remembered him. And you kept a picture of him. A picture I saw. A picture is not as good as a person. Nor is a memory. But I needed you not to shoot me on sight," Damon said.

"Why aren't you eating me? Carrying me off?"

"We aren't your enemies unless you make us so."

"If you're not our enemies, why invade and eat us?"

"Because you keep faith with our true enemies," it said. He said. "And we needed to remember."

Gods below, what's happening?

"There's a rotten core to this city's people," Damon said. "But you are different. Her memories told us so. Ali. They told us how you hated him. Your enemies are our enemies. So there's a chance I can make you understand. Understand what we once were."

"You were human," Iaz said. *Steffi, you were right.*

"None alive now," it said, as if it had listened in on her call moments before. It was like an optical illusion, snapping back and forth constantly. Damon and not. "But our ancestors were."

"How?" Iazmaena asked. "How is that possible?"

Damon shrugged awkwardly. "Memory has degraded with time and generations. We needed to sacrifice many to remember," it said, gesturing at itself. "But there are some in this city who understand."

"Who?"

The incredulous look it gave her was so patently Damon, she could have wept. "You know who. Please, we just want you to understand."

"Understand what?"

"What you did."

"What *we* did?" The words blurted free from Iazmaena, barreling their way from her lungs. "Your kind invaded my city! Butchered my people! If you want us to *understand,* why do you keep *killing and eating us?*"

Damon smiled sweetly, and her defenses crumbled anew. The lopsided grin, the twinkling secret of his eyes, the uneven dimples. They were *perfect.*

Oh Damon. I'm so sorry. I wanted to help you, and I wasn't there when you needed me.

A blinding flash and thundering roar shook the room, and the right side of Damon's chest became scorched, meaty pulp. He fell hard. Iazmaena's cry was boundless denial, rage at watching him die his second death. How could one world be so cruel?

As Damon struck the floor, Iazmaena was moving. Some part of her mind still functioned with cool, detached rationality, and it was this part that leveled her sidearm and fired in one smooth motion, discharging into the darkness gathered in the shape of a person lurking just inside the door. There was a groan of surprise and pain then a second thump as the assailant followed Damon to the ground.

Instantly, she was at her poor Damon's side, watching those magnificent eyes begin to glaze, watching his hacking attempts at breath.

"Had. To. Devour. So. Many. To. Remember," it wheezed. "To. Relearn. To. Return. While. There's. Still. Time."

"To being human," she whispered, speaking to a revenant, thinking of her dead lover. *Don't leave me again.*

"To. Reclaim. What. You. Stole." He practically spat the last word then lay still.

The world closed in around Iazmaena, muting the weakening groans from the bleeding shadow across the room. Her eyes remained fixed on the body of the thing in front of her, and she nearly blacked out with the force of the memory it evoked. His face was not swollen and purple this time, but it was every bit as still.

It took some time for the change to begin, long enough that the groaning form of Damon's killer finally went still. It was not what she expected. In humans, Mutagen Prime acted with random, monstrous whimsy, all cloudy eyes and spines and slimy, thick muscle attached to nothing. In the case of Damon the revenant, Prime obviously behaved in a wholly different manner. Primed to look for it, Iazmaena could see it.

She could see the traces of humanity rising from its rapidly warping form. A humanity lost generations ago.

But how? Why?

Gradually, Iazmaena's attention was pulled away by the spreading pool of blood from the darker part of the office and the horrid things squirming about its edges. Her breath caught sharply as she understood she'd killed a human, surely a lancer trying to protect her. She stepped forward, fumbling for more light. The light came on with a flick of the switch and one last, fateful moan of involuntary despair slipped past her lips.

Karl Yonnel lay still on the floor beneath her feet, his eyes pinched closed in a final moment of agony, his body curled into a tight ball around his middle.

Horror bleached the color from Iazmaena's sight, draining everything to stark grayscale. Denial was already rewriting this nightmare play into something Iaz could bear. The two emotions warred for control of her.

Karl, her loyal lancer.

Karl, who had been looking at her strangely ever since she'd announced her intentions to dismantle Gene Sequencing.

Karl, who had shown up here, uninvited and unannounced.

And, Iaz now wondered, to what purpose?

Maybe, just maybe, he'd written this fate himself. For not trusting her. For planning to turn on her. Yes, that made the sight tolerable, but not enough to remain. She had to get out of the room, out of the building. She couldn't remain in this place a moment longer.

She ran, hurdling Karl's body, sloshing through his watery boot prints until their trail curved back around to the service entrance hallway toward the back. Iazmaena opened Heart Hall's front door into the downpour, and the only thing that stopped her flight was an unfurled umbrella placed above her in time to prevent her total drenching. An unexpected retinue awaited her.

Iaz's cop eyes, so trained in observation, immediately picked out the strange details of the group. They carried themselves with the same wrongness to their joints and idle movements that Damon had shown. These were Damon's fellows, then, dozens of them. All wearing human disguises. All regarding her expectantly.

Not one of them asked what had become of Damon. Not one of their stares were accusatory. The nearest one, the one holding the umbrella, was the spitting image of Ali. Ali smiled at Iaz, gesturing at the gathered crowd. So many reinforcements. It felt as if they'd always been waiting for Iaz, waiting for her to see.

She pulled out her handheld to issue a final order to the besieging lancers.

BREAK SIEGE IN ONE HOUR. RETURN TO BARRACKS TO AWAIT
FURTHER INSTRUCTIONS. CONFIRM UPON RECEIPT.

The response requesting authentication was so swift Iaz almost laughed. The lancers were clearly desperate to get out of the wet weather. Well, they had earned their rest. Order confirmed, Iaz stepped out and over the two lancer corpses without glancing down once.

"We're going to Gene Sequencing," she said to Ali. Ali turned and made a forward chopping motion, and the rest of the crowd began to move, making way for Iaz until they could form a protective ring around her. And why not?

She was the archon of Coldgarden, and it was time to get what she'd paid for.

CHAPTER 51

GENE SEQUENCING'S headquarters was almost as unassuming as their warehouse had been. Three stories and windowless, it looked more like a prison than the heart of empowered malfeasance it was.

The last of the lancers departed while Iaz and her retinue stood at a distance, Iaz not wanting any close contact between the two groups. She should have waited longer to be certain there was no possibility of a clash, but Iaz lacked the self-control.

The lancer rear guard lingered, packing up the broadcast equipment into waterproof containers and throwing Iaz and her retinue long, curious looks, as though waiting to be called over. Finally, they jogged off in the direction their fellows had gone, looking dejected. Perhaps they'd thought something astounding was about to happen.

They were right.

Iaz forced herself to wait another five minutes. Her new army in miniature made no complaint, scarcely moved at all. It was an obedience she could grow to like easily.

The mental clock in her head wound down to zero.

"Take prisoners where possible. Palo Hayasun in particular. Go," she said.

It turned out that watching revenants attack your enemies was far more thrilling than horrifying. Iaz could barely suppress a giddy smile as a pair of vicious kicks stove in the barred double doors like they were made of real glass. Doing so while still holding their human forms just enhanced the uncanniness.

The pair flowed into the gap to scout the way, their movements gaining a scuttling quality as though they remembered how to deal out violence only in their true form.

Iaz itched to follow them in. She had waited so long for answers, for retribution. She might never get the former, but the latter would be total. Ending Teodori and his cronies had been gratifying but not visceral enough to sate her. Something inside her stirred, something she had never before felt, though she knew with certainty it had always been there.

It wanted death.

"Soon," Ali said beside her.

She placed a restraining hand on Iaz's wrist, her grip gentle for all that the skin didn't feel quite right. Iaz turned to look at her friend's winning smile, seeking a familiar sight to ground her.

A dim red flash in Iaz's peripheral vision, a searing sense of heat, and she watched Ali's beautiful face burn away, crisping to black char and crumbling as the rest of her thumped heavily to the ground.

Gene Sequencing was shooting back and with more than lances. But the thought barely registered as rage and grief swallowed Iaz, all the worse for being the second time that day.

She didn't even lift her own gun. "Everyone inside, now!"

The mass of them began to surge forward, and Iaz's blood sang with the promise of revenge.

"Let me go first," said Ali, stepping over her own hypermutating corpse, her face unblemished and grimly set. "Stay behind me."

Iaz was so glad to see her friend alive and unharmed again that she didn't argue.

As one, they crossed the threshold just as the screams began from inside.

The resistance was stiff but over quickly. Gene Sequencing was hers.

Lab-coated figures slumped everywhere she walked. Ali distracted Iaz whenever she tried to look too closely at any of the bodies. It had not been bloodless on their side either, of course. Aside from the first—second?—Ali, three others had fallen. But the remainder of the revenants, in their human forms or otherwise, had not shown any great concern over this. And the Gene Sequencing personnel, as monstrous in spirit as any revenant, had paid dearly for each death.

Based on her lone visual conversation with Hayasun, Iaz had expected Gene Sequencing to be a glittering palace, as decoratively advanced as it was scientifically. Instead, she stalked through drab, gray hallways branching haphazardly into cramped offices and scattered labs with no seeming rhyme or reason.

And everywhere, those labs now lay in ruin.

Bodies drained bubbling blood into sample trays. Shelving units lay collapsed, their contents dumped onto floors that would have to be incinerated. This hurt Iaz to see, mainly on Steffi's behalf. Her friend would not be happy when she saw how much information must surely have been lost.

I'll make it up to her. Somewhere in here is the data or the person she needs to make sure Ella is safe.

Though there didn't seem to be that many scientists remaining. It was hard to make a count with Ali constantly pulling her gaze toward something else anytime she tried to see. There were still some moans, at least. Given the number of the dead, the scientists had been equipped to put up much more of a fight than she'd assumed.

We're lucky they didn't attempt to break the siege.

Deep into her self-guided tour of the building, Iaz at last found one of her most-sought targets. Dr. Palo Hayasun sat behind the same desk she'd seen when speaking to him, in a room that was clearly meant to be the only part of Gene Sequencing any outsiders ever saw.

Two of Iaz's people held him pinned to his chair with iron grips, their blank smiles directed at Iaz, awaiting her orders.

She took her time in her approach, wanting to savor the impotent rage on Hayasun's face for as long as possible. She wandered slowly around to the far side of his desk, the better to remove any sense of hierarchy he might still possess. A bank of screens greeted her, all showing various images and looped videos, but it was Hayasun's rage-contorted face that held her attention.

"Dr. Hayasun," she said languidly, sticking out her hand despite knowing he couldn't move his. "I'm Archon Iazmaena Delgassi. It's such a pleasure to finally meet you, though I wish it were under circumstances in which you'd been more cooperative when I first called."

"You're insane!" Hayasun spat. He struggled to get free, but his captors were far stronger than he could ever hope to be, whatever form they held.

"And you're going to be much more receptive to my questions now, I'm sure," Iaz said. "I have a lot of questions, Dr. Hayasun."

"Enjoy this," Hayasun said, defiant. "You won't be in power much longer. We've already sent evidence of what you did to the *real* archon to the other magistrates. We have the recording of his call to us from the shelter. He states exactly where he was and that he intended to call you next. So they know what you are."

A chill ran through Iaz at this. Suddenly her worry that the silent acquiescence of Graysteel and the others was an act did not seem so paranoid.

"Well, then," Iaz said, keeping her voice calm, "I'll table my questions for now and begin with a demand. Show me the records of the kill order that was issued on me before the election." If nothing else, it would muddy the waters of the situation, give her surer footing on the moral high ground. Self-defense was self-defense. "If you're cooperative enough, doctor, you'll fare better than your colleagues out there."

"No one issued a kill order against you, Delgassi, you psycho—"

"Tell me who ordered Damon Blackburne to visit Gene Sequencing instead of his normal doctor."

Hayasun sagged. "Archon Teodori gave that order, but—"

"See there?" Iaz said. "Prompt honesty. Let's build on that. Where is Dr. Kyne Libretta?"

For all his accusations, Hayasun's laugh was the thing that sounded insane. "I don't know."

"I'm close to losing my temper, Hayasun," Iaz said. "And then this will stop being friendly. Why was my election being targeted by Gene Sequencing and the archon?"

"Because the archon thought losing the buffer in his voting majority would be inconvenient, and he didn't think you had what it takes to be a good magistrate." Hayasun's look left little doubt to his opinion on the matter.

"So he was willing to kill first Damon and then me for an *inconvenience*?"

"Neither of those accusations are true! We barely cared at all about you after the election disruption effort failed. Not until you seized control of the whole fucking city!"

Iaz stepped back. The man's selective honesty was infuriating. No longer leaning in, she finally got a good look at the screens on his desk. "You care about me now, though, don't you?" she taunted. "Why else would you have Rieve Revolos front and center on your monitor?"

Hayasun frowned and glanced at where Iaz gestured. The picture of Rieve looked like a cross between an ID photo and a mugshot, but it was unmistakably her.

"Her?" Hayasun asked. "You recognize her?"

Iaz had to suppress a laugh. "You don't know as much about me as you think if you don't know I've been working with Rieve Revolos since almost the moment I took office."

Hayasun laughed. It began as a bark but became almost hysterical. Even his captors looked to be having trouble holding him in place.

"What," Iaz asked, a feeling of uneasiness bubbling up in her, "is so funny?"

"You," Hayasun said around fading chortles. "Asking where Kyne Libretta is when you've apparently been working with her for weeks now."

CHAPTER 52

DR. KYNE LIBRETTA watched the entire hilarious scene from the dedicated feed in her Underlab. She'd set it up specifically for this purpose, using every bit of her remaining backdoor knowledge from her time in Gene Sequencing, all the little protocols they wouldn't have thought to change. Though she didn't lack for talent, she was not quite the wizard with compromising networks her assumed identity had been. She wondered sometimes where the real Rieve Revolos, or the mutated mass that had been her murdered corpse, had wound up. Some alley somewhere, transformed past all hope of identification.

It was indulgent, she knew, both the video feed itself and remaining here a moment longer than necessary now that she was discovered. She knew it was indulgent. Palmieri could only be chased away by Kyne's obnoxious behavior for so long. But the look on Delgassi's face when that idiot Hayasun delivered the news ... perfection.

Still, she felt the itch of her window of escape closing. Her supposed betters were dead, captured, or fled. She mustn't succumb to hubris, not this close to total success. She had the information she needed now, the information to do properly what Delgassi had been fumbling at. She spun her chair around suddenly, a nervous tic, a reflexive check to make sure she was truly alone. It had been an easy thing to annoy an already upset Stefani Palmieri into seeking some fresh air, but there was no telling how long she'd stay away. There was no sound of the hatch above. No footsteps on the stairs. Kyne wondered, now, if this fear of being watched was truly a human reflex. How not to wonder?

Truthfully, she didn't know why she wanted to gloat over Delgassi's comeuppance so much. The woman had been a far more versatile tool than Kyne could have hoped for when this desperate farce began. Kyne ought to be thanking her. Revenants walking the halls of Gene Sequencing. The cache unlocked, its secrets at last laid bare.

But Delgassi wasn't likely to accept any gift from Dr. Kyne Libretta. And the only wealth Kyne Libretta possessed was knowledge which she very much intended to deny everyone else. Her copy, fully decrypted, was safely downloaded to her handheld. For the copy which remained on the Underlab system, Kyne had written a script which would re-encrypt the data, erecting even more barriers to legibility than it had begun with. She could have just deleted it and destroyed the drives, but that felt too pat. Give them some vain hope of eventual understanding. Let them know even a taste of the suffering she had labored under for years. Savoring the moment, Kyne reached out to key the script to life and leave them all trapped in ignorance forever.

She froze in this awkward posture as the cold circle of a gun muzzle pressed itself against her neck.

"Don't. Move." It was the voice of the rat, Marri, and it was unnervingly steady.

Hubris, Kyne chided herself. *Hubris and one thrice-damned ghost of a girl.* She should have arranged for an accident for the whelp after their very first meeting, when she'd sneaked into Delgassi's office without so much as a sound.

"I don't know what you're doing," Marri said. "But I know what I heard on that monitor just now. You're the one she's been after all this time."

"Don't do anything foolish, girl," Kyne said, but despite her attempt at calm, the child couldn't miss the sweat now plastering her hair to her face. "I can make you very sorry."

"Not dead you can't."

But the rat had erred. *She means to kill me whatever I do,* Kyne told herself. It didn't matter if it was true. She just had to believe it was to summon the wild recklessness she needed. *If I'm dead either way ...*

She spun, moving as fast as she ever had. Juking to the side to get clear of the shot line. The gun barked once, painfully loud in the confined lab, but Kyne lunged into the space opened up by the recoil and grabbed Marri's wrists, pushing them above her head and twisting. Though she was no paragon of strength, Kyne Libretta could certainly overpower a gawky waif of a girl. In short order, the gun was in Kyne's hands, and Marri was the terrified one.

Most satisfying.

Secure in her position now as master of this situation, Kyne took a moment to study the weapon. She was surprised to find she recognized it. It was the very one she had provided to Damon Blackburne for his failed assassination attempt. She'd been so irritated that she'd misjudged his response to the treatment. It had cost her dearly. Her position, her access, and very nearly her life.

But looking back, it had all worked out in her ultimate favor.

"Now," she said, savoring the way the girl cringed. "I believe it's *your* turn to d—"

The hatch to the Underlab creaked open above, and footsteps descended rapidly.

Kyne cursed. Was *everyone* going to show up? All right. Kill the intruder. Kill the girl. Spare the infant. No sense in being needlessly cruel. Then be gone. At least it wasn't Delgassi and her pet revenants. There hadn't been nearly enough time for that.

Kyne turned her head just enough to see Palmieri descend. Kyne grabbed the brat and pulled her in front to serve as a shield. Palmieri's eyes flashed with fury.

"I just got the call from Iaz. I always knew there was something off about you," the woman said, all bile and bluster. Then she saw that Kyne had her adoptive brat at gunpoint, and that flawless, tawny skin went very pale indeed.

"If you felt that way, you'd never have left me alone with your infant all those times," Kyne said with vicious triumph. "So my bet is you actually had no idea."

"Let her go," Palmieri said, and to her credit, her voice was iron. "Iaz is on her way. She said she's bringing help, so the lancers will be coming too. You might as well give up now."

She knows so little. Hardly a surprise. Only one of them had possessed the intellect for Gene Sequencing.

"Is that really what you want?" Kyne asked. "Delgassi to be here? Weren't you and your overly friendly lancer commander plotting a coup as recently as a few hours ago?"

"Now I know who's been speaking poison in her ears," Palmieri said. "More importantly, so does she. She'll listen to reason, now."

"I'm not so sure about that," Kyne said. This was taking too long. Kill Palmieri. Kill the girl before she could respond. Kill the infant too, because now Palmieri had pissed her off.

Marri squirmed in Kyne's grip as though sensing her distractedness from the moment. Kyne tightened her choke hold until the girl's struggles took on a more desperate character.

"Let her go," Stefani said, tears in her voice.

"I tell you what," Kyne said, struck with sudden inspiration. "Pick which one you'd rather keep. This brat or the one you birthed yourself? The infant is your own blood. But she's also flawed, isn't she? I don't see that getting any better. Not with what I've been reading about, oh, everything."

She'd been wrong before. The look on Palmieri's face topped the look on Delgassi's by several orders of magnitude. Kyne had to stifle a laugh of delight. "No, I'm only kidding," she said. "I'll be killing all three of you now." By the sounds Marri made, she was halfway to dead already.

Kyne decided she wanted Palmieri to suffer more before dying. She applied slow pressure to the gun's trigger so that Palmieri could wonder if the world had slowed down to draw out her agony.

Metal squealed behind her, and abruptly Kyne was flying through the air, her grip on the girl lost to an arm gone numb with the impact. She landed roughly on the sofa where she'd spent many a night. She'd only imagined it was hard before. Hitting it at speed taught her better. Breath left her in a painful whoosh.

The girl was less fortunate. Kyne saw her collide with the table leg next to the sofa. She went limp, into unconsciousness or death, Kyne didn't care. Across the room, Palmieri's shrieking matched the baby's, and Kyne at last turned to see what had sent her flying.

Through a newly made hole in the Underlab's wall emerged a revenant, black death with a ruby sheen. Then it began to change, and Kyne shortly found Damon Blackburne's likeness staring down at her. It was remarkable. If they'd passed on the street, she'd have never noticed what was off. At least, not if he was wearing real clothes. The simulacrum the creature produced out of some misplaced memory of modesty wouldn't fool anyone, even at a distance.

Still, they'd come so far in so short a time. So far back toward where they'd begun.

"Dr. Libretta," Iazmaena Delgassi said, entering behind her revenant, her face a twisted mask of hate. "Do you remember him?"

"She does," said another voice, a not-quite-human voice—which was very nearly a joke. A second revenant, already wearing a human disguise and actual clothing, had entered beside Iaz.

"Damon and I can handle things here, Ali," Iaz said. The chaos and insanity she'd brought were belied by her prosaic tone. *Take the kids to practice. I'll clean up dinner.* "Go back, tell the others we've got her. Keep the rest from causing trouble. I'll be in touch soon."

Stefani Palmieri watched all of this in naked horror.

Stefani Palmieri. Kyne's ticket out of this mess.

CHAPTER 53

"IAZ," Stefani began, pushing through the numb shock that suffused her. The Ali-thing had stepped back through the hole from which the three had entered, so she pointed a shaking finger at the Damon-thing. "What the fuck is that?" She knew the answer. She had watched the transformation. The answer wasn't the point. The point was to give Iaz a chance to explain herself.

It's a revenant. And it came in with Iaz.

Something snarling and savage swelled in Stefani, pushing rational thought to the side. Even the horrified sense of violation over Rieve Revolos being Kyne Libretta seemed muted and distant. Instead, a primal thing took up residence behind Stefani's eyes. The only thoughts she could muster were a steady stream of Ella's name, blurring into one endless cry in her mind.

Stefani moved before Iaz could respond, surging forward without thinking, twisting, pulling muscles she hadn't exercised in years. She first reached under the desk and pulled free the lance Karl had left for emergencies. Resuming her full height, Stefani then placed herself between the creature and her child, leveling her weapon at the thing's chest.

It didn't move a muscle.

"Steffi ..." It was Iaz that spoke, her voice strangely devoid of emotion.

Stefani's voice had no such deficiencies. "What is this, Iaz? What the fuck is this?"

"Easy, Steffi, they're helping me."

"*Helping* you? In case you don't remember, Iaz, they just ate an entire ward of this damned city!" Her eyes never left the Damon-thing. How did they do it, assume the shapes of those that people cared about?

"They were human once, Steffi. You were right!"

"I said their ancestors *might* have been human once!" Stefani snarled back. "Do you remember being a fish? They'd have no memory of it now."

"They want answers," Iaz said, a note of pleading entering her voice. *Pleading for what? This thing's life? Or forgiveness?* "The same as we do."

"We know. Answers." The Damon-thing was impassive. "Helping. You to. See." It was too much.

"And you're *talking* to them now?" Stefani accused, shuddering in revulsion. "Negotiating?"

"One of them came looking for me!" Iaz's voice finally, *finally* betrayed some anger, something that made her sound herself again. "It came in Damon's shape."

"This one?" Stefani asked, aghast.

"No. It's dead now. Karl ..." The pause after that word was heavy with meaning, a horrid emptiness, but not empty at all. Something lurked in that pause.

"Karl killed it," Stefani said. "Karl was with you." Neither was a question, and Iaz did not dispute. Stefani's gut lurched. "Iaz, where's Karl now?"

Iaz's face crumpled just for an instant before snapping back to rigidity. She couldn't entirely purge the emotion from her voice though. It came out in a whisper. "He'd turned against me, Steffi ..." That trailing off was full of menace. *I hope you haven't too,* it implied.

Grayness swooped down upon Stefani, dimming the light. *Karl. No, no, no. Oh gods below, Karl. Please, no.* How far gone was she? *That's for later,* urged a stern part of Stefani's brain. *My best friend invited a revenant to stand five meters from my daughter.*

"Steffi," Iaz began again.

"Iazmaena, you brought one of those things here knowing full well my daughter is here?"

"It's not going to hurt anyone," Iaz said, sounding distressingly sane while speaking impossibilities. "Who do you think took down Gene Sequencing for me just now? It wasn't the lancers."

An army. She had a damned *army* of revenants. How many of them looked like people now? How long before they could pass perfectly for people and blend into the city unnoticed?

Iaz eased herself into Stefani's line of fire, disrupting her spiraling thoughts. "It's a fragile truce," her friend said to her, as though calming a hysteric. "I can't have you disrupting a chance for peace. For *answers.* Don't you want answers more than anything?"

Stefani's finger tightened spasmodically on the trigger for a moment, but thankfully not with enough pressure. For a horrible instant the thought was there, the notion that Iaz's reign must be ended, that no price was above paying.

It was an insane fear for Ella that filled Stefani's head with such thoughts, her mind dutifully rationalizing. But discharging the lance in here, so close to Ella, would be almost equally insane. Stefani released the trigger.

And Kyne Libretta took her moment.

Lunging, she caught Iaz's ankle, and Iaz stumbled.

"Kill it!" Libretta hissed.

Stefani charged as though down the barrel of a gun. Her mind raced to catch up. She couldn't shoot, but there was another way. White-hot rage carried her as she rushed forward. Using the lance like its ancient namesake, she drove the Damon-thing back, and it went sprawling into the open door of the nearest test chamber.

Stefani arrived an instant later, and she hit the button to slam the hatch closed automatically. She'd made some modifications after they'd determined the creatures' interest in radiation, and she depressed the buttons in their predetermined sequence to trigger the radiation bath. Nothing precise or calibrated. Full power across the ionizing spectrum.

And not a moment too soon. Iaz was distracted by Kyne's attack only long enough to allow Stefani to act. The little woman was no match for a former cop in a fair fight. Using the battered Kyne as leverage to get back to her feet, Iaz took in the radiation chamber and let out a wordless, stricken wail of anguish.

The gunmetal walls of the chamber were instantly rendered transparent as its interior cameras, radiation hardened, began transmitting. A deep thrumming began as the Damon-thing writhed underneath a boiling tumult of invisible rays. Human-looking skin blistered and burst, oozing blood and a sludgy ichor. The creature within appeared to be screaming, neck working as great chitin armor plates stood out beneath the darkening and mottling skin. It thrashed, battering itself against the interior walls of the chamber, leaving streaks of those thick fluids with each impact.

With a horrifying rapidity, it reverted to its revenant shape as the radiation forced it to unclench whatever held fast its human disguise. The skin was either subsumed by the chitin beneath or peeled away in great stiff strips. Variable, shifting limbs sprouted. The creature's separating, scorpion-tail spine with its split egg of a head lashed about madly. The Underlab rattled with the impact of its blows. Wherever it struck, cameras went dark, rendering portions of the chamber opaque again. Gripped by a primal fear deeper than any she'd ever felt, Stefani moved without conscious thought to scoop up Ella from her bubble and hold her close, shielding the baby with her body.

But she couldn't help but watch, her scientific curiosity momentarily overtopping her horror. The thing was *still* changing. An uninformed observer might assume that the process they had just witnessed was somehow reversing itself. But the radiation, tearing away portions of whatever had caused these creatures to stop being human, forced its transformation to move in only one direction.

It's true then. This is what they wanted access to the reactors for, an energy source to allow them to overcome the threshold necessary to revert to what they once were. But it wasn't enough, and they settled for these crude human simulacra instead. The test chamber put out far more energy than those reactors did. Maybe it was too powerful, and there was a happy medium somewhere that would have granted them the transformation they wished without killing them. Or maybe there was no way it could have ever worked and left them alive.

The chitin plates of armor, interlocking in impossible ways, were sloughing off, falling to the floor of the chamber in what Stefani imagined was a deafening clatter. The effect diminished the creature, like the easing of an indomitable force. Stefani watched, trapped in this abject nightmare, as the quartered head opened wider and wider, the petals finally falling away to reveal the torn-asunder human skull within.

The creature continued to shrink, as though the ceaseless bombardment was physically crushing it into a smaller size. Whatever remained of its shape-changing properties kept at work, attempting to reassemble its pieces into a semblance of order even as the ability itself was stripped away. The skull fused partly shut around its slackened brain as it failed, and the gap-toothed jaw opened in a scream beneath empty sockets.

When it finally stopped moving, Stefani could breathe again. It was dead, the chamber readout promised. It had a great deal more preliminary data as well, but Stefani didn't need to read it to see what was right in front of her.

The revenants had unquestioningly descended from humans. The burned-black form knelt as if in prayer or supplication was entirely too familiar to be dismissed.

"Before I came down here," Iaz said, her voice a whispering thunderclap in the gnarled silence of the room, "they helped me uncover the rot at the heart of this city." She reached behind her back and pulled out a set of police-issue handcuffs, then bent and roughly bound Libretta's wrist to the leg of a worktable bolted to the floor. "I told them to stand by at Gene Sequencing. It was a truce, Steffi, and they held up their end."

Stefani at last tore her gaze away from the burned thing to stare into Iazmaena's eyes. They were, in their own way, equally scorched.

"I hope to all the gods below that you haven't ruined that."

CHAPTER 54

STEFANI TRIED TO SPEAK. No words came out. What could she say? What words could possibly convey what she was feeling?

"Keep an eye on her," Iazmaena commanded without looking at Stefani, then she moved around the corner toward Kyne's section of the lab. "It's time to see if ... so she did unlock it." A note of grim satisfaction entered her voice. She sat down at Kyne's workstation, stared fixedly at the screens for several moments, then lowered a large pair of headphones over her ears.

Stefani's gaze returned to the burned-up human husk staring out at her through sightless eyes, before suddenly recalling Marri. She rushed over to the girl, who was just beginning to stir.

"Are you all right?" Stefani asked her, checking the girl with one hand for signs of broken skin or blood, while keeping Ella on a hip away from possible contamination. Marri's answering nod meant nothing. The girl would likely refuse to admit if she'd lost a limb.

"You did the right thing," Kyne said to her back. "Delgassi can't be trusted. She's become too unstable."

"And whose fault is that?" Stefani responded coldly. Satisfied there were no external injuries, she peered into Marri's eyes, lifting back the lids to check pupil response. Mild concussion. Other vitals normal. Not ideal, certainly. But Marri would be all right.

"I know I've wronged you all," Kyne said, testing her restraint. "But you need to listen to me. You call her a friend, but whatever else you may think of me or what I've done, our illustrious archon can't be trusted to behave rationally. What she needs is help, and what she has is near-absolute power."

It was too close to what Karl had said just a few hours gone. "She's exactly what you made her," Stefani snapped. "You've manipulated her into this!"

"Listen. To. Me," the woman repeated. "Those buildings she destroyed? One of them wasn't empty. Her predecessor was in it, along with her aide, Johe, and several other magistrates. She had me lock out their communications so no one else would know. Then she blew up the building with them in it."

"You're ... you're lying," Stefani said, and she hated herself for how her voice shook.

"I have the evidence right here. Recordings of their conversations. I'll give it to you. You can view it over there. You'll see I'm right!" Kyne's voice rose in pitch to match her desperation, as Stefani lifted Marri to her feet and checked that she was steady.

Stefani winced at the sudden increase in volume, wondering just how much noise those headphones Iaz wore would block. She realized with a sudden, horrific lurch that she was afraid of Iaz. Afraid of her oldest friend. *Is she still my friend?*

"I see it in your face," Libretta said in hushed triumph. "Tell me honestly that you haven't had doubts about her mental state."

"I can't trust anything you say. Everything you've said from the moment we've met has been a lie."

But once the thought was in Stefani's head—*I am afraid of Iazmaena Delgassi*—it would not leave. It hardened her resolve. Her instinctual action, the action she was taking even now, was the right one. A mother's action. She'd been ignoring her duties as a mother for too long. With her free hand, she bent and picked up the gun from where it had fallen and pocketed it gingerly. She wouldn't leave that where Libretta might contrive to get hold of it.

"We three are leaving," she said of herself, Marri, and Ella. "What Iaz decides to do with you is up to her. But I won't have any part of this anymore. We'll find Karl, and he'll know what to do."

"She all but admitted to killing Karl!" Libretta cried.

"Goodbye, *Rieve*," Stefani said, determined not to listen. "I suspect I won't see you again." She gathered up a reluctant Marri and her lance. After a moment's thought, Stefani handed Ella to Marri. The lance was no one-handed weapon. Then the three of them made for the hatch.

"Palmieri! You let me out of here right now! Palmieri!" Kyne's cries paradoxically grew louder the further away from her they got. As the hatch door slammed shut, Stefani could swear they hadn't diminished in volume at all.

CHAPTER 55

THE HEADPHONES FIT DOWN around Iaz's head snugly, cutting off the world. The first thing she noted was that Libretta had placed the fully decrypted files under her own, multi-layered encryptions, but had failed to lock them. *We got here just in time.* Iaz immediately took the initiative presented to her, adjusting Kyne Libretta's password to something only Iaz knew.

That the little woman had perused the entirety of the files, Iaz had no doubt. But that wouldn't matter soon. A part of her worried that Stefani had perhaps had a chance to view the files herself. Once, this wouldn't have been a concern. But Stefani had proven as untrustworthy as the rest. *Too friendly with Karl.* But Iaz didn't want to think what that might mean right now.

One file had been placed at the top of all the others. It was titled only HEARME. Using the unfamiliar interface, a cruder affair than she was used to, Iaz selected it and instructed it to open.

A man's voice, strangely accented, immediately began speaking. Iaz's heart hammered within its prison of ribs. Everything she had worked for, sacrificed for, had crept close enough to smother her. This data cache had come from Gene Sequencing. Hayasun had explained all about Libretta's theft of it. That made it even more precious than something simply dug up from beneath the city. It was a secret; one they were protecting with all their insidious methods. And it was hers now.

"To whomever may be listening," the voice said, "I am called Matteo Cairanus, as far as such names mean anything at all."

As he spoke, a new window opened in the terminal display and text appeared over images that began flashing up on the screen, synced to specific times in the audio file. *Whomever Matteo Cairanus was, he had a talent for presentation.* He was also a ghost, a man speaking to her out of a past thought destroyed in the Loss. The enormity of this threatened to overwhelm. The man continued speaking.

"I was not yet alive when the invaders came to our world. None live who remember that day, but all agree that the intruders arrived within a burning sphere of brilliance that scorched the very ground around it and left a vast ring of broken metal in its wake."

Only moments in, and already he rewrote Coldgarden's history. It was commonly accepted that the revenants had arrived on-world not long before their invasion of the city then known as Calgary, renamed Coldgarden after the resulting Loss and the rise of Mutagen Prime. But if Cairanus's story and the data behind it were true, the revenants had been here many generations prior to those events.

"We were as animals to them at first," he continued, "considered dangerous to those foolish enough to wander from their places of safety. They even captured a few of us for study. I do not have to imagine the shame of it, the indignity, for such shame is written upon my flesh. We are being asked to heap that shame upon ourselves now, only this time, voluntarily. But I get ahead of myself."

Iazmaena frowned, perplexity dulling her excitement. Something more than just the timeline was odd here.

"From the very beginning, the invaders underestimated us. They never learned otherwise. Not even at the end. We have never been ones to remain wary for long."

Images appeared of the city Coldgarden in sunlight. A Coldgarden of the past. Calgary, then. Iaz recognized some of its landmarks, all considered among the oldest structures now. *Those that still stand.* But she squinted in confusion when the captions named the city *New* Calgary. New. She'd never heard that modifier used.

"Our way has always been," the voice went on. "Watch. Learn. Consume. Mimic. The invaders learned this to their sorrow. They took to calling us 'gobblers,' trivializing us even as we hunted them. They did not know we used the feasting to learn, to become. It has ever been our way.

"They adapted too, of course, hunted us in turn. Tried desperately to drive us from their places of imagined safety. It was their great mistake, repeated over and over." Pictures rose of armored men and women wearing backpacks and brandishing hoses. Liquid fire sprayed from the hoses' tips. Iaz furrowed her brows in confusion. "No matter how we adapted, they still refused to believe we possessed intelligence."

"What the hell?" Iaz whispered. *What is this?*

"But we learned, while they failed to. We learned how to act out the behavior they expected of us while following other paths entirely. It was not long before we dared the borders of their fledgling colony."

Pictures of remains, gory and unrecognizable. Blood both red and a sickly, iridescent green. Smears of pasted flesh staining sidewalks. Cordons of police tape were the one constant in the photos, except for the few that were obviously taken beyond the city limits. Iaz's frown deepened.

No, this makes no sense.

"So even as they swept the sewers and the alleys and the forgotten, abandoned buildings, we had already learned enough to infiltrate them and spread.

"I have lived my entire life under the same patterns as all the rest. Infiltrate, consume, replace. Until I conceived of a better way. For there would be no need for the hunt if we could simply breed them out of existence. Their method of reproduction was new to us. As changeable as we have always been, we had no need to combine genomes for fitness. We adapt not across generations but across individuals. But if we pantomimed their archaic methods, we could infiltrate the invaders, select them as mates, and pass our budded children off as their own.

"Thus did I assure the humans' ultimate failure."

Iazmaena allowed the words to wash over her. She strove to absorb their magnitude and multitudes, but she was too shallow a vessel to contain such knowledge without brimming over. It was impossible, it *couldn't* be true.

You wanted answers, Damon's voice said in her head. *You'd pay anything for answers. For why I died.*

"Freed of our need to hunt and consume, we vanished from their searches. Perfectly disguised, our kind mated with the humans, those posing as females passing off their own offspring as products of that mating, like the cuckoo bird of their own world, while those posing as males ensured each pairing would produce no offspring in turn. We thus swelled our numbers while diminishing theirs.

"Eventually, they learned their mistake. Too late. The genetic plague—their last, desperate attempt to save themselves—was a replicating mutagenic compound derived from our world's biology and keyed to *our* biology. We would have no immunity to it because it was the very essence of us but distilled and strengthened. It would accelerate our own mutational prowess uncontrollably, precluding any further reproduction. 'Hyperspeciation' they called it."

New images flew at the screen, complex chains of atoms and molecules that meant nothing at all to Iaz.

"But they did not know that we had infiltrated the team concocting the plague. We made changes, and so the plague targeting us changed them instead, warping them as our own bodies are capable of warping, but without the control we have learned over the eons. Weakened as they were, we cast those few survivors out of this city and into the wilderness that had once been our home.

"If we are lucky, these wandering human revenants will never achieve the requisite control to trouble us again. I do not believe in such luck, but those who lead us must. It is the only way I can explain these insane new dictates."

Iaz teetered dizzily, struggling not to tilt off the chair. There were more pictures, even full videos, but she could no longer concentrate on them. She was burning up, sweat slicking her entire skin. *I can't be hearing this.* But the voice continued, horrific and inexorable.

"Always we have mimicked our prey in order to hunt our prey. Never did I think that we would stoop to *become* them. Yet it happens now all around me. Many have altered themselves to such a degree that they must now breed in the disgusting manner of the humans, with two progenitors. Everything we have held sacred is being transformed.

"We desire their technology, I am told, and to understand their technology we must commit wholly to their being. So the leaders say. We desire to travel back to their home world, their Earth, to other worlds, to spread ourselves throughout the stars. But these concepts are still so new, so raw, and all gleaned from the records of those we have displaced. How can we know what to make of them? This world is our home, and even now we turn our back upon it and the ways it has made its mark upon us."

The words wouldn't stop. The voice kept droning on and on. It was so much worse than Iaz's wildest imaginings. *This* was the secret that Teodori and his ilk and all their predecessors had pulled strings from the shadows to protect? But why, why keep it a secret at all?

Because, Damon whispered, *we believed too strongly in our own lie, became so human that to think ourselves anything else would unravel us. Destroy us. How long can you pretend to be something before you can't see yourself any other way?*

And he was right. Even having heard the truth, even *believing it,* Iaz found herself horrified and denying it still with a fervency that frightened her. Denying her very existence. *My whole life.* Not just her life. Everyone's life. Everyone in the entire city. Every life for almost a hundred years. *All a lie.* Stefani was right. The revenants had indeed been human before being driven from their city. And all those that thought *themselves* human now, every single person in the city, everyone Iaz had ever known, were descended from beings that had been ... something else.

"As I record this," Matteo Cairanus said, "the final preparations are taking place to purge all record of what we have done. As the humans tried to do to us, we will now do to ourselves. But it will not be our lives that are lost, merely our whole identities.

"It is madness. So I have decided to leave this recording hidden in a secret place. Perhaps by the time it is found and decoded, we will have forgotten why we were ever so foolish, and we will be ready to remember ourselves again.

"I can only hope that you, listener, are one who takes pride, and not horror, in this knowledge. If we have forgotten that we were ever not the humans we now pretend to be, then I fear for the future of our race.

"Hear my words, listener. Your human form is a lie. Your kind was not always as it is now. Once you were the proud apex predators of this world. Deadly hunters feared by all other life. Do not allow this history to pass from all memory."

Iazmaena was riven, cored out, lips curling in rage and trembling to fight back tears. And when the picture of a horrid green-black monstrosity appeared on the screen, revulsion rocked her anew at the six spindly, bony claw legs poking from a thickly muscled, worm-like body.

Worse, a human man, half-swallowed, protruded from the thing's wide, toothless gullet as it slurped him down with what Iazmaena could only imagine was gusto. The picture was still, slightly blurred, and yet both forms seemed to writhe within it.

Is he saying that's what we are? That monster ... is us?

She shuddered, first from that toxic revulsion, but then from something much worse. For she felt a sudden kindred with this thing in the picture, an *appetite*, a sense of predatory lust for the meaty flesh the creature was guzzling down. The taste of hot blood and of muscle fibers dissolved by acids. On some impossibly deep level, she recognized the monstrosity in that image and felt a deep affinity toward it.

It's true, then. Her thoughts rang her head like a mourning bell. *That thing is us.*

Iazmaena bent over in her seat, fighting the urge to vomit. Of all the compromises and indignities her election had forced upon her, the horrific truth displacing the world she knew was the last and worst of them. This, this was what Teodori and his ilk worked so hard to protect: cursed knowledge. A lifelong burden, either in the form of a secret to keep, or the guilt of revealing that secret and so damning the rest of the city to understanding of their collective crime.

The world pinched down in Iaz's vision, narrowing to a tunnel with gray and fuzzy walls. Feeling suddenly constricted by them, Iaz pulled off the headphones just in time to hear footsteps approaching from behind.

Steffi. What was she going to tell Steffi about what she had heard? And would her friend even listen to her anymore?

CHAPTER 56

IT TOOK A FRUSTRATINGLY long time for Kyne to bring herself under control after Palmieri and the two brats left her in the custody of her would-be murderer. It seemed her days of successfully manipulating her ragtag team of marks were at an end. This probably shouldn't have surprised her, given her cover being blown, but as ever, failure did.

The only reason she wasn't dead already was likely because Delgassi wanted to question her about what she knew regarding the recording and her boyfriend. Kyne's answers on that score would prove disappointing. There had to be another way out of this.

A cursory examination revealed how haphazardly the table leg had been bolted to the floor. The composicrete was riddled with cracks. *The price of too-rapid construction.* She felt it again, as she always did, that uplifting surge of the world aligning itself to her needs. She exulted in the feeling. It was so rare that she couldn't simply will her wants into existence. Perhaps that was why the stone wall presented by Gene Sequencing's innermost circle had been so galling, so unacceptable.

Well, they'd paid what they owed in denying Kyne Libretta access to their darkest secrets.

With constant upward pressure applied by her shoulder—painful, but what was a little more pain?—the table corner sprang loose with a puff of crumbled 'crete. Kyne stood and waited for the sounds to raise some alarm from her workstation, but no sound came. She'd procured those headphones to block out the Palmieri brat's incessant wailing, and now they were going to save her life. Palmieri had taken both gun and lance, but that was all right. Too quick. Too clean. Kyne took tentative steps then rounded the corner to her workstation.

Delgassi faced away from her, still wearing the headphones, posture slumped in a feeling Kyne remembered well, though she'd mastered the impulse better. Then Delgassi shuddered a breath that sounded half a sob and tugged the headphones from her ears, looking as though gravity was doing most of the work.

No time to dither.

Kyne moved as quickly as she was able. Approaching from behind, she whipped the free loop of the cuffs around Delgassi's throat and pulled the chain tight.

Instantly the woman tried to rise, hands slapping Kyne's workstation console as she drove herself up and backward on powerful legs in an attempt to relieve the pressure on her airway, but Kyne did not let her get to her feet where her height would give her the advantage. She kicked out at Delgassi's legs, and the woman's low heels slid out from under her, her weight nearly bearing them both to the floor.

Snarling and laughing, Kyne pulled even harder, cinching tight the chain around Delgassi's throat. After a few seconds more of struggling, Delgassi slumped unconscious into dead weight, sprawling out prone on the floor.

CHAPTER 57

"WE SHOULDN'T HAVE LEFT them alone," Marri said, and Stefani was at a loss to respond, because she wasn't sure the girl was wrong.

"She's chained up," Stefani said brusquely.

They wended their way through the knot of alleys which made the entrance to the Underlab such an easy thing to hide, sidling around recyclers that ought to have been ground up and fed into their fellows by now. Stefani wasn't certain where she was going, in truth, and the feeling was expanding to take over an ever-larger portion of her thoughts.

Ella. Ella and Marri. They come first. There was no telling when the next revenant, answering to Iaz or otherwise, would show up in the Underlab.

"You're supposed to be her friend," Marri said, anger serrating the words. Her tone set Ella crying again, and Stefani reached down and took the baby back into her arms, quietly shushing her before responding.

"As soon as I get you two somewhere safe, I'm going back," Stefani said, unaware she'd been going to say the words until she did. She'd been right to leave, but Marri was also right that she couldn't stay away. Whatever Iaz had been driven to become, it had happened while Stefani was watching. *I was her last living friend, and I let her down.* She'd let that snake Libretta insinuate herself into their lives, even vouched for Rieve Revolos's skills. If she'd been more skeptical of a woman she'd never met, maybe none of this would have happened.

Despite all this, Kyne Libretta's parting pleas haunted Stefani. What if her claims had been true? That was the worst part, because despite knowing how thoroughly the woman had deceived them, the degree to which Iaz had changed meant that Stefani could not dismiss the awful woman's accusations. A shameful part of Stefani hoped that bringing the children to safety would take long enough that Iaz could deal with any proof of those claims before Stefani returned.

The bliss of ignorance, of simply not knowing if it were true, felt almost as powerful as proof of Iaz's innocence would. Ella squirmed in her arms as Stefani hugged her tight.

"Where are you taking us that is safe?" Marri asked, and the old suspicion was back in her voice now.

"To Karl," Stefani said, and again, the words were automatic. Karl epitomized safety. *But Iaz said* ... No. Iaz hadn't said anything. She and Karl had argued. That was all there was to it. Karl was fine.

They were all going to be safe, especially the children. She would bring them to Karl. She would call him right now to find out where he was and go straight there. Or ... or perhaps she would just take them straight to safety.

"Come on," Stefani said, realizing she'd stopped moving. "We're going to Lancer Headquarters." If Karl wasn't there, the other lancers would know where he was. And if he was there, she could warn him about the revenants that looked like people now. She could also call and warn him, but ... no. No, this was a conversation better had in person.

It was not because she feared he might not answer.

Marri didn't respond. Annoyed now, Stefani turned, intent on browbeating the girl into following her no matter how sullenly she resisted, only to find herself staring back at an empty alley. While Stefani had dithered and warred within herself, Marri had taken the opportunity and run off.

Back to Iaz. Stefani took a step in that direction, then froze. She stared down at Ella, a squirming bundle in her arms. *Marri will be okay until I can get back. I have to make sure Ella is out of that place forever.* It was like pulling her own teeth, but Stefani turned back to find her bearings and make her way to Lancer HQ.

Only to find a figure blocking her path.

He was tall, this man, dressed in an expensive, tailored suit that was much too dapper to be wearing out in the rain. Clearly one of those people who ostentatiously spent to keep up with the latest fashions.

Her annoyance sharpening—annoyance was always better than fear—Stefani moved to push past him, expecting him to reluctantly shuffle aside. Willing him to, really. She poured all her will into the notion that he was just a strange man, randomly encountered, who meant her no harm. She did not meet his strange, not-quite-right eyes.

He did not move to let her aside. What he did do was begin to change.

In a sudden panic, Stefani lowered the lance tip, taking shaky aim with her one free arm. The man's transforming hand moved like a blur, batting it from her grip.

Clutched tight in Stefani's shaking arms, Ella began to cry.

CHAPTER 58

KYNE WASTED NO TIME. The keys for the cuffs glinted at Delgassi's belt. Smiling ferally, Kyne deftly freed herself of the second cuff. She examined the console, then engaged the encryption she'd meant to set in place before being so rudely interrupted.

Kyne turned next to her would-be victim, considered stomping Delgassi in the throat until it was all pulp, then applying the cuffs, but discarded both options. The former was too quick a death, the latter pointless if she moved fast. Now seemed like the perfect time to see the recording's revelations in action.

"It wasn't personal, you know," she said, as she set about dragging the woman away from her workstation. It didn't seem like a long trek until she had a fully grown adult's dead weight working against her. "I was assigned to derail your election. They told me if I pulled it off, they'd finally trust me enough to let me into their inner sanctum.

"They screen you very thoroughly before admitting you into Gene Sequencing. More thoroughly still before you can be told everything. You need the right genes, ones expressing for the tendency to keep secrets well and submit to authority, in order to be trusted. I scored very high on the former, and, as you can imagine, not so well on the latter. Looking back, I don't think they had any intention of admitting me, but I had to take the opportunity to learn all the secrets you just heard. You're welcome, by the way."

The bruising the revenant had gifted her made the dragging even harder, but Kyne persisted. Slowly, she made her way toward the one vacant chamber in the testing apparatus.

"None of this would have been necessary if they'd just listened to my recommendations. It's their fault, really. They swore to me your Damon was susceptible to authority, that he would submit to suggestion at a normal dose of therapy. Treat him properly, they said, and he would act in some publicly shameful way that would ruin your reputation just in time for the election. That failed spectacularly, of course, but since when has a man like Teodori let something like failure adjust his expectations of results? So I pushed the treatment harder, but it was too late to get results before the election. That was when the idea occurred to me. Even better than having you lose would be to have you die."

Depositing the false archon's limp form at last, Kyne stepped out and sealed the chamber, the hiss of its mechanisms echoing especially loudly. Or maybe that was just the blood roaring in Kyne's ears, a song of her final victory over both her enemies and the useful idiots whom she'd co-opted to achieve it. It was just a pity she couldn't toss Palmieri and the brats in as well.

"Can you imagine?" Kyne laughed, rendering the chamber transparent. "Your triumphant victory, and then, at your celebration, your own lover shows up and shoots you dead before killing himself? Pity only half the suggestion took. Even bigger pity Teodori was too much of a coward to approve it. I've never seen a person so livid."

Delgassi stirred in the chamber now, recovering consciousness, but it didn't matter. She was sealed in. Kyne tapped on the transparent wall, trying to get her attention like a fish in an aquarium. "The death order I showed you? It wasn't for you. It was for me. Teodori issued it after I'd escaped Gene Sequencing. Which makes it kind of funny that you killed Teodori when he thought what I'd done to your Damon had gone much too far."

Delgassi was struggling to her knees, clutching her throat. Her breaths sounded like croaks. Her face was flushed nearly purple. It was possible Kyne had broken something there. "No one gets fired from Gene Sequencing and lives, so that should have been the end of me," she said. "But I scored very highly in keeping secrets. And they had no idea, no idea at all how long I'd considered that threat a possibility. My plan was already in place. And I knew where they kept their precious data drive. Once I knew for certain that I'd never get at it legitimately, it was no trouble at all to slip away with it." She shrugged, satisfied that her tale was complete.

Having watched once before, the radiation chamber's operation was easy to decipher. Delgassi looked to be fully conscious now, and Kyne's smile grew to painful proportions, her breath ragged with anticipation as she activated the radiation bathing sequence. The emitter hummed as they began the surprisingly appropriate ending of Delgassi's reign of stupidity. Kyne watched, giddily awaiting the transformation.

CHAPTER 59

MARRI FELT bad sneaking away from Steffi while the woman was distracted by her own thoughts, but she was in less danger up here than Magistrate Delgassi was down in the Underlab with that evil woman, chained up or not. Later might be too late, and Marri could not risk anything happening to the only source of stability her mice had.

Her decision made, Marri wasted no time. She ignored her throbbing head and raced back the way they'd come, instinctively retracing their path as quickly as her feet would carry her. Steffi had been in such a hurry she hadn't bothered to hide the hatch, so there was no need to push the recycler clear.

A creepy silence greeted her from the bottom of the spiral stair. Maybe that was good. They'd left with that woman shrieking at them, but surely she'd given up by now, and Magistrate Delgassi had been engrossed in listening to something on those big headphones.

Marri ran down as fast as she dared. When the tunnel opened up near the bottom, she leaped down the last few stairs, but there was no sign of the Rieve-Kyne woman, only the table to which she'd been chained, one leg worked free of the composicrete below. Escaped.

Worse, there was no sign of Magistrate Delgassi either. No sign at first. But the second radiation chamber was no longer empty, and there was a horrible *something* inside it, something Marri's brain would not classify and urged her to look away from. It was the shredded clothing that caused her despair. It lay in torn swatches around the misshapen thing, and she instantly recognized it. It was the suit Magistrate Delgassi had been wearing.

Marri began to cry as she forced herself to behold Magistrate Delgassi. She pounded on the clear metal of the chamber, shrieking in rage and fear. *She helped me; she helped us all; she kept us alive.*

At first, she wondered if the thing inside the chamber had eaten her.

Then the thing *moved.*

Its skin was tough and rubbery, covered with muscular ridges and knobs. It was oily black with green highlights. Fat and massive, it was like half a worm with bone bug's legs slumped about it, flexing mindlessly. Two lines of three eyes alternated milky white and gleaming black. They joined a pair of stumpy arm-like claws in bracketing a huge, toothless mouth. Out of that mouth slopped something that Marri could only imagine was a bulbous tongue.

The tongue moved. There was *hair* attached to it. Long, auburn hair. Magistrate Delgassi's hair. Not something that was partially swallowed. The hair was *growing out of the tongue.* As if the tongue had been a head not long ago.

Magistrate Delgassi's hair. Magistrate Delgassi's head.

Marri's mind was a humming blank. Yet as terrible as it was, she was strangely fascinated by its shape. It awoke something inside her. She felt something within stir in sympathy with the great dying thing before her.

The thing surged forward suddenly, claws scraping against the chamber walls as though trying to pry them apart. That gluttonous mouth flexed. That horrible, hairy tongue pressed against the wall. Then the thing slumped and was still.

From above, the hatch opened.

Steffi. Marri felt the absurd urge to somehow hide what had happened here. Steffi had forced Marri to abandon Magistrate Delgassi, and because of that, the magistrate was dead. Marri had only begun to explore the depths of anger she felt for that, but a part of her still wanted to shield Steffi from this horrible truth and everything it must mean.

But it was a man's groan Marri heard as footsteps descended the stairs at an uneven gait. And Marri recognized that gravelly voice.

Karl the lancer boss staggered the last few steps down, only barely catching himself on the railing. He was in bad shape, gray-faced and caked in blood around his middle, which sported a wound plastered with cryobands. Marri flinched back, fearing the hypermutation that might begin at any moment, particularly in someone as old as him.

But Karl remained himself. He took in the test chamber with a mixture of confusion and disgust, then turned to Marri. Whatever answer he was looking for he seemed able to read on her face.

"Too late, then," was all he said. Then he sagged to his knees with another groan.

CHAPTER 60

THEY HAD CLIMBED one wall and lowered another. They had devoured a ward, sacrificing thousands, all to remember. They had made an unlikely ally and had breached the city's rotten heart. Now they feasted on corpses, glutting themselves on the past, while screaming memories, meals to be, begged them to stop.

They waited, then, for new orders, willing to see this alliance through to its useful conclusion.

Gradually, it became clear that no new orders would come. Something had gone wrong. Wary of being caught by surprise or betrayal, they abandoned their new alliance as easily as they had formed it. It had always been an alliance of opportunity. Their original plan was still intact.

They ate the begging ones, devoured them all. Fed upon glorious memory. The newly purged halls of Gene Sequencing grew quiet. They completed their transformations, discarded the parts of themselves now rendered vestigial. Then, one by one, they left the gore-strewn facility, disseminating out into an unsuspecting city.

They had a schedule to keep.

CHAPTER 61

SOMEWHERE CLOSE, something was crying.

She woke by degrees, staring at the crumbling side of an alley wall, a place that looked simultaneously familiar and alien. It was cold and wet on the ground, growing worse as water rained down upon her, and with these twin revelations, she became aware she was naked.

She stood, apparently unhurt despite being unconscious in an alley, which something inside her whispered was strange. Much in her mind was strange. She felt like things she had recently known were lost to her, while new things kept revealing themselves.

She looked around for her clothes. *That is what one does when they found themselves naked and outside,* these new thoughts whispered wordlessly. The clothes were there, torn in places, bloody in others, though the rain had washed some of that out before it could set. That was good. Blood might mean questions that were difficult to answer. Ultimately, she judged them good enough for now, if uncomfortably wet. She put them on. The motions of getting dressed were both familiar and alien.

The crying was growing worse, so she set about resolving that next. Finding the source was easy. It was a small creature—*a baby,* the thoughts whispered—wrapped in a sodden blanket and laying on the ground not far from where they both must have fallen. This baby seemed unhurt, merely upset. There was no blood on it. Cushioned by the blanket maybe. Or maybe, some dim recollection whispered, set down in a last-ditch attempt to draw attention from the baby and back to herself.

But attention from what?

From me, her mind answered automatically. But that made no sense. Why would she attempt to draw her own attention away from this baby? How would that even work? Voices old and new in her mind warred for a few moments over this but provided no answers.

This stalemate achieved, a part of her, a deep part, whispered that she should eat this baby. That it would help her to remember. But the newer whispers, which strangely felt older at the same time, clamped down hard on this idea. No, she must not do that. She remembered all she needed to. This was *her* baby. *Her* offspring. This was Ella.

She was Stefani Palmieri, and she was human.

EPILOGUE

IT HAD BEGUN WITH AN ELECTION. Now it would end with one as well, and all that had happened in between was that Stefani had become both a mother and bereft twice over.

In contrast to packed streets and hollow-eyed, hungry stares, the inside of the hospital lobby was well-kept. Stefani sat with Ella bobbing in her arms. She'd found that if she kept swapping Ella between herself and Marri, the girl was never anything but happy. That was a blessing, after all they'd been through and all the neglect Stefani had felt forced into.

So perhaps it was appropriate that on the day of this new election, a friend was pronounced "recovered." Whatever that meant. Or perhaps it was all the product of a wearied mind, trying to contort coincidence into meaning, trying to prove to itself that this had all been worth something.

Anything.

Between Marri's explanations and the Underlab security footage, she'd pieced together most of the story of Kyne Libretta's subterfuge. She had then meticulously purged that footage from all storage devices, answering to a deep-seated urge she didn't fully grasp. It was the same urge that compelled her to see to it that Iaz's remains disappeared from the Underlab as well.

Marri presented another difficulty. In the beginning, she had spoken nonstop about the revenants that could look like humans now and might be anyone or anywhere in the city.

"Let the grown-ups worry about it," Stefani would say every time the girl insisted upon bringing it up. Gradually, Marri's obsession had lessened. Stefani hoped she'd soothed Marri's worries, though she feared the girl had simply learned the topic wasn't worth mentioning in Stefani's presence.

Stefani often felt strange since the day Iaz had died, sometimes unlike herself at all. When those times passed and her sense of self returned, she always had the feeling she had forgotten a great deal of information she'd only just recalled moments before. It happened when Marri talked about disguised revenants. It happened when Stefani thought too much about what had happened to Iaz in that radiation chamber.

She tried not to think of either very much.

With much coaxing, she'd convinced the girl to come forward with her hideout's location so the children could be given homes, then lobbied hard for Graysteel to take a personal hand in ensuring them placement in good homes. Graysteel had resisted until Stefani had agreed to run for magistrate of Illuminance if Graysteel's own appointment to acting archon became official with the election. With the virtual destruction of Inkwell, there were enough broken families that the prospect of re-homing all those children suddenly seemed very doable.

Which means my days of doing real science are likely over. If it had ever been such. Stefani knew she shouldn't be so ungrateful. It was a far better fate than being implicated in Iaz's misdeeds, which had very much been on the table. Graysteel had vouched for her character personally there, and that seemed to have calmed matters. And perhaps, if Stefani won, she could get access to whatever records of Gene Sequencing remained after Iaz's assault and the resulting purge.

Another dissociative surge swept over her at this thought. *I am Stefani Palmieri. I am Stefani Palmieri.* It was a litany she'd adopted to deal with these episodes, as she'd taken to thinking of them. It seemed to help. Usually, it did.

The feeling subsided, and she tried to exist in the moment to help it along. This was supposed to be a good day. This *was* a good day. They were going to have a fancy dinner tonight to celebrate Karl's convalescence.

The double doors of the recovery ward slid open, disappearing into their wall-mounted recesses, and Karl hobbled out.

Stefani didn't recognize him at first, out of uniform and in civilian clothes, without even his hat. But it was his gait that threw her off the most. He walked slanted to one side. There had been no damage to his legs, but he'd suffered nerve damage near the spine. He would likely never walk normally again. He used a cane to help steady him now.

But he was smiling, as he was wont to do in all but the direst of times. That was what convinced her he was, fundamentally, the same person. Marri ran up to greet and help him.

"Mouse!" Karl roared jovially, which startled some of the nursing staff scattered around the airy lobby. Then they saw who they were dealing with and alternated between fond smiles and exasperated head shakes.

"You're notorious, I see," Stefani said as she approached with Ella. The words and tone were warm and familiar, even if the emotions behind them were muted. Stefani often found she knew how she was supposed to feel about a given thing, and how that feeling was supposed to sound. She could go through the motions convincingly, even though she seldom really *felt* these things. That should have upset her, but that feeling too was muted. This threatened another dissociative episode, which nearly did upset her until she fought it down.

I am Stefani Palmieri. I am Stefani Palmieri.

"They can't wait to get rid of me," Karl responded, then tickled Ella, who giggled and squealed in turn. He looked down sheepishly at his cane. "I guess I'm officially old."

"Good thing you have kids to help," Stefani replied. Perfectly timed. Perfectly pitched. Utterly false. "Kids keep you young."

"We'll see about that," Karl laughed, eyes twinkling. It was not as bright a twinkle as it once had been, her memory informed her. He had lost something, maybe something as profound as she had. It was hard to say, given that she still didn't understand what she'd lost.

Except for the times she did and then couldn't remember.

I am Stefani Palmieri. I am Stefani Palmieri.

He leaned in close, and for a panicked second, she thought he meant to kiss her. "You're going to have to tell me what's being done about the revenants. The ones who can disguise themselves as humans."

Oh, not you, too. "Not tonight," she said, pleading. "Tonight is supposed to be a celebration."

"I just need to know. It would ease my mind."

"Tomorrow," Stefani lied. For a moment, Karl looked stricken. But then he nodded.

"I don't know about any celebration," he said in a normal voice. "I'm not worth any fuss."

"Hush," Stefani said. "You're worth what we say you're worth. You'll eat a ridiculous amount of food and you'll like it."

"Yes, ma'am," Karl said, snapping off a dapper salute somehow made more so by the presence of his cane.

"Marri, you'll run and get the Mice. They need the food even more than Karl, I'll wager."

With an uncharacteristic grin, Marri darted through the front door, vanishing into the crowd in that uncanny way she had.

The day was cold and clear. Canopy clung to its last vestiges of red and gold above them, and Stefani knew she should have felt something. Contentment. Love. Anything. The dissociative episode that followed was one of the worst yet.

I am Stefani Palmieri. I am Stefani Palmieri.

It wasn't enough. She felt detached from her body, as though she was no longer in this place, this city. As though she roamed the wilderness in a strange form that both was and wasn't her. All she could think about was trials in her past, deprivations going back generations, with the worst still to come.

She teetered at the brink of losing herself and had to fall back on something more basic. It was a litany from a deeper, older place, a mantra she somehow felt as though she'd been repeating her entire life, impossible as that seemed.

I am human. I am human. I am human.

It worked. This time, it did.

ACKNOWLEDGMENTS

This weird little tale of mine has waited patiently for a long time for its turn at publication. A lot of people were kind enough to read it and give feedback and encouragement. Many thanks to Andrea Stewart, Ben Leonard, Garret Bonnema, Joe Silber, Ken Hoover, Marie Moler, Matt Cullen, Megan Walker, Molly Leonard, and Mom. Special thanks to Eric Flint for convincing me the manuscript was worth pulling out of the trunk and dusting off. Extra-special thanks to Sara George for suffering through what I like to call the Gregory D. Little Proofreading Experience. Extra-super-special thanks to Kelly Lynn Colby, whose insightful developmental editing skills enabled this book to achieve its final form (and who decided to, you know, publish it).

ABOUT THE AUTHOR

Gregory D. Little is the author of both the Mutagen Deception series and the Unwilling Souls series, the concluding volume of which, UNFINISHED DEAD, will be available in June of 2022. His short fiction can be found in THE COLORED LENS and the A GAME OF HORNS, DRAGON WRITERS, UNDERCURRENTS, ECLECTICALLY SCIENTIFIC, and MISSPELLED anthologies. He writes the kind of stories he likes to read, tales of human failure and redemption set in strange worlds where, be they magical or technological, everything is not as it seems. And spiders. He's fond of spiders.

Join Greg's newsletter and get a free story:

facebook.com/gregorydlittleauthor
twitter.com/litgreg

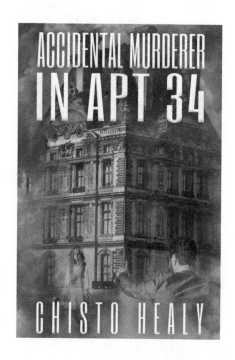

Some mistakes haunt the guilty,

while others seek revenge.

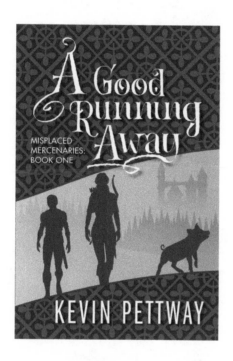

Stealing the cash box of your mercenary unit as you run away probably isn't wise, but it sure is funny.

CPSIA information can be obtained
at www.ICGtesting.com
Printed in the USA
LVHW041939010422
714992LV00002B/73

9 781951 445270